Apathetic Knight

Part 2
The Burning

Opening Dedication:

This book is dedicated to all of the Lovely Madness in this world. The mad love, the mad drama, the mad trauma, and all of the insanity in between.

Let me bring you into my Lovely Madness...

The Apathetic Knight

Part 2 – The Burning

Written by Kristen Elizabeth

Table of Contents:

Opening Dedication:..2
Table of Contents:..3
The Apathetic Knight Muse Playlist–....................5
Disclaimer Notice: 7
Author's Warning:..8
Special Author's Note:..9
Previously, in The Apathetic Knight......................11
Now, we continue… 15
Kyeareth Ashland… 17
Kyeareth… 24
Cinder Ashland… 39
Cinder… 51
Cinder… 69
Cinder… 82
Kyeareth… 100
Kyeareth… 113
Kyeareth… 130

Kyeareth…	146
Kyeareth…	162
Cinder…	178
Cinder…	189
Seryn Leonhart…	198
Kyeareth…	217
Kyeareth…	236
Kyeareth…	254
Seryn…	270
Seryn…	280
Kyeareth…	302
Kyeareth…	332
Book 1.5 Excerpt…	348
Books by Kristen Elizabeth	353
Acknowledgments	356
About the Author	358
About this Book	360
Reader's Observing Questions:	363

The Apathetic Knight Muse Playlist—

(Alphabetical Order)

Book 1.0 theme: Jeris Johnson & BOI WHAT – Battling My Demons

1. ASTAROTH theme: Somaticism – Symphonic Planet
2. Breaking Benjamin – Breath
3. Breaking Benjamin – Rain
4. CINDER theme: Flames in the Sky – Virtuocity
5. Citizen Soldier – Through Hell
6. Disturbed – Divide
7. Disturbed – Leave it alone
8. Duncan Laurence – Arcade
9. Ellie Goulding – Beating Heart
10. Evanescence – Bring me to life
11. Evanescence – End of the Dream
12. Evanescence – Like you
13. Gabbie Hanna – Dandelion
14. Hawthorne Heights – Dandelions
15. If Not For Me – Blameless
16. KYEARETH theme: Finding You – Symphonic Planet
17. Linkin Park – Pieces
18. Linkin Park – Pushing me away
19. Linkin Park – Runaway
20. Linkin Park – Sometimes I remember

21. Madonna – Frozen
22. Ruth B., (sped up and slowed) – Dandelions
23. SERYN theme: Warrior Theme – Avenged Sevenfold
24. WINTER theme: Bangalore – Symphonic Planet
25. WITCHZ – The Magic
26. Within Temptation – Blue Eyes
27. Within Temptation – Forgiven

Disclaimer Notice:

Disclaimer Notice:

All of the art in this novel series is drawn by the author, Kristen Elizabeth.
By no means am I a professional artist, nor do I claim to be, but I've always enjoyed the hobby.
I hope the drawings help you to integrate even further into this novel's world.
Thank you for reading!

Kristen Elizabeth

Author's Warning:

This book contains trigger warnings and material, including:

Abandonment/Neglect
Bullying
Sexual Harassment
Trauma/Extreme depression
Incestual themes
Miscarriage
Witch Craft
Attempted Murder/Murder/Gore

Please proceed with caution, and if triggered by any of these themes or by the story, please seek the appropriate help or resources. Be safe! Thank you!

Special Author's Note:

This novel saga uses an entirely different Calendar system, with different names of the months and days of the week. So, the Months and Weekdays are as follows:

January – Blizzard's Reign (30 days)
February – Nivis's End (20 days)
March – Seed's Sewn (40 days)
April – Rain's Fall (40 days)
May – Veras's Height (40 days)
June – Veras's End (20 days)
July – Solaris's Gifts (30 days)
August – Solaris's Reign (40 days)
September – Solaris's End (20 days)
October – Moon's Dance (27 days)
November – Folias's Blessing (30 days)
December – Year's Fall (20 days)

Sunday – Sun's Dawning
Monday – Morning's Stars
Tuesday – Seed's Rising
Wednesday – Sun's Reign
Thursday – Sun's Falling
Friday – Twilight's Reign
Saturday – Moon's Height

Spring – Veras
Summer – Solaris
Autumn – Folias
Winter – Nivis

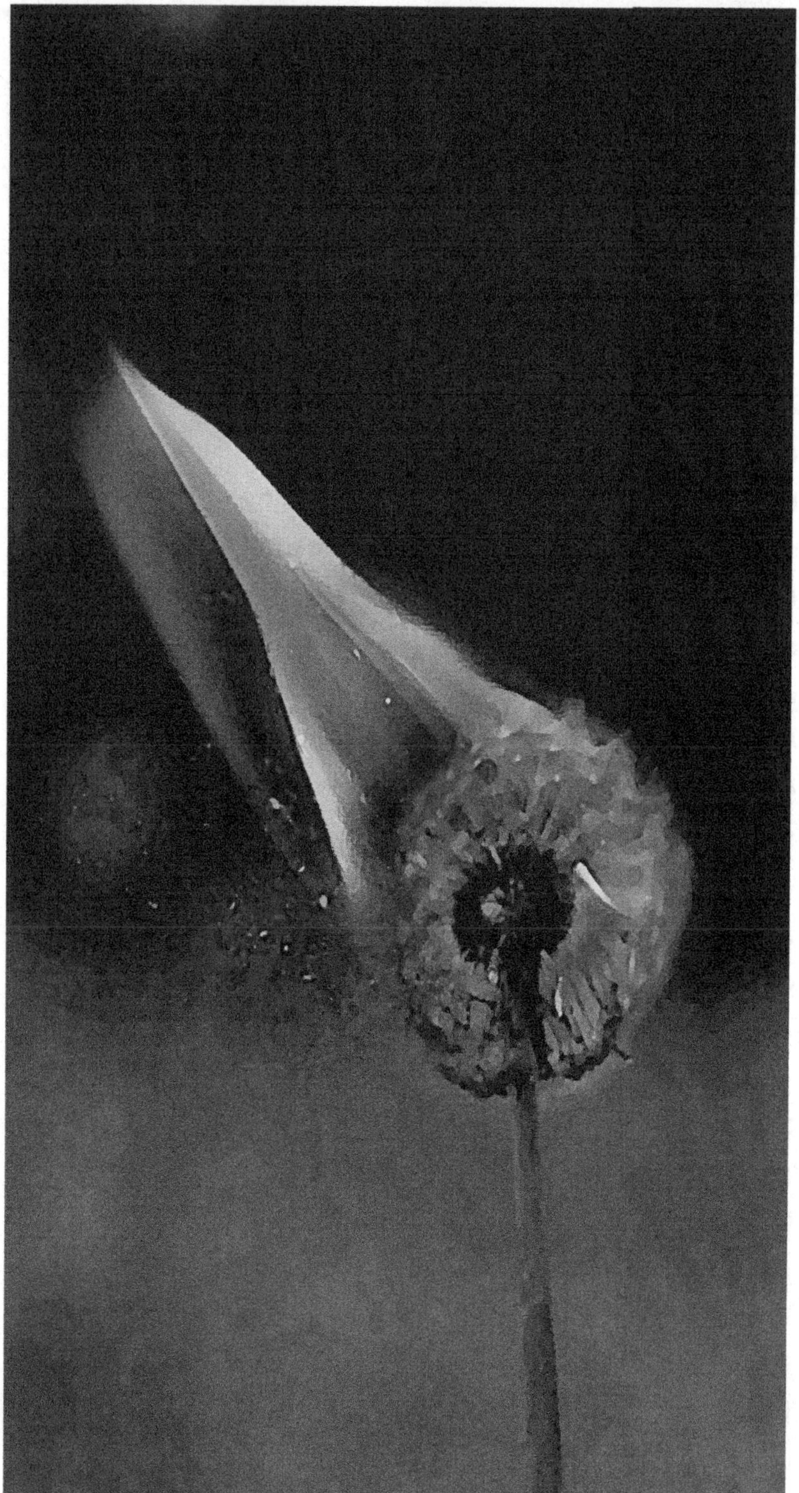

Previously, in The Apathetic Knight...

"Do you...understand, wife, the etiquette-ruled meaning of each of these gifts?" Cinder asked me, serious.

I hesitated, watching his eyes dart around the room, nervous.

He was actually nervous, afraid that he'd misunderstood my intent.

That in itself bolstered me with some confidence, and I smiled. "Of course, I do. Why do you think that I prepared those items, together, specifically?" I asked, hugging my fox pelt to my chest.

He startled, gaping at me in shock. "What...? So, then... your...'special gift'—?"

I then did something else with deep, deep-rooted meaning in the etiquette rules;

I turned, back facing him, and let my hair down, before pulling it over my shoulder, leaving my back clear.

He gasped, and as I glanced over my shoulder, I could see that I had completely stunned him.

He watched me with wide eyes.

"Crowned Princess—"

"You can just call me by name, your highness," I said, soft. "From now on...you don't have to be so formal and cold with me. You don't need to be so stiff."

"I...I don't know what..." he trailed off, looking a bit lost.

"Your highness..." I said, softly and as seductively as I could manage to do so. "Come to me."

He hesitated, at first, but then...

He took a tentative step toward me, and I felt his hands pause at the top of my gown's ties.

'Tell me, wife...before this even begins...are you positive that I do not misunderstand your meaning? Are you absolutely certain...that this is what you want?"

Kynareth & Cinder

I nodded. "I know it might sound silly, but I want more between us than the silence and avoiding one another...how can we possibly get through this marriage with any sanity, if we only sit together quietly when we are together? If we are to be married...shouldn't we be at least a bit closer?"

"Then...you actually care to grow closer to me...?" He asked, surprise in his tone.

I didn't know how to respond to that.

"I thought...I thought you hated me. You're afraid of me. You actually...want to be closer?"

I glanced at him again. "...Isn't that better than the alternative? Would you rather hate one another forever? I don't, nor have I ever hated you...Cinder," I whispered.

"You don't?" He asked, genuinely surprised.

"Really," I said. "Feared you, perhaps, and disliked you, yes, but I never hated you. We both had little choice in this. I just hated the circumstances. What about you?" I asked, needing to know. "Do you...still hate me?"

He paused, hesitating. "No," he said, finally. "I don't hate you. I don't necessarily like you, but I don't necessarily hate you anymore."

"Then, yes...I am sure about this. I don't want things to remain this awkward and stale and uncomfortable for us all our lives. Shouldn't we be on good terms? At the least, let's try?"

He trembled, nodding. "Let's try," he murmured, and began undoing the ties to the back of my gown. He gently pushed the material down before he set to untying my corset.

The moons in the sky outside of our bedchambers made a stunning backdrop as he undressed me.

"I do have...one request, your highness..."

"What is it?"

"Please...prince Cinder, I beg you...please do things properly with me this time. Don't hurt me. Don't just—"

As my shoulders became bare to him, he slowly leaned forward, pressing his lips to the skin of the junction where my shoulders and neck met, and my words fell off into thin air as I moaned.

I gasped, leaning back into him, and shutting my eyes.

He moaned softly in an approving manner, pushing my clothes the rest of the way down and leaving me in just my underwear.

He shucked off his shirt quickly, and I felt my body heat up even more.

Tingles ran down my body with the heat of his touches.

His fingers left fire in their wake as he raked his fingertips across my skin.

He turned me gently to face him, lifting my chin with his finger and gently pressing his lips to mine, even as he pulled my hair out of its bun and let it fall freely around me, like a veil.

I felt his tongue sweep against my lip and I opened myself to him, letting our tongues dance and mesh in a new, exciting dance I'd had yet to feel with him.

Then, oh, then...

Then, his mouth moved to my neck and shoulder, laving me with his tongue there, and I trembled...

Now, we continue....

Chapter 1

Kyeareth Ashland...

While he took his time kissing down to my neck, he undid the fastenings of his pants, and slowly became bare to just his underwear as well. I could make out the hard bulge where his...*extremity* was. I couldn't stop staring at it, both fearful and in anticipation.

"Do you like looking at my cock, Kyeareth?" He asked me in a chuckle, and my cheeks flamed.

The crude language was something I was unaccustomed to, but it heated me and did magical things to my insides...

Who knew I was such a dirty girl?

He slid his underwear down, the thing springing to life and bobbing before settling heavy between his muscled thighs before my eyes. I hadn't ever seen one this close, this intensely, and been able to really *study* it.

It was a fascinating specimen, in my mind.

I felt myself heating as I blushed, looking at the smooth curve of him, the smooth, swollen, almost helmet-like head.

He was long and thick in my eyes.

I would guess him to be around seven inches long? His thickness was a thick as two and a half of my fingers pushed side-by-side.

It was hard to wrap my hand around it as I experimented with touching it.

I tried to be gentle and gave a soft squeeze, and as a bead of fluid wept out of the head, he groaned.

I let go, startled and jumping back.

I looked up to see his eyes again, giving a timid nod and twiddling my thumbs. "I can...appreciate it for what it is," I whispered, glancing at it again. "It is...alive...and I want to look at it," I admitted. "I want to touch it..."

He leaned back with a chuckle, taking a good look at *me*. "You are beautiful...Kyeareth."

I felt my heart beat harder, and I blushed, taking in his physique.

He wasn't as muscular as Seryn, but he was a bit more built than my brother.

Though, he was admittedly several years older than we were, so of course, he'd be more built than us.

He had a good physical body, and you could tell that he was active and strong.

I had known that, during the tournament, Seryn had thrown the match for him, but they had been fairly closely matched, really.

Seryn was a year older than Cinder, and had been in combat much longer, so it made sense that he would actually be stronger.

The Crowned Prince had a beautiful body, with tan skin that was smooth.

I reached out, running my fingers along his abdominal muscles and he groaned, trembling.

When I let my fingers graze the velvety steel of his "cock," as he named it, a rush of heat began tumbling in my body when he hissed out a sharp breath.

"Princess..."

I gazed up at him, my cheeks burning, before he took my hand, leading me to the bed.

He lay me down, pressing kisses to my lips, my neck, my collarbone, and then down to my shoulders and chest.

"My Crowned Princess..." He murmured, heating me.

He gently undid the bindings around my chest, and I shivered when I became exposed to him.

He took me in with heated eyes, before he used his mouth on my flesh, massaging with his hand.

"If only you had been so gentle during the first night," I laughed softly, and he paused.

"I had thought that you wanted it to be over as quickly as possible...I should have prepared your body better, and hurting you hadn't actually been my intention, even if I hated you."

I smiled, pressing a kiss to his forehead. "I appreciate the thought of that," I said, soft.

He chuckled, returning to his touches and kisses, and I gasped when he reached my naval.

Soon enough, he had come to my lower regions, and I flinched as I remembered how much it had hurt before.

He undid my clothing there, and removed it, stroking lightly with a finger and lifting his finger for me to see the slickness of my hidden place gleaming in the light of the room.

I felt my cheeks heat up.

He grabbed my chin in one hand, and grinned at me as his other hand was held between us, showing me my own juices.

"You are already quite thoroughly prepared," he chuckled. "Just look how wet you already are for me," he said. "I think I should get you a little wetter, though," he said, thoughtful.

I cried out in surprise when his mouth and fingers were on me.

The lewd sounds that came from what he was doing...

The lewdness, the heat...combined with the airy cries my body released all on its own...

The things that he was doing to my body, and the way my body responded...

I didn't know what to do or how to act.

"How is it?" He murmured against me, the vibrations oozing through to my belly. "You like my tongue working in your pussy? Licking your clit and your hole?" He hmm'ed out against me, digging his face back in to feast, and I nearly came off the bed.

I felt his tongue flatten against me, and the area came to life.

I felt my body heating rapidly, building toward something that I didn't understand.

His lewd, filthy words were just spurring on the burning in my belly and privates.

"Am-am I alright?" I asked, panicked. "I-I feel tight, I feel like something is almost tickling me with a *pang*—"

"Shh," he whispered against me, putting himself back to work immediately, and finally, I gasped, thrashing as I fell over something.

All of that gathered tightness exploded, and I felt fluid gush around his fingers as he continued thrusting them in and out like a piston inside of me.

I cried out as he kept going, coaxing out more shots and streams of fluid and my cheeks flushed at my cries.

"Give me that come, *fuck*," he groaned against me.

I felt like I had just broken or something, but it felt so good.

It was hot, it trembled and pulsed, gushing...

He slurped and sucked, making me want to crawl off of the bed almost, but he finally finished, lifting a hand, and wiping his saturated mouth and lower face.

It was so...sexy.

Chapter 2

Kyeareth...

"How do you feel?" He asked.

It took me a good, long moment of silence to even comprehend his question, let alone find my voice to answer him.

"That...what...?" I asked, out of breath and overwhelmed.

He chuckled. "Your physical peak. I made you orgasm, or 'come.' It comes from physical stimulation and love making. It is the height of physical pleasure...you, my sweet, innocent little lion, are a gusher...and I am quite pleased."

"Oh," I whispered, in awe, not knowing what that meant. Were there women who weren't "gushers?" Did he have experience with other women? How many—

All my thoughts died as he brought my hand to his shaft, and I gaped as I unconsciously wrapped my hands around it, stunned by the heat and the thickness. It twitched and throbbed in my hold, and I studied it, before glancing up at him.

"What...what do I do?" I asked.

He threw his head back, letting out a shuddering, chuckling breath, before he looked at me again. "Touch me, put your mouth on me. I will show you along the way."

I gave a tentative nod, before I flicked out my tongue to taste him, the little bead of fluid coming out of the slit on the head.

It tasted a little salty, but not bad. We had been a bit sweaty from dancing, so it was to be expected, I guessed.

I opened my mouth, taking him into my mouth, and he hissed when one of my teeth grazed him.

He jumped, and I was afraid that I had messed up and hurt him or done something wrong. He gently stroked my hair.

"Watch the teeth. Gently…yes, good girl," he said when I used my lips to block my teeth. "Ah, *fuck*," he groaned, hips thrusting up a bit. I hmm'ed as I bobbed my head a bit, and he moaned and grunted softly in his thick tone as I worked him. He directed me once more. "Cup the sack beneath—*fuuuck*, **yes**," he drawled out as I cupped his sack below the shaft. "Good girl, such a good girl for me. That's where my seed comes from, so take good care to be good to it, alright?"

I cupped and squeezed the smooth sack lightly, fascinated by the two egg-like things inside even as I continued working with my mouth and tongue on him.

I felt his hands grip my hair, and I startled and gagged as he pushed my head down a bit.

"I need you to do something, okay? I need you to suck hard, and flatten your tongue. Just breath through your nose, and focus on breathing. I promise, I won't go too deep...I just always dreamed of...*this*," he said, and he gently thrust into my mouth.

He didn't go very deep, but I wasn't used to anything like this. It took work not to gag, fighting the reflex over and over again.

He finally gasped, before he pulled himself out of my mouth.

I gasped for air, struggling, but I felt

"If I don't stop, I will finish in your mouth and I don't want to do that to you...not *yet*." He put me on my back, crawling up me and positioned himself between my legs, and I clamped down, flinching and tensed.

I whimpered. "C-Cin—"

"*Shh*," he whispered. "Relax your body, or else you will feel pain. You *must* relax."

I took a few deep breaths, regaining my composure, before I gave a nod. "I'm alright..."

Gently, he pressed forward, and I found that...there was no pain.

I reached up for him with one hand as he leaned over me, and my legs raised to encase his waist.

I felt stretched and a little twinge of initial discomfort, but this was nothing compared to the first time.

He gasped when he was fully encased inside of my body, trembling and struggling to hold himself still.

He gave me a good minute to adjust, before I gave him my permission to move. *Slowly*, in and out, in and out...

It was...*good*. It was much better than it had been before.

I gasped out, noises beginning to escape from me even as they escaped from him.

"Fuck, *yes*," he said. "You feel so damn *good* wrapped around me, sweet girl, oh—yes, yes, *shit*!" He said. "Are you close? Please tell me that you are, because I won't be able to last long," he said desperately, shoving a hand between us to stroke over my nerve center rapidly.

"Ah, *Cinder*—" I gasped, feeling myself climbing up, up, *up* again.

"Your body seems to enjoy mine," he said. "You like me deep inside you, don't you? I can feel you flexing on my cock like a little vice," he grated out. "Let's see if I can make that tight little cunt of yours come for me again," he said, voice tight and strained, the gravelly tone sending me up all the higher.

It was so guttural and wanton that I wanted to hear that voice all the time. He grinned down at me, before picking up his pace, and it wasn't long before I was falling again. "Be a good girl, princess, come for your prince," he growled out. "I want you to come on my cock like a good girl," he groaned.

That did it. That brought me to that ultimate bliss.

I cried out and slapped my hips up to slam against his as I met him thrust for thrust, shuddering and spasming around his hot length.

He gasped sharply and let out a long, deep groan as I felt him swell and he let out a string of curses as he filled me up with himself.

The noises of our fluids slushing and mixing and slopping together was so lewd, it almost made me come again.

I felt warm, full, and sated...

This...this was what the first time should have been.

How had we waited this long?

I knew, right away, that I would never be the same again. I could never wait this long again; I could never go a long period of time without feeling this again. There was no way that I could.

I felt that my happiness was dependent on this feeling, and if I couldn't have Astaroth...I would just have to chase after it with Cinder.

When we were finished, we lay still as we took deep, thick breaths, and I heard him chuckle into the night air.

"Oh, heavens," he groaned, still inside of me. "Once will *never* be enough. I hope you understand and are prepared to take responsibility for what that means, 'wife,'" he said, glancing over at me.

I gave a soft, minimal smile, almost asleep already. "As long as you will, too," I murmured, before falling into a deep, restful slumber.

I heard him chuckle as he slipped out of me, bringing me into his side and grasping me.

Year's Fall, 314 AR

My stomach churned sickeningly; despite that I was so hungry.

We were at the Heaven's Gift Holiday feast with many of my favorite foods, celebrating with my family and the other highest nobles...and I looked down at my plate with disgust.

I was so hungry, but I just couldn't stomach it.

It had been around five weeks since that first night of passion with Cinder, and we'd had several instances of it occurring since then.

"Darling?" Cinder asked me, concerned.

My cheeks still burned with blushes to hear him call me endearments like that.

He had been calling me endearments like that when we were in front of others, ever since his birthday, and it had really increased our popularity among the nobles.

Unfortunately, rumors of what had happened at the tea party from before had spread, and I had accidentally really negatively impacted our social standing by admitting that to the noble ladies.

So now, we were trying to fix our relationship as well as our reputation...and honestly...

I actually kind of...enjoyed it.

Our time together was no longer always silent, either.

We still had a lot of quiet time, and he told me that it was because his days were filled with work and meetings and he enjoyed having the time to just sit and relax in the quiet peacefulness...

Still, we were beginning to open up to one another, just a little, and he was making much more of an effort. Things were starting to improve and feel better. The physical intimacy was, indeed, bringing us closer together.

Slowly, *marginally*, but still.

Now, he would initiate conversation with me. He would ask me things, and I would ask him things. We had learned several things about our likes and dislikes, things that we were afraid of, things that brought us joy and comfort...

I looked to the prince as he said my name, trying to get my attention. I vaguely remembering asking him to repeat himself, and he leaned closer to me, murmuring. "Are you feeling alright?"

"It's just...the *fish*," I whispered. "It *smells*..."

He startled, before taking a deep whiff, and then he gave me a confused expression before taking a bite of my food himself.

"It smells and tastes fine, Kyeareth," he whispered. "What's the matter? Are you feeling *sick*?"

"I haven't felt good today," I told him. "I feel...I feel bad..."

He looked concerned. "Please, go and get some rest, then, princess."

I stood, and I managed to get almost completely out of the banquet hall...I just couldn't, however, make it all the way out.

Of course.

"My lady!" Seryn sprang into action as he moved toward me when I suddenly collapsed.

"Kyeareth!" I heard several voices cry, and as I fell into the darkness, I saw my family appearing, blurrily, in my vision, worried expressions on their face.

When I came to sometime later, my family stood by my bedside, with many different, varying expressions.

The king looked overjoyed while the queen looked a little concerned.

My father looked a bit warily, cautiously happy, while mother looked on with a warm, tender smile.

My brother looked completely *shattered*, but his wife looked overjoyed and elated.

The second prince looked excited...my sister-in-law, the princess, was strangely...*absent*...That struck me as particularly odd, but I foolishly pushed that out of my mind.

Then, there was my husband.

Oh, my husband, who I had originally been so fearful and wary of. *Cinder*.

Cinder looked very emotional, with concern and worry, but hope and joy as well.

He had tears in his eyes, and his cheeks were flushed.

"W... what's going on?" I asked. "What happened?"

"You lost consciousness," the doctor said, walking over to us. "However, with lots of rest and good food, you should be just *fine*." He paused. "Your family has just received some very exciting news, and I think they're all wondering how *you'll* take it," he laughed.

"Take what...?" I asked, completely dazed.

"...*Darling*," Cinder said quietly, almost...*tenderly*. It was odd, how soft he spoke. He may have been growing more tender and gentler with me as of late, but he was never *that* gentle...

"What is going on?" I asked again, looking at Cinder.

He leaned forward, whispering the news into my ear. "You're carrying my heir, Crowned Princess," he said. "You are pregnant...darling. Is it alright, if I call you that?"

I felt my heart thump wildly as my emotions fluttered, tears filling my eyes. It took a moment for it to hit, but when it hit...it was like a wave of feeling overtook my being.

Pregnant. I was pregnant.

I was carrying our child inside of me, surely conceived on that fateful night that I'd given myself to him.

"Truly...?" I whispered, taking his hands in mine.

He beamed a smile at me, the first ever of its kind. My heart thumped wildly, mesmerized by his joy. I had never seen him with this expression, and it sent butterflies spiraling through my belly.

"Yes. You are carrying our child, my dear. We are now connected in a new way."

"Are you...happy?" I asked.

"Yes," he said, pulling my hand to his lips and kissing it. "Are you? Happy, I mean...about the news?"

Joy flooded through my heart, overwhelming me.

"Yes," I smiled at him. He kneeled at my side, wrapping his arms around my body, and pressing his face to my torso.

I didn't feel prepared or ready, but...

Just to know that something so wonderful, so beautiful, was happening inside of my body...it was so much to take in.

I was terrified, but so, so happy.

I might not be sure how things would turn out between me and Cinder, but this child wouldn't be just his.

They would rely on me, need me...love me.

They would be my—*our*—child.

"A baby," I whispered, resting my hand over my belly. "*We* will have a baby. And yes," I said, whispering into his ear. "You can call me endearments. We must grow even closer...for the baby."

He rested his forehead against mine. "Mmhmm," he murmured, a pleased sound. A gentle, warm smile spread on his lips, and I felt my heart throb.

Kynareth & Cinder

We were going to be parents...

"Well, I for one am absolutely *thrilled* at this news!" The king said, excited.

I was excited, but I was also a bit shaken. I just...was timid to hope.

"Be careful though, princess," the doctor warned, and we turned our attention back to him. "You need to be absolutely careful not to be stressed or strained. If you become too upset or stressed, it could cause serious problems with the baby."

"She won't be having to worry about that," Cinder said, firm. "I will be putting some of the load of my work onto you," he said, looking to the second prince. "I am sure you understand that."

The second prince just smiled. "I understand, brother, you can count on me,"

My husband lay his head, gently, on my abdomen, humming a sweet tune. Perhaps, maybe, I could build on that tune to create a lullaby, in honor of our child.

Our very own little prince or princess, conceived of the tenderly and slowly budding friendship between Cinder and I that we had freshly began cultivating together. Even as I thought that, I felt guilt and pain build in my heart. I knew that Astaroth was upset. I was, too...

I had to come to grasp reality, though.

This was my reality...and the reality was, I was going to be a mother.

The mother of a prince or princess.

Chapter 3

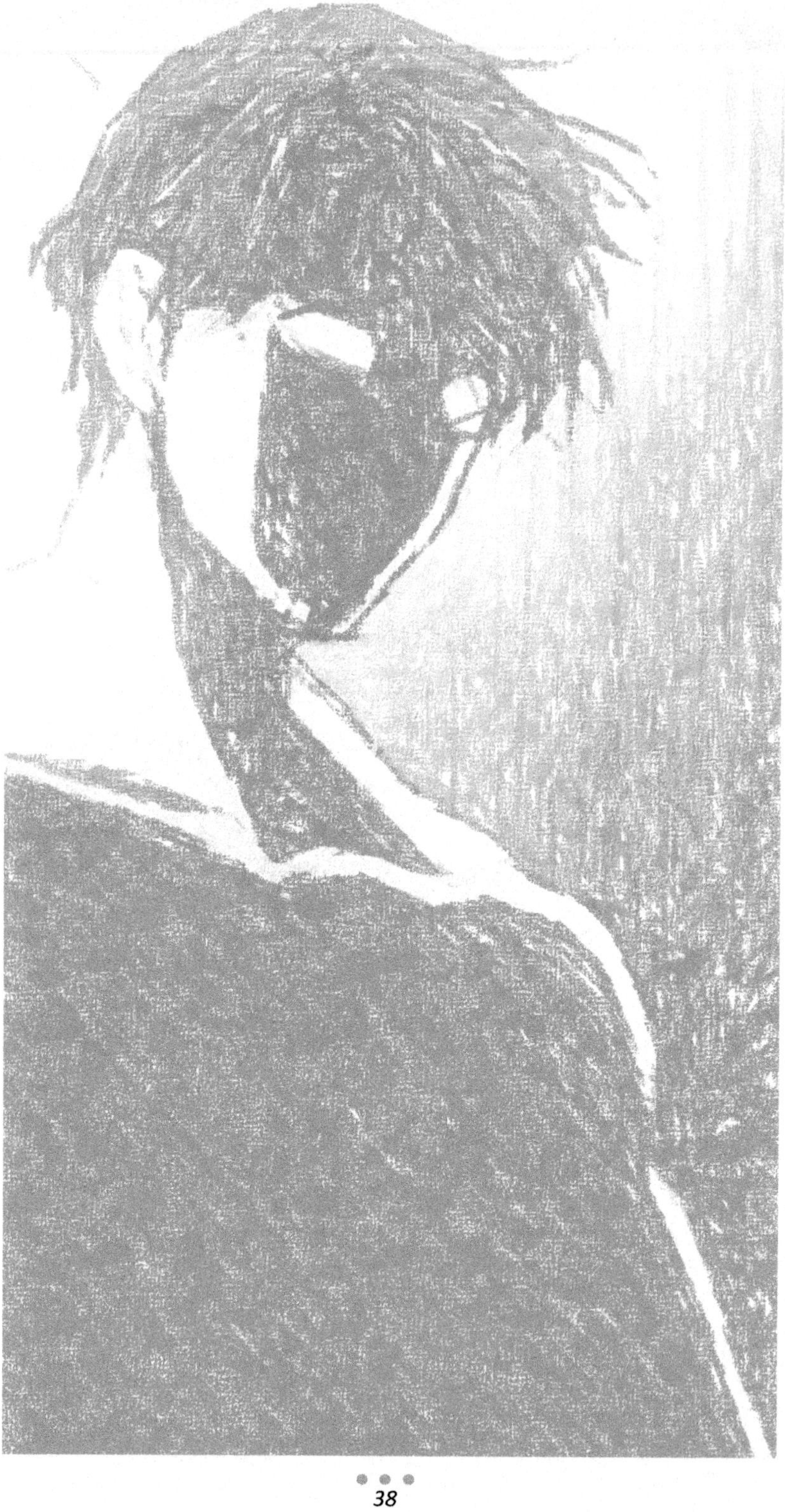

Cinder Ashland...

Seed's Sewn, 315 Ashland Rule

I was cuddling her, kissing her.

I was taking in the changing shape of her body and pressing kisses to her shoulders.

I wanted to make love to her.

I wanted to be in her body, almost more than I wanted anything else. How had I come to depend on this so much?

Was I a wild beast?

Still, I tried to focus and calm myself

I was stroking her swelling belly.

Cinder & Kynareth

She groaned. "Aww, please...stop," she said, sounding distressed. "My body is so gross..."

"No, it isn't," I tried to assure her. "You are just growing a new life within you, and it is perfectly natural."

"But I feel horrible," she said, sighing.

She'd had quite a bit of morning sickness, and was just now able to keep down food.

She had been so miserable with herself that she would hardly let me touch her, let alone make love to her.

She was finally starting to feel somewhat better, though, and I hoped to use that to my advantage.

"Darling," I said, my tone a bit whiny. "I...I want you," I said.

She looked up at me. "...R-really...?"

I licked along her collarbone, and she gasped and threw her head back.

This...this was the closest I had gotten to having her intimately since the doctor had told us about the pregnancy!

"Please...?" I murmured, sucking her earlobe into his mouth.

She moaned, weaving her fingers over the back of my neck and upward into my hair, gripping the strands.

"Please...let me have you. I cannot bear to go any longer without being encased my you, having you wrapped over my cock like the sheath on my sword," I murmured. "Please, darling."

"...You really...don't think my body is disgusting...?" She asked, her voice tiny and small.

"Of course, I don't," I said, kissing her jaw. "You are beautiful, and your body is filled with my essence. You are the most stunning, powerful woman in my heart. You are growing the life my seed supplanted into your womb," I told her.

She trembled. "C-Cinder...oh..." She moaned as I sucked hard on her shoulder.

"What?" I asked.

"Pl-please. Please," she gasped. "G-give it to me, please...I need it," she squeezed my hair.

I made short work of her nightgown, my mouth on her breasts and kissing over her rounding torso.

I kneeled in front of her.

I dipped my tongue in her belly button, and swirled my tongue over her belly until I reached her center.

I worked my fingers, massaging her legs, knees, thighs...before I spread her pussy lips and delved into her.

She gasped, throwing her head back, and quickly took to the bed for support.

It only took just over a minute, before she was gasping out and crying in abandon as her hips thrust forward, pressing her pussy into me and she was squirting all over my face.

I drank it all, not letting a single drop escape, before I lay her back on the bed, at the very end.

I maneuvered her onto her knees, haphazardly covering her with a blanket and pushing it up so that I could reach her center, pressing the tip of my cock to her sweet, tight little hole from behind.

I did this because she immediately threw a tantrum as I tried to have her the usual way, so I opted for this position.

I obliged, all too happily.

In fact, I loved this position.

The view was nice, as an added bonus.

She was tighter and hotter than I remembered, and even wetter than usual.

I thrust gently, and she gasped as her toes curled. I loved the feel of her beneath me, on her knees, taking my cock into her warm, wanton little body.

"It has been so long since I felt you around me," I murmured.

"It's been too long since I felt you inside of me," she gasped. "S-so good! Good heavens, so good! So good!"

She gasped as I rolled my hips, stirring myself within her.

"Yes, darling," I murmured.

I felt her flutter over me, and after a few more minutes, I felt her throb and pulse and she cried out as she squeezed over me, crying out as she came.

That was it. That was all I could handle.

I groaned, leaning over, and kissing her deeply as I spurted out my release into her waiting body.

"Fuck, yes, darling," I whispered, kissing her. "So good."

"Cinder," she gasped. "Cinder..."

"Yes," I kissed her.

"Cinder," she whispered, her pussy still fluttering over me.

"Kyeareth," I murmured, sucking her bottom lip into my mouth, and nibbling it.

I thrusted again, softly, and her gasping moans spurred me to keep going.

I gradually started to get stiff again, and I made love to her all over.

Veras's End, 315 AR

It was at the six-month mark, back in Veras's Height, that we told the kingdom about the pregnancy.

That was a cautionary detail, to ensure that the baby was well-developed and safely out of the most dangerous period of the pregnancy, before anyone found out about it. Now, during the seventh month, Kyeareth began to nest a lot.

The doctor said that it was natural, like a mother bird, building a nest for the arrival of her eggs. She was much like a bird these days, as I often found her in the gardens or on her terrace, humming a beautiful and familiar tune. The first time I had heard it, when she had been just coming out of the first trimester,

she had been knitting as she sang the tune aloud, no words, just the melody itself in her voice.

She was a beautiful singer, with an angelic, airy, soothing voice that I had quickly grown to love hearing.

It was still strange for me to admit that to myself. Over the last several months, I had made much more of an effort. She was to be the mother of my child, so it was a necessary thing.

I listened to the tune, taking it in.

I had known the tune, remembering humming it against her belly several times, and I had chuckled at how she had taken it and made it her own.

Now, she had even added words, and it was a song of praise and beauty and blessing upon our child.

It did odd, warm, tingly things to my belly to hear her praising the child that I had cultivated inside of her body. It made me feel things to know that she was happy with the idea of having a child from the both of us.

Things may not have been as bad as I had initially thought, in the beginning...

Our relationship had changed a lot, thanks to her initiative at my last birthday, and especially since we were now expecting parents. We were doing better now, as we began to take walks together and rest together, discussing our futures and imagining life with a baby.

Since the night that she had given herself over to me, I had made an effort to try to be a bit friendlier to her, and to actually open my heart to her. Now, it wasn't strained or awkward, not forced, not pushed.

We felt...natural.

Even in our silences, it felt so natural to be together and just hold hands and be close.

I had gone from hating her outright, to strongly disliking her and avoiding her.

Now, I no longer strongly disliked her, either.

In fact, I didn't dislike her at all, anymore...

It was very odd, indeed.

She was a sweet girl, kind and giving.

Since her sister-in-law's tea party, she had been receiving a few invitations to events here and there, as an obligation, but she hadn't attended many.

The first that she'd attended after that tea party, there had been an incident where someone "accidentally" spilled some tea on her lap.

Seryn had made quite a scene over it, and informed me as soon as they had returned.

After I had filed a formal complaint and revoked the girl's father's title, people had been avoiding inviting her—or insisted in their invitations that she didn't have any obligation to attend—and so, she hadn't been to many events since.

However, the moment that we had announced the pregnancy to the public, that had changed, drastically.

Getting on her good side meant getting on the good side of the future king, and so, everyone wanted to become her best friend.

In good spirits and trying to make a good impression, she made a great effort in the city and in charity events, banquets, tea parties and the like.

She had even hosted several, now, as the Crowned Princess.

The first had been awkward and uncomfortable, but with my help and assigning the maids and chamberlain to help her plan and make everything grand, they got better. As her husband, I had made it my job to be sure that I sent the invitations to all of the appropriately aged and ranked ladies, ladies in other arranged marriages to other noblemen…

I found her friends and connections and was sure that everything worked seamlessly for her.

I made sure that her brother was welcomed and that his letters found their way to her safely.

I made sure that she was able to enjoy her visits with him when he came to visit, though

I felt the need to look after them both by telling him that he frequented our palace and sent letters too often.

She was upholding her duties as my wife well, and the people liked her. In the process, she was showing me that she was taking this position seriously, and that she loved this nation as well.

I could see her being a good queen, and I hadn't been able to before. She had grown and matured a lot in the last several months, with impending motherhood leading her down a stronger, wiser mindset.

I could see myself ruling this nation with this woman at my side, helping me...and that was the most important thing.

I was beginning to cherish her.

She would soon give birth to our child, brought to us through this new love that was beginning to blossom.

When had I even started thinking of this tingly sensation as love?

I didn't, originally, actually *want* to love her.

I had really *wanted* to dislike her...but I *couldn't* dislike her.

Not anymore.

I couldn't say that I really *liked* her, but I didn't *dislike* her anymore. I felt all muddled and confused, not really knowing where to turn in my mind.

I tried not to think about it too much.

I wondered what the child would look like; *would he or she have my raven locks of hair?*

Or would they have her beautiful, platinum, wheat-shaded mane? Would he or she have my piercing, golden-green eyes, or their mother's soothing, clear-blueish-gray eyes?

Would he or she have her dimples? My thick lips? Her cute nose?

It drove me mad wondering. I could hardly contain myself.

Chapter 4

Cinder...

Solaris's Gifts, 315 Ashland Rule

It was the twenty-third day of the month that we held the baby shower for Kyeareth.

The day happened to be the day of Morning's Stars. My mother-in-law and my sister had planned everything.

I was initially wary of my sister planning the event, but she had come to me saying that she had been jealous of my wife, but wanted to show her sincerity and start over with her now that she was to be an aunt.

She had *seemed* sincere, and all of her arrangements and planning checked out with our safety team. Kyeareth and I enjoyed a wonderful meal with everyone—which had been tasted and checked for poisons, so we hadn't suspected anything...

We all gathered and listened to her sing her completed lullaby as she held her hands over her belly affectionately, eyes closed and smile in place.

We cheered and congratulated her, giving thanks and blessings to our baby inside of her.

All was going so exceptionally well...

Though...that was always when tragedy seemed to strike the hardest.

It was shortly after the opening of gifts that Kyeareth began to complain of cramps. It grew to be severe cramping, so badly that she was struggling to breathe.

Fear had plagued me, watching her suffer and not knowing what was happening. I was agonized over her pain, fearing for my child inside of her. What was going on?

The doctor arrived just as she began to scream, doubling over in pain, and we rushed her to the medical room, panicked and afraid.

I was confused.

If this was labor, she was still almost a month early!

She wasn't due until the latter half of Solaris's Reign, after her birthday...

I got behind her on the bed, letting her lean back against me. Seryn was on one side and, somehow, her brother was on the other, sobbing and crying as he listened to her agonized screams and telling her she'd be alright.

His wife had been in attendance, I remembered in my mind.

Had his wife done this? I knew that she wasn't fond of Kyeareth. Had his wife...done what?

I didn't even know *what* was happening, but I was already looking for someone, somewhere, to put the blame onto, because *this wasn't natural*. It now no longer seemed like labor.

The doctor said that the pains and signs didn't indicate a normal labor.

Something else was at work here, but what?

The doctor had a grave look on his face, not wanting to say anything until his suspicions were confirmed, I guessed.

The men had been enjoying cigars and brandy in another area of the palace while myself and all of the ladies had been opening gifts, and I hadn't suspected anything to be out of place or out of order.

When had this happened? What had happened?

The others waited outside of the room, pacing and worried, confused...

She began to push, gasping for air and crying, blood going everywhere.

The doctor, startled, began giving her direction and jumping into action, prepping the nurses to help us with delivery.

Was my child actually being born right now?

Perhaps this was just a very early delivery, and nothing was actually wrong? I hoped, against all odds, that everything was actually okay...

Soon, the doctor was reaching to her center, pulling out a small, limp, *lifeless* body.

I froze, my blood running cold.

No cries. No wails...Not even a whimper.

Please, *please*, **please**, I begged in my mind.

A few moments passed in silence, staring at the lifeless little body in the doctor's hold even as he waited with baited breath for a moment.

We were too frozen to react.

The baby was purple and stiff, *cold*...Dead for a good bit of time, it seemed. Kyeareth groaned incoherently, and we finally breathed again, life coming back into the room.

The doctor examined the child, his face almost blue with the loss of blood, but he gave a solemn, negative shake of his head.

"C-can I see my baby?" Kyeareth asked, eyes closed...still not aware of what was happening.

Fearful pain speared me, gutting me like a pig.

How would she handle this?

She was already so fragile. So young, so tender. She was so sweet, so caring and loving.

She had already been so attached to our baby...

What was I supposed to do now? It had taken her *so long* to open up to me to begin with, it had taken *us* so long to reach this point.

Could I even help her through this?

Would she trust me? Would she even *try* to look to me for strength? Would she even *think* that she could lean on me at all?

We had only *just* started to let love in, giving it room in our space together, *just* started to grow a bond of a romantic nature.

Could she bring herself to face me after this?

What if she didn't? Would I have to divorce her and subject myself to growing love with another woman? Would I even be able to?

On the other hand, what if she *did*? Would we be able to get back in a good, decent place and have more children?

Would she be able to handle that? Would she look to me to help her through this tragedy?

Was I even strong enough for that...? My child was dead...

The doctor glanced up at me, and clenching my eyes tight for a moment, I sobbed, but I gave a nod.

I saw Kyeareth look back and up at me.

"What's wrong, Cinder?" She asked. "Is the baby too beautiful for you?" She laughed in a joke.

"Sister..." Astaroth whispered, clutching her hand tighter.

She heard the sad, serious tone of his voice and sat up a bit, opening her eyes as the doctor handed her the freshly cleaned, lifeless body of our child, wrapped in a blue blanket...

We had a son.

We would have had a *son*.

On his head were his mother's thick, light blonde tufts of hair...and *that was all we would ever know about him.*

She went still, unmoving, as the truth began to hit her.

I could see the blood drain from her face, see the light fade from her eyes, see her happiness *shatter* into a million pieces.

It was written all over her face.

Her body was rigid.

"Kyeareth..." I whispered; my voice thick. "Darling—"

Stunning me into silence, she opened the boy's mouth and began to blow desperately into his body, before using two fingers to press his belly.

Kyrareth & Asfaloth

    She repeated the process, again and again, begging the heavens to return her boy.

    She was trying to revive him...

    Tears blurred my vision, watching as she worked over him.

    It wasn't until after five entire minutes of this, without a single change, that I had to end it.

"Kyeareth, darling, *stop*...please. It is over. He is *gone*," I told her. "It's too late..." I wrapped my arms around her, placing a kiss to her temple. "There is *nothing* we can do."

A sad, heart-wrenched wail slowly crept out of her chest as she took our son in her arms, hugging to her in a tender but frantic hold that splintered my heart.

"My...my *baby*," she choked out, struggling to breathe.

Tears stung my eyes. Just that frail, pitiful, broken sound from her was enough to break whatever was left of my splintered heart.

"*Our* baby," I whispered in her ear. I looked up at the doctor. "I want an explanation."

"Sire, from...from the coloring of the infant, his current state...she had been feeling fine and the baby had been very active this morning...the cramps began over an hour ago, just after the meal..." He paused. He looked up at me. "The *meal*," he repeated, eyes wide.

"*Poison?*" I whispered, confused. "But the taste-testers—there were no ill effects! Even I feel just fine!" I said, upset. "What—"

"Perhaps not *poison*, but *rather*..." He met my eyes, and I took me a moment...and then, I realized that I knew what he meant.

He was being careful of his words, knowing that he could cause her to snap.

She was still stiff and crying.

From the looks of things, however, evidence pointed to abortion medicine.

I glared at Seryn. "My *sister* and your mother were the ones in charge of the entire baby shower. Send someone to bring in Duke and Duchess Severing, but first...bring me my sister. *Now*." I ordered, and wordlessly, he set out to do my bidding.

Astaroth stood, going to cry softly in the corner. I wanted to join him...but I had more important things...I wrapped my arms around my wife, adding an extra set of arms to the hug that held our son.

"What shall we name him?" I asked her, and she flinched. "He *deserves* a name. He is the prince, and our son. What shall we call him?"

She gazed upon the child before the name tumbled from between her lips, and I froze.

"*Asfaloth*," she whispered. "I had...intended to give a son a similar name to Astaroth...in honor of our sibling bond...if the boy looked like *me*."

Astaroth fell to his knees in the corner, clutching the wall desperately as he sobbed, begging the heavens to have mercy upon his sister and nephew and brother.

I was almost flattered to be in his prayers, even though I knew of his odd affections for my wife, his own twin.

His sobs were gut-wrenching, harsh, and guttural.

He gasped, struggling to even get the cries out as he almost choked on them, the force of his sobs so heavy. It was an extraordinary honor to have a child named in your namesake. He was being so highly honored by his sister.

I didn't resent the name.

After all, the two being twins, they held a special bond to one another, and I knew that he was my wife's first love.

I could live with that.

Since the baby looked like her, it was sort of a funny joke, almost, to name him similarly to his uncle, who he would also look like. I wasn't offended. I just hadn't been anticipating it.

"*Asfaloth Blaze Renard Ashland*," I deemed him, and Kyeareth began to tremble and cry, pressing kisses desperately into the baby's hair and cheeks, almost as if it could bring him back to life.

I wished that it could.

The door flew open to Seryn, holding my sister by her wrist, and he slung her at us. "I apologize for the intrusion...but I felt that you deserved to know of this treason."

"*I didn't do anything!*" My sister cried, holding her arm. "*You* will die for this!"

"Tell me the truth," I ordered Seryn. He nodded.

"She consorted with a knight at the Severing duchy, who obtained abortion medication, and paid a maid to slip it into the *entire* feast."

"W...what...?" I asked, gaping at him. "What are you talking about? What are you saying?"

"It gets worse."

"How could it get *worse*?"

"...The maid was found dead, bled out through biting her tongue, in her quarters. The knight also killed himself this morning. A dagger to the throat, at an angle that determined it was self-inflicted. What do you want me to do, your highness?" He asked, snarling down at my sister even as she continued to plead her innocence.

Anger ripped through my body, and I struggled to contain myself. "Get my father."

Solaris's Reign, 315 AR

It had been a month since that fateful day...

The day that my son had been born, dead.

When my father had come in, we told him what had happened and gave all the evidence, and we found out that *Kyeareth* had *not* been the *only* one to lose a child that day, in fact.

One other noble, the wife of a count, had lost *her* baby as well, in almost the exact same fashion as my wife.

The poor mother had filed a formal complaint against the royal family for the abrupt, violent, and unexpected ending to her pregnancy, which had led to her husband wishing to divorce her...

Before the truth had been revealed that it had been a successful assassination attempt on the new prince's life.

It seemed that it was, indeed, the truth, and my sister didn't even try to deny it.

Thankfully, my mother-in-law had been completely unaware of my sister's actions, and cried when she found out what had happened.

My sister was the one whom was guilty.

She even wrote a formal apology to the lady had filed the complaint...confirming her guilt.

My sister was imprisoned and our father, even now, was still mulling over whether or not to have her executed.

It would have helped if Kyeareth had an opinion...

The first night after his death, while his body had been prepared, she had been completely inconsolable.

I didn't know how to approach her in this situation. However, since the stillbirth of our son, she had hardly left his graveside.

She even stayed at the grave at night.

We'd had a large funeral in his honor, and he had been buried in the garden right behind the palace, among Kyeareth's favorite flowers.

It was only a temporary place, while a formal mausoleum was being built in his honor, but it felt better to at least give him a proper burial, since he was a prince.

Since that day, things had spiraled out of control for my wife, and I had no idea what to do about it.

Where did we go from here?

I watched, in lonely agony, as my wife sat by the headstone all day each day, with no expression on her face.

She wouldn't speak. She wouldn't eat.

She wouldn't sleep until she literally passed out from exhaustion, and then she would continue her vigil over his resting place the moment she had awoken.

Even in the rain, she sat by the grave. She literally only left to relieve herself, before stumbling back out to the grave.

I'd had a beautiful mausoleum built for our son, but I couldn't even move his remains because she wouldn't leave the graveside.

I needed to at least get her out of the rain.

Seryn stayed at *her* side, a silent vigil over her at all times, bags under his eyes from the lack of sleep...but he wasn't willing to leave her.

I had to admit that I respected his loyalty and dedication to his mistress. She hardly could stand for me to be around her.

All she saw when she saw me was our dead child, I supposed.

I knew that he was just as agonized as the rest of us, *horrified* that he'd been unable to save the baby, and thus save his liege.

He had taste-tested the food she had eaten, but because *he* wasn't pregnant and because he wasn't the *target*, he had been unaffected.

The abortion medication was flavorless and scentless, thus undetectable.

I could certainly understand why Kyeareth didn't want to eat anything...she was *traumatized*.

The only ones at fault were the ones who had set this into motion.

I hadn't even seen my sister since that day. I hadn't been able to look at her.

I hadn't been willing to.

All I wanted to do was kill her.

It was an early morning, when I startled awake from the recurring nightmare of my child's death, and I washed my face and hands before I turned to my shadow guard as he swept silently into my room.

"Is she in her chambers?" I asked, and he kneeled, shaking his head.

"No, sire. She is by the grave."

I sighed, exasperated. "Of *course*, she is. I don't know why I even *bother* asking, the answer never changes unless she's relieving herself. What time is it?"

"Still before dawn."

I glanced out the window, my window overlooking the garden where our son was buried and she was, indeed, sitting out beside the headstone.

Thankfully, a coat made of a lion's pelt rested over her shoulders to keep her warm...but a navy-blue, knitted baby blanket was clutched in her hands.

She wouldn't even let go of it.

I sighed. "Has she *still* not eaten of her own will?"

"No, sire."

I thought again of what the physician had recommended, after the first entire week had passed after the tragedy and she'd refused to eat...

I had been desperate, begging for an answer, when he'd given me a horrible, *foul-feeling* "solution" that didn't feel like a solution.

Now, however, she was starting to seriously drop weight. She was starting to randomly pass out from starvation.

She was, slowly but surely, killing herself.

"How long has it been since she was *forced* to eat?" I asked. "I hate to resort to that method, but I...I can't lose her."

He glanced up at me, "Four days, your highness."

Pain speared me. We really tried not to do that if we didn't have to.

What was I supposed to do?

"Have Seryn force it again," I said, strained. "She *must* eat."

He nodded. "I shall do as you command, sire."

I turned. "I don't know what to do for her, Maxus..."

"Sire?"

I glanced at him again. "What can I do for her? This has *shattered* her, understandably. And now, I am even frightened at the prospect of even being intimate with her again. I am frightened to get her pregnant again. Maxus, we had only *just* started to let ourselves get closer."

"Your highness..." He murmured.

"We were just starting to let go of our discomfort for one another. We were so... nervous, to grow together, grow as a new family. And honestly, I'm just as fucking shattered as *she* is! So, how do I....how *could* I possibly help this poor girl?"

He hesitated for a long, still moment. "I don't know what to say, sire," he said, soft. "Perhaps she just needs some time to return to a healthier state," he comforted me. "I am sure, by the time your coronation arrives, she will be in better condition."

I would be turning twenty this year, in three more months.

That meant that in just over a year, I would be crowned king, upon my twenty-first birthday.

"I hope so. It has already been a month, and she has hardly moved from her spot. It is like she isn't capable of normal function ability anymore."

"Excuse me, your highness," a maid said, coming in. "Your guard outside told me you were already awake."

I sighed heavily, turning my attention to her. "Yes, come in," I motioned her, and she stepped inside.

"Your father has requested for you, your highness."

I sighed again, but I pulled on a house coat and some slippers, before I made my way to my father's office.

He stood there, back facing me as he watched a painter working.

I didn't pay any heed to what was being painted.

"Is her condition still the same?" Father asked me as I arrived to his office. He didn't look at me. He knew that I was still testy, lately. The last that he had looked at me, he had commented on my ragged appearance and I had practically snapped his head off. I didn't blame him for not wanting to look at me.

I gave a nod. "It is."

"I see." He considered this. "I hope that time will heal her," he said sadly. "This is a terrible tragedy that has taken place, and I am still conflicted on how to handle this." He glanced at me before looking away again. "What do *you* wish to do, Cinder?"

I sighed. "Let me speak to her," I said. "I want to talk to Ember myself, and find out *why* it was that she did this. She was the one who took my child from me."

My father gave a nod. "She still hasn't told the interrogators anything, but she has been asking for you since the tragedy happened. Maybe, perhaps she may speak to you." He turned to face me completely, and I could see how tired his eyes were, in that moment.

"I just...don't know anything anymore...."

"You have no idea, my sorrow for you both," he said. "I know how excited you had both been. Surrow," he addressed the painter.

The painter stood and gave a bow, before he turned his painting to me, and I felt the wind knocked out of me.

It was a portrait of a boy, with my wife's hair, arms wide in a shower of falling flower petals, eyes closed, a peaceful smile on his face. He looked to be about five years old.

A brilliant light shined from his back, almost in the shape of wings.

*It was a **stunning** painting, but it hurt me so just to look at it.*

"What is this?" I asked in a choked voice.

"Forgive me for being so presumptuous, your highness," the painter said, bowing. "Your father asked for me to paint an angel...*your* angel."

I glanced at my father, and his eyes were full of tears.

"Please forgive me for this," he said. "But I wished to gift it to you. I thought...perhaps *she* would like it."

I nodded. "She may, though I have no idea when I will be brave enough to allow it to be gifted to her, herself. There is no way that she is in any condition to receive such a gift at this time. It would destroy her. I am sure that you can understand...However, I will give you permission. Just wait until the right time."

He smiled. "Thank you for granting permission."

I looked away, giving a sigh before I turned to walk out of the room without another word.

I needed to speak to my sister.

I had never hated her before, I had always gotten frustrated with her easily because she was haughty and so, so clingy to me and to our other brother.

Now, I had to wonder how I would feel when I looked into the eyes of my baby sister...my son's murderer.

• • •

Chapter 5

Cinder...

"I was starting to think I would never see you again."

Her haughty tone made me immediately want to kill her. "If you tell me why you did this, I may agree to grant you a *quick* death. If you don't, I will make it as drawn out and painful as possible, even if I have to have father imprisoned to get it accomplished."

She scoffed. "You're *that* angry over a child you didn't even know, with a girl you don't even love?" She laughed, but she cried out and gaped up at me in stunned shock when I backhanded her. "You...*you*—"

"Did you think that I *wouldn't*?" I asked, snarling, "That was not just '*a child*,' it was *my* child...and I *did* know him. I knew him for *eight months* as he grew within his mother. And I may not be in love with my wife, but we were finally getting onto good terms together! You have ruined everything I had worked so hard to gain. So, tell me, '*sister*,' why would you do this?"

"*She* shouldn't have *been* your bride. Everyone knows that even the knights of her home duchy weren't fond of her. It was the knight who approached me."

I paused. "What...?"

"I—"

"A knight approached you? You are sure? It was a knight from the Severing Duchy?"

"Yes, yes!" She said, thinking she was convincing me that it wasn't really her fault. "He came to me, confiding in me and informing me of her inferior and dirty Mage-Born mother and the truth behind the twins. They were born of a glorified *concubine*, which is against the law in our country!" She shouted. "She wasn't born from the legal duchess, and thus she is an illegitimate girl with a name she wasn't truly born for!"

I hesitated. "So, because the duchess was unable to have children and *our* father *ordered* for Duke Severing to marry a lady from another nation to produce an heir, then had him divorce the woman and compensate her once she had birthed him the twins, you decided to kill *my legal, fully legitimate* heir?" I asked, and she startled.

"*What?*" She asked.

"You didn't even *know* the *full* truth, did you? You knew a *half-truth* from a knight who was discriminatory toward his former lady." I scoffed.

"But the duchess has a child now—"

"She didn't get pregnant until the twins were *eleven years old*!" I shouted at her, and she flinched. "If he had waited eleven more years for an heir, he would not have been able to keep the duke's seat in the first place, you *fool*. Father knew that, and commanded him to marry a foreign lady who would be outside of our legalities in the first place."

"But—"

"Father legalized it, so even though the twins were not born from the duchess, they were still born *in marriage* and thus legitimacy *is* in their blood. Half Mage-Born or not!"

"What?! But—"

"The knights of the Severing Duchy are partial to the *duchess*, strongly favoring her, and they *hated* the twins...especially the girl, who was just seen as an extra, unwanted child who couldn't and wouldn't even become the heir."

She gaped at me. "But that knight—"

"Was completely biased and had a grudge, and convinced you to commit *treason*. He used you! He knew that you are a prideful princess, and that you wouldn't wish to stain our family with the blood of illegitimacy. But he only fed you half-truths that he knew that you, at your young age, would be too ignorant to look into. *You* killed *your nephew* for such an absurd reason. I hope you're proud of yourself. I have already decided, to comfort and bring peace to my bride, as my son's mother, to get justice for our murdered son and have you executed...but since you were honest with me, and since you were ignorant and lied to, I'll see if I can convince my bride of a lesser sentence...but in the end, your method of demise is up to her. I remove my hands of you."

I turned, striding out of the prison as she screamed and cried, and I glanced to the guards of the prison.

"Inform my father that she fully answered my questions, and that I am demanding a public execution by whatever method my bride chooses."

• • •

The guards startled, but one bowed and rushed off to do my bidding as I made my way through the halls and out to the gardens.

I found Seryn there with her, still by the grave, and he had her pinned to a chair, forcing food into her mouth and closing her nose and mouth off as he forced her to chew and swallow to be allowed to take breaths.

I cringed, but the pained look on Seryn's face reminded me that this had been an order from me, and that this was necessary.

I stepped over to them, looking at her as she glared up at me with eyes burning with rage even as they filled with tears. She was practically snarling at me with her mouth full.

"I don't *want* to force this," I told her. "But I already lost my son. I will not lose his mother, too." I sighed. "My sister finally told me the truth. She told me why she did it," I told her.

Her body flinched, and she stood on shaky legs, shoving Seryn away, startling us both.

"Why?" She croaked.

For the first time since our son had been born, I saw real emotion stirring in her eyes. Not sorrow or anger, but true confusion and fear over the answer to this question. This was the first time in *weeks* that I had seen her stand on her own feet...the first words I'd heard from her lips. I knew, in that moment, that I *did* love her. It hit me with a sudden sick, devastating realization.

It was heavy in my heart.

I might not be *in love* with her, I couldn't admit *that* yet...but I cared about her, *I had grown to be moved by her.*

I could no longer say I disliked her, nor could I say I only somewhat liked her.

Watching her wither away the last month had done more emotional damage on me than perhaps I had originally thought...

Even as joy flew through my entire being, I also reminded myself that she had asked me a question, and she deserved to hear the answer.

I brought myself back to where I was, and answered...even though I knew the answer would really hurt her.

"A knight from your duchy reached out to her with prejudiced feelings and told her that you weren't the trueborn daughter of the duchess, that you were illegitimate. He manipulated and convinced the princess that you were a stain on the royal bloodline. My sister...did what she thought she had to do to protect the bloodline. But when I told her the full truth...she seemed to finally understand, and felt remorseful. I have already sentenced her to public execution, to take place this afternoon. The method is entirely up to you, but—"

"*No*," she said, her tone hard and sharp, like a dagger dripping in poison.

I hesitated. "...*No?*" I asked.

She shook her head. "I want...for the princess...to *suffer*."

I jerked in surprise. "Kyeareth..."

"She...killed *our son*," she grated out, hoarse and thick, tears filling her eyes as her entire body trembled. "A quick execution? For the murderer of our baby, before we even had a chance...to see his eyes?" She shuddered. "No. No, she is not good enough for that. A quick death...is too good for her."

Even as father and mother rushed out into the garden—obviously to question me about what the prison guard had told them—I, for the first time in my life, *kneeled* to my wife. It had taken two years—a year of being engaged, and a year of being married—for her to finally bring me to my very knees.

Not once had I, the Crowned Prince of the Ashland empire, ever kneeled for anyone...but now, I had.

I kneeled for her.

"How shall I punish her then, darling?" I asked, looking up at her with a pleading gaze, desperate to appease her.

Something in me drove me, some need at the base level of my being, something that *pushed* me to fulfil her every whim.

This woman, the mother of my child, my wife...the wife I had hated, the wife I never wanted...

In a single moment, coming back to life to exact justice upon the murderer of our son...Something snapped within me, caving to her will. She now owned my authority.

The king and queen startled, realizing that for the first time in over a month, my wife was speaking.

*She was **living** again.*

"I want her..." She deliberated for a long moment before it seemed to dan on her. "I want for her to be forcibly mounted," she grated. "I wish to see her...*defiled*...pulled off of her pedestal. I want...to see her fed poison afterward, then given an antidote. I want...to see her in *pain*, agonized the same way that I was in agony when she forced me to miscarry our child," she forced the words through a cracking voice. "Then..."

"Then...?"

"Then, I want to watch as she is publicly banished, with no one...not even her knight...I want to take away her everything, just as she took away *my* everything...I want to see her pay the price of our son's life."

Though startled with the force of her demand, the sheer animosity and horror of what she was wishing for...I couldn't feel any will to deny her.

I knew how wrong it was.

I knew how dirty and despicable this was...but I couldn't stop it.

My mother wailed in the background, falling to her knees and begging for mercy, but my father stood there, silent; a sorrowful, hesitant gaze on his face.

I glanced at my father, forcing all of my anger and rage, all of my heartbreak, onto my face.

Finally, after a long moment, my father gave me a nod, tears running down his face.

I looked up at my bride as she panted, clutching onto my shoulders with her effort to remain standing as she shook, struggling to remain on her feet, but eyes full of desperation.

"I shall see it done as you wish it so," I told her, smiling up at her. I kissed her arms, still by my face as she held my shoulders for support. "*I will carry out vengeance for you*, my princess."

She smiled down at me sadly, before her eyes slid closed and she gasped as she collapsed into my hold.

I could see just how much my promise relieved her, taking the tension from her entire being.

She *needed* this to move on.

Pressing kisses to her hair, I lifted her into my arms and strode past my parents, taking my wife back to her chambers even as they clutched to one another, shaking and crying.

I couldn't imagine how much this broke their hearts.

When I had lay my wife back in bed, I kissed her cheek before I returned to my father, even as my mother stumbled her way back to her chambers with the help of her's and my father's personal shadow-knights.

"Father." My tone was serious, my voice thick with emotion.

He hesitated for a long time, but finally gave a nod. "You are both owed the payment of the life that was taken from you," my father said, voice cold and void of emotion. "And it was *my* child, whom took your child from you. I will give you the compensation you both deserve. I...I won't intervene. I truly feel that my heart is dying this day, but I will grant you this vengeance...this justice."

I gave him a hug, and though his feelings were forcibly reigned in, his body trembled.

"I *must* give her what she has asked of me, father. For the first time in a month, she spoke up. She stood on her *own* feet, and she *spoke*. It is not a choice...not for me."

He gave me a serious look.

"I understand. If I were in your position, I...I would do the same," he admitted. "I would do it, if my queen asked it of me. I...I am only angry that I must suffer this, because of my own child."

"I am sorry, father," I told him.

Folias's Blessing, 315 AR

It had been three months since the sentence had been carried out against my sister.

She screamed and cried even as I watched the sneer on my wife's overly-invested face, pleased by the sounds.

I cringed as I thought of it now.

I watched my wife, after my sister was out of sight, collapse to her knees, shrieking and sobbing into the evening air, crying out our son's name and gripping her head in her hands even as tears ran down her face.

She was so thrilled by the vengeance, and yet so agonized over the passing of the sentence. She truly was a kind girl.

Since then, I hadn't had to have meals forced on her.

She ate regularly and stayed hydrated, and though she still spent almost all of her time at the graveside, there was an improvement; now, she let herself cry.

She didn't just sit in numbed, dead silence. She no longer starved herself or tried to force herself to stay awake at all hours. She even went to her own bed to go to sleep, which was a vast improvement. She hadn't allowed herself to cry at his graveside until Moon's Dance, so I knew that forcing herself to function normally and having exacted her vengeance on my sister *was* helping to heal her.

On our one-night a week sleeping in the same room together, she would request to spend at least half the night at the graveside, and then we would spend the rest of the night with her lying in my arms, though she still didn't initiate intimate touches or kisses as I did.

She didn't seem to have any will to do anything other than to eat, drink, and hold vigil over our son's grave, but even *that* was enough for me. I couldn't argue.

I couldn't ask anything more of her, at least not now. She had come so far already from the lifeless heap she had been.

Now, it was the annual hunt, and this year, I had a special surprise for my bride. I'd had more than double the usual inventory of the hunting grounds imported in, and I had given strict instructions for all of the Keeper Knights of the royal family to dedicate their hunts to my son, in his honor.

After all, I was having the special tomb built especially for him, a building that was made with beautiful stone, beautiful stained-glass windows lining the walls, decorated with all of our hunts. To honor him, and her.

In the center of this indoor garden, was a stone pillar where our son's coffin had been built into, becoming his true resting place.

The room would be decorated with the pelts of the pray that was dedicated to him this year.

Astaroth and his Keeper Knight had already asked me for permission to hunt on Kyeareth's behalf. This was an unprecedented thing, a husband and his Keeper Knight not hunting for his wife, but I couldn't refuse him, or the determination in his eyes.

The announcer came onto the stage, giving me a nervous glance before I nodded to him, and he bowed, before addressing the crowd.

"This year is an unprecedented circumstance," he said. "Rather than having allowing the Keeper Knights of the royal family to hunt on behalf of their masters, the Crowned Prince has decreed that their hunts would be dedicated to the mausoleum of the late prince, Asfaloth Blaze Renard Ashland," he announced.

Kyeareth startled, standing in surprise, shocked eyes whirling to find me.

I smiled, bowing to her as I stepped up to her, even before the king and queen.

"I dedicate my offering to *you*, along with Seryn and Maxus...but the rest of the Keeper Knights of the royal family hunt in honor of Asfaloth," I told her, kneeling.

"My prince," she whispered, touched.

Astaroth and Sir Varo stepped up to her, kneeling at the same time.

"*Sister*," Astaroth said. "This year, I would be honored to offer my hunt and my Keeper Knight's hunt to you, in honor of Asfaloth. My most gracious brother-in-law has given his permission for us to do so."

Seryn kneeled to her. "And, of course, my hunt is dedicated to you as usual, my liege."

Tears welled in her eyes, and small, soft sobs bubbled their way out of her as she wiped her tears away, crying softly.

"Thank you," she whispered in a croaked voice. "Thank you...all of you," she sniffled, smiling.

We all wrapped her in a warm, loving group hug, comforting her and helping her together.

She had not been expecting this, but it seemed to deeply touch her, and that was all that mattered to me. I just wanted to be of comfort to her.

That year, the largest hunt that had ever happened in our history took place.

Many offerings were received for Asfaloth, and many offerings were received for Kyeareth who, in her good will, donated most of the meat and pelts to the citizens...a truly benevolent thing to do, as the Crowned Princess.

Even in her grief, she still sought to be kind and gracious.

I knew that she still felt guilty for the sentence she had passed upon my sister...but she had earned her vengeance.

Now, she was quickly earning her title as the Crowned Princess, and I felt my affection for her growing ever still.

Chapter 6

Cinder...

Seed's Sewn, 316 Ashland Rule

It was late evening, on a night of Sun's Reign, when we received the news that my sister's body had been discovered. My wife had agonized over this, crying and whimpering into her pillows, begging for forgiveness for her soul and my sister's soul...

She struggled desperately with this.

There was no funeral for her, not *formally*...though my parents held a small service for her on their own, devastated by her death. *It was a tragedy for all involved.*

I found my wife in the mausoleum that night, washing the podium that our son's body rested in.

"Kyeareth," I called her softly, and she turned to face me. "You know that this isn't your fault."

She hesitated. "I didn't say it was..."

"You always clean when you feel bad," I laughed. "Asfaloth's podium is perfectly polished, and yet you are here cleaning it as if it's filthy." She startled, taking in the wet cloth and the polish in her hand, and she gave me a soft, humorless laugh.

"You know me so well..."

I sat on the bench nearby, patting the open space beside of me to have her come sit with me. Seryn stepped over to the entrance of the building, giving us a little privacy.

"I don't...I don't want you to blame me for *this*, too."

I startled. "What?" I asked. "What have I blamed you for?"

She glanced at our son's podium suggestively, and I stood, appalled.

"*What?!*" I exclaimed. "Kyeareth, *no!* Not *once*..." She flinched, trembling, and I sighed, calming down. "Not once have I ever blamed you for what happened. Please..." I kneeled before her, taking her hands in mine. "*Please*, don't ever think that I have blamed *you*."

"But if I had been born from the true duchess, if I didn't have Mage-Born, then our son—"

"*Stop*," I said firmly, squeezing her hands. "Don't you dare do that to yourself. Don't put that on *your* shoulders, or *mine*. Don't put words in my mouth."

"Isn't it the truth?" She asked. "I..." She trailed off, looking away.

"Kyeareth...have I not been patient with you?" I asked, and she jerked in surprise, looking at me. "Did I not wait patiently for you while you refused to live? Have I not been patient while you spent months crying by his grave, and now, as you spend most of your time *here*, blaming yourself for everything?"

"Cinder—"

"Have I not been patient with you, in your grief, even as I have been lost in my own?" I asked, incredulous.

She froze, eyes wide and glassy, her face horrified. "Your...your *own*..." She paused, a sob breaking free.

"Kyeareth?" I asked, cautious.

"*Your own!*" She sobbed. "You...you were...you were his...he was your..." A wail wormed its way out of her as she clutched her abdomen. "I am not the only one lost in grief...you lost *your* son, too..." She choked out in a whisper.

I reached out, hesitant, before I embraced her. "Oh, my princess," I said softly, comforting her. "You carried him within you. My grief...it just seemed less than your own. I wanted to take care of you, first."

"But...why?"

I pulled back, meeting her gaze. "Do you truly not realize?" I asked. When she shook her head, I chuckled. "I care for you," I told her. "You seem to think that I still hate you."

"Don't you...?" She asked, hesitant. "You used to," she whispered.

"I haven't hated you in a long time. Disliked you for a long time, perhaps, but even that dislike has faded. I was angry and bitter, but I grew to understand that you were just a young girl, and that for me to be so angry over those things was immature and not entirely appropriate. That, and your irrational fear toward me...I was offended by it."

"I am not afraid of you anymore..."

I smiled. "I know. I would like to think that...I would like to believe that we've become closer, at least as friends if nothing else. Then, you...you opened yourself to me, giving yourself to me on my birthday, and I truly began to see you; not just as a girl I had obligations to, but as a *woman* who would be with me for the rest of our lives, as my wife. You aren't just *my* wife; *I* am *your* husband."

"So, what are you saying?" She asked, a nervous laugh bubbling from her. "Are you saying you have feelings for me?"

I met her eyes with all seriousness. "Maybe not in love, but...romantic feelings, in general? What if that is so?" I asked, and she startled.

"W-what...?" She asked.

I smirked. "I am not certain how I feel, really. So much has happened the last few years. But I know one thing that is certain; you have become an important piece of my heart."

She clutched her hands in the material of my uniform, eyes wide and surprised, and then she leaned forward, pressing her lips into mine.

I kissed her gently, reveling in the fact that she had kissed me first.

I glanced over to Seryn, who stood with his back to us.

I knew that he had feelings for Kyeareth; I had seen it in his gaze enough times to know it. However, he always put her before himself, never imposing his feelings onto her, never stepping out of line. He was a true knight.

Apathetic, perhaps, but he was good at what he did and he was a perfect match to take care of her.

I believed that he knew that he'd never have her. Were it not for me and for Astaroth, perhaps it could have been so, but with the both of us in her life, Seryn would never be hers and she would never be his.

I was aware enough, though, to realize that a man could not be as closely devoted and attentive to a woman as lovely as Kyeareth without developing romantic feelings.

I knew he meant no harm and would never act upon them.

So, I was entirely unperturbed by them.

"Sir Seryn," I said, and he turned to face us with a bow.

"Yes, your highness?"

"Please escort my wife to her chambers. I'm going to spend some time here alone, for some self-reflection."

He gave me a nod, before he offered her his arm, taking her back out of the mausoleum.

I sat there for a while, alone, thinking about my young wife.

She was fixing to be sixteen in a few months, and I would be twenty-one this year.

We had come so far since we had met.

She was right, I had hated her at first, and had not been particularly fond of her for a good while.

I had felt distasteful toward her for a long time, strongly disliking her before I had simply accepted her presence in my life and tolerated her.

Soon, I had grown to not dislike her...and not long after that, I had actually started to put effort into *not* disliking her, trying to care more about her feelings.

I grew, slowly, to like her.

That like grew into a care, and now...

She was irreplaceable to me.

I wanted to make her happy. I wanted to please her, in an almost illogical way.

I wanted her to be...happy with me.

When *had* she become this for me?

Solaris's Reign, 316 AR

  I was made aware, by my chamberlain, that it was Kyeareth's birthday, which had fallen on the day of Seed's Rising this year.

  In quiet honoring of her, I took the day off of work, and together, we spent the entire day out in the gardens, relaxing and eating snacks and treats rather than working.

  Since I had come to understand my growing feelings for her, I wanted to spend a lot more of my time with her...but she wasn't, mentally, in a place to deal with such things...not yet.

  I had to be patient, since she was fragile, but I found that I enjoyed the challenge of getting closer to her.

  She still didn't laugh or even smile often, but she wasn't as quiet anymore.

  She had finally started accepting my presence near her on a more intimate, more-present level.

  That was enough for me, for now...

  It had to be.

  "You know that I will be coronated, soon," I laughed, glancing at her. "You will no longer be the princess, but the queen. How do you feel about that?" I asked her.

  She glanced at me, a bit weary, but she gave a small smile that didn't quite reach her eyes.

"It will be different for me, but I am undergoing lessons on how to be a good queen, and mother-in-law has been being very thorough. It doesn't seem that it will be too hard to get adjusted. There's...really only one thing that worries me."

I gave a nod. "I understand," I said, soft.

I did, truly, understand.

We still hadn't had intimate relations since Asfaloth had been stillborn.

It had been a long time...

It had been well over a year since we'd been intimate, and I was nervous for us to become the king and queen...because then, it would be *expected* that we produce an heir, quickly.

Could we really do it?

Kyeareth was so deeply traumatized by the past events, and honestly, I was as well. It was still hard just to think about.

It was hard to imagine trying again, and especially hard to imagine actually getting told that I was going to be a father again.

"How...how soon is an heir *required*?" She asked, subdued. "I know that my father was made to take a different wife because of my infertile step-mother...is there also a time limit we are subjected to?" She asked.

I gave a solemn nod. "We would need an heir within five years. If, within five years, you have not had a single successful pregnancy...they would either bring in a new wife to complete the task, or I would be forced to pass the throne to the next in line for the throne, my brother."

"I see..."

  I smiled at her. "I am sure that everything will turn out alright. What happened before...I won't allow for it won't happen again. We have nothing to be concerned about, I promise you. I will protect you, and our child, from now on. We would keep things much more secretive this time, as well, as an extra precaution."

  She gave a nod. "Yes..." She trailed off in thought.

  "I know it is hard, but please…trust me."

  She let me pull her into my arms.

  For the rest of the evening, we sat out under the stars and fireworks, just enjoying one another's company in a peaceful quiet.

Folias's Blessing, 316 AR

I glanced at the bouquet of dandelions sitting on the dresser.

Astaroth had sent more today. He had gone from sending them once a week, to every day—a single flower each day.

The bouquets built quickly, and Kyeareth would let them dry by pressing them in books.

All of her novels on the shelf smelled of the flowers he picked.

I had learned quickly that this was a long-standing, childhood tradition between the twins; that he would gift his lovely sister a dandelion whenever he was worried for her—which was *every day now*, apparently.

I didn't take offense to it. They had a special bond, and it always made her smile to receive them. Even Seryn would get a smile on his face when they arrived, seeing her light up over the flowers.

It was one of the few things that gotten her smile won easily.

I sighed, thinking about the month.

My birthday finally arrived, and it was time for the coronation to become the king.

We had a large celebration, a giant feast, and everything seemed to be going off without a hitch.

Kyeareth was happy enough, smiling minutely even if the smile didn't touch her eyes and her eyes didn't twinkle.

Still, she was functioning and actually conversing with her family, and it was nice to see her living normally again.

She and I wore matching outfits, our usual color scheme, and she stood tall and proud to be by my side, holding my hand.

She made a beautiful queen.

It was at the gift-giving ceremonial part of the celebration that things took a turn for the worst.

A visiting dignitary, a king and queen from a neighboring country, was visiting on behalf of establishing good relations with our country's newest king. They stepped up to us, a small box in hand, and the queen smiled warmly at my bride.

"I wish you two a long and happy, fruitful future!" She smiled, clapping happily.

Kyeareth opened the box that was handed to her, and as I thanked them for their blessing, I was startled by the crash as the box hit the ground, the sudden shriek that pierced through the room as my wife began to shout.

She was suddenly holding her head and thrashing, wrenching herself backward so hard that she tripped over her own foot, stumbling and falling into her throne, hitting the back of her head.

"Kyeareth! My queen, what is the matter?!" I cried, rushing to look at the gift, when fearful rage roared to life in my blood. "What manner of sickness lies in your hearts for you to gift such a thing to *my* queen?!" I snarled, throwing the box back at them and unsheathing my sword even as my queen continued to tremble and cry.

Seryn took an offensive stance beside of me as he blocked my wife from their view. They sputtered and gasped, seemingly stunned by the reaction to the knitted baby-booties that they had gifted.

"I-I only wished to wish you a fruitful marriage and a healthy heir!" The foreign queen cried, clutching her husband. "It is a tradition to gift this to a new king and queen, to wish them a healthy line!"

"If you had done your *research*, as you *claim* that you had done in order to 'build a bridge' between our nations, you would have known that this was the *worst* possible thing that you could have given to my queen!" I snarled. "Do you not know what happened?!"

They shook their heads, still confused even as whispers flooded the room.

"The queen was fed abortion medication at her baby shower last year," Seryn stepped forward, and they startled.

"W...*what*?" The king asked, stunned. The foreign queen looked horrified.

"Did you study our kingdom before your arrival? Learn about our culture, learn about recent events?"

They nodded. "Well, somewhat, but we already knew a good deal, so we just—"

"You just assumed that was enough?" Seryn asked, enraged.

I gave a nod. "*We* are not honored to receive such harsh, *hurtful* gifts such as *that*," I spat through grated teeth. "It is highly offensive to give such a thing to a queen who has experienced such a trauma. You should have done your research, fully and in great detail, before you travelled here."

"We're sorry—"

"I understand you meant no offense, but what an ignorant gift," I said, still baffled.

The king and queen bowed. "We are truly sorry, Queen Kyeareth...we were not aware of the circumstances. We didn't know, and we apologize for this grave mistake. Please, please forgive us for this blunder."

"I-it is alright, just please...please, just go," my wife choked, struggling to catch her breath, and I sheathed my sword.

"Just know that, in the future, such willful ignorance about something so important in the family that is even common knowledge among the commoners in the kingdom, will be met with severe confrontation."

They gave murmurs of understanding before I stepped back to my wife, hugging her.

"Are you alright, my queen?" I asked softly.

She shook her head. "I...I need to rest." She turned to leave, but I caught her hand, turning her back to face me.

I glanced at her. "You...you understand that, as the king and queen, we will be...officially...in the *same* chambers, now?" I asked her.

She blushed a bit. "Oh...that's right."

I looked away, my cheeks burning. "Don't worry, I won't bother you with such a thing. Do not concern yourself. I just wanted you to...be aware."

She nodded. "Yes..."

She stood, letting Seryn lead her back to the newly renovated King and Queen's chamber, a room that my parents had once occupied but now they had moved into the side palace since I had been crowned king.

It was prepared beautifully, and I knew that Kyeareth would enjoy it. We had a brand-new bed, and everything.

After the celebration came to a close and I dismissed the party so that everyone could retire to their lodgings, I strode through the halls with speed to hurry and get to my wife.

I knew that tonight had hurt her deeply.

Such a thoughtful gift for any *other* couple, but such a heartless gift for my bride and me.

I sighed, feeling the need to check on her.

As I began to approach, I noticed that there were no guards posted at the door, and a maid came out.

When she saw me, she blushed, scampering off quickly, and I couldn't understand what was happening.

Where were the guards...?

I rushed into the bedchambers, and I froze when I saw her.

She stood, bathed in the moonlight by the window, a beautifully scented perfume permeating the air and a light, sheer lingerie on her body.

"*Kyeareth...*" I whispered, surprised.

She turned to face me, stepping up to me. "My king," she whispered, coming and draping herself onto my body oddly, giggling.

"What—"

"*Shh,*" she interrupted, pressing a finger to my lips. "No talking, your majesty. I am ready to have you, sire."

I held her at arm's length, cringing at the embarrassment of her acting in such a way.

"Kyeareth, what on earth has gotten into you?" I asked.

She giggled. "I asked the maid...to give me *something*...something to help me, your majesty, to help *us*. I wanted to...give myself to you, but I was afraid. But I'm not scared *anymore*!" She smiled up at me.

How long *had* it been since I had seen this smile...?

"What did she give you?"

"It's a seeee-creeeet," she giggled, acting silly.

"Kyeareth," I said, pinching the bridge of my nose.

"Fine," she pouted. "An aphrodisiac," she admitted.

"Aphrodisiac!?" I cried, exasperated. "Oh, Kyeareth..." I chuckled, sighing. Even as annoyed as I felt for doing something so silly, I felt my cock swell in my pants.

I sputtered when she attempted to take hold of it through my trousers, not even bothering to try to undo them.

"I want you, my king...besides, you *need* me," she said, shoving me onto the bed and straddling my hips.

I grabbed her before she could kiss me, shoving her down and switching our position so that I was above her.

"I can't do this..." I said. "You aren't in your right mind. We can discuss this lat—"

"No!" She cried. "I...I don't know when I might be able to...to...in my right mind," she said, a heavy blush on her face. She began to sweat lightly, her hips grinding up into mine. "I'm scared...so scared..."

I sighed. Her wanton behavior wasn't helping me to get any less turned on.

I was barely containing myself, and I could only hope she would respect me more for this restraint later.

At least, that was my hope.

Would she be offended, instead? I knew she was doing this for me, but still...

"Kyeareth, I...I *appreciate* what you are trying to do...but *this* isn't the right way. I don't want our first time together in over a year to be because you had yourself drugged to do so."

Tears welled in her eyes, and she lifted her hands to her face, hiding her face from my sight.

A pitiful, weak wail rose out of her as she sobbed.

I lay down beside of her, hugging her into my arms. "Shh," I told her. "I am grateful that you want to make me happy, and that you want to do your duty. But we have plenty of *time* for that. You don't need to push yourself."

She gave a weak nod, and we lay there in silence for a long time before I heard her breathing even out. I glanced down at her, seeing that she had fallen asleep, and I gave a sigh of relief.

I knew it then. I loved her.

I had just turned down *freely offered sex*, because her mental health and her feelings were more important to me.

I had just denied my cock some amazingly tight pussy for her sake. I had just fucked myself out of an orgasm, and I sort of hated myself for it...but I knew that was just my dick-head thinking.

I loved her too much to let our first time together after the tragedy happen while she was drugged. Even if she had initiated, even if she forgave me...I wouldn't be able to forgive myself.

As she slept, I quickly sprang myself free of my pants and had a fistful of cock in an instant, stroking myself to thoughts of her mouth and body wrapped over the tender, swollen flesh.

• • •

I came to thoughts of her crying my name, as she once had.

I loved her...more than I loved even myself.

I knew it in that moment, breathless with the truth behind it, the powerful force of that truth.

I was in love.

Chapter 7

Kyeareth...

Solaris's Gifts, 315 Ashland Rule

A few priests came into the room, and Astaroth rushed over to speak with them off to the side, whispering to keep them from disturbing my moment with my newborn.

He startled before throwing a panicked look over his shoulder at me...not that I noticed, really, so lost I was in my son and the situation.

He stepped over to me softly, sitting on the bed beside of me, wrapping his arms around me and his nephew.

"Love," he whispered into my ear. "You have to let him go, now. The priests want to prepare him for the funeral."

"What?" I asked, gaping at him. "N...*no!*" I cried, burying my face into Asfaloth's chest. "No...no, no, they can't have him. I won't let them take my baby away!"

"My love," my brother choked out, swollen and red-rimmed eyes filling with tears again.

"He's my baby! He's mine! I already lost so much! I finally had things going alright, and now..." I choked up.

His bottom lip quivered. "I know he's yours. I know, my love..." He hesitated. "But he's gone...you have to let him go."

I shook my head violently.

He gestured to the priests to go out, and they followed a nurse out to wait outside of the room. I could vaguely make out a priest waiting by the door, but I wasn't paying much attention.

I did, however, relax a bit when they were gone.

"Please," he whispered after several minutes of mournful silence. "May I...may *I* hold him? He was named for *me*, wasn't he?" He asked. "He's my nephew. He's my love's child. I'd like to see him." His voice was thick as he trembled.

In my grief, I couldn't see the truth behind his intentions, and I finally let go of my son's tiny body.

My brother held him for a long moment, hugging the tiny body to himself and whispering loving things into his ear, despite that he was dead...

It was in a split instant, as I wrapped myself deeper in my blankets to get warmer as I was feeling so desperately cold...I didn't see Astaroth nod to the priest who had his head poking inside of the door, and I didn't catch him as he rushed to the door with haste. He quickly handed my baby off to a priest before he shut the door, gasping, and clutching his chest as he looked at me with a sorrowful, guilty expression, his back pressed against the door as he stared at me.

"No!" I shrieked, trying to leap up from the bed but getting tripped up on my own throbbing legs and blankets, falling into the floor. "Asfaloth!" I sobbed, reaching out toward him.

He trembled even as his face showed his grief, but I glared at Astaroth.

"How...*how could you?*" I whispered with venom. "How could you do such a thing and still claim to be my brother? Claim to *love* me?" I whispered.

He flinched, trembling harder. "It had to be that way, Kyeareth. They needed to prepare him for the funeral—"

That got my attention.

Now that my baby was out of my arms and out of the room, I had to admit that I could actually focus a little more on my surroundings.

I needed to be there. The funeral would be a mandatory need for me. I would want to go, need to go...have to go. No matter how much it killed me.

"When...when is it?"

"They will hold the funeral in a few hours," he told me.

Pain struck my heart. "That...*that quickly?*"

He came and tried to lift me back to the bed, but I slapped his hands away. He flinched, gaping at me.

"Si-sister..."

"*Don't* **touch** me," I snarled. "Just...leave me..." I whispered.

"What?" He asked. "Kyeareth...my love—"

"Stop it! I don't want to be loved anymore! I don't want anything! Give me back my baby!" I sobbed. "Leave me here to *die*! *I just want to die!*" I wailed, flinging myself onto the floor, sobbing and wailing.

He tried to touch me again, and I wrenched my body away from him.

He, himself, fell to the floor, sliding down against the nearby desk as he broke down.

I couldn't bear to think how badly it hurt him for me to refuse his efforts to comfort me...

I just wasn't in the proper state of mind for that.

"**Leave me!**" I shouted.

I could hear him breathing hard, sobs coming out of him as he pled my name in sobbing whispers and cried.

I ignored him, too wrapped inside of the spiraling abyss of my mourning, as he tried to soothe me...

Soon enough, though, he stood and rushed out of the room, and I was *finally* left alone.

I loved Astaroth...but I simply couldn't be around him right now.

I had already lost him, now I had lost my child...

I could not be surrounded by what I had lost any further in that moment.

I awoke in my own bed, no longer in the medical room of the palace.

I glanced around, and I saw my knight sitting by my bedside.

He noticed that I had awoken.

"My liege," he whispered, kneeling by me. "I was waiting for you to wake up. Thank goodness. We still have *time*," he told me. "You woke up *just* in time to go to the memorial service."

So, it had only been a few hours since I had passed out, then.

I didn't speak, and he hesitated as I stared at the wall nearby. *"Crown Princess?"* He asked.

My only response was a shaky breath and fresh tears...but he understood, and he reached out and took my hand.

"I understand," he whispered, his eyes gazing into mine intensely.

He helped me put on my robe, getting it fastened over my nightgown that I'd been changed into at some point during my unconsciousness, and slid slippers onto my feet.

He brushed my hair, braiding it loosely and laying the braid over my shoulder, before he placed my tiara into my hair.

"Even in grief, in mourning, in loss…you are the Crowned Princess. Never forget that. You have been through too much to forego that now, my liege. Mourn, but do so proudly and with dignity. You are stronger than this…and I will be here with you through it all."

I gave a nod. I still had my dignity, and I was thankful that Seryn had reminded me of that.

Then, he lifted me into his arms, carrying me through the halls and to the balcony that overlooked the throne room.

I was thankful that I could still watch the service without having to go down there and mingle and be part of the ceremony.

I wasn't strong enough for that. The loss was simply too fresh.

When we arrived, I could see the table that had been set up in front of the throne, with my son's beautiful, tiny body lying there on a luxurious pillow inside of a too-small casket, a blanket covering him from the belly down.

My husband sat upon his throne, crying, even as everyone else did, too.

A priest stood over the casket, reciting a prayer.

He was praying, lighting candles...

The room filled with the sound of a hymn for a few moments.

Everyone walked by the presented body, paying respects, and laying a flower at his tiny feet.

He wore a beautiful white suit with navy and sky-blue embroidery, and even a cape of the richest blue underneath him.

He looked stunning, with his thick blonde hair.

I could only *imagine* who's eyes he had gotten...having never seen his eyes open. However, I liked to think that he would have gotten his father's bright, vivid golden-green gaze that smoldered me.

He would have been a very handsome man one day.

Tears ran down my face silently as I gazed down upon the scene.

"Do you wish to go closer?" Seryn whispered into my ear, but I turned my face into his chest-plate and sighed softly, giving a small grunt in response as I clung to him. I barely shook my head in the negative, but he caught it. "I understand," he whispered. "I know where they are burying him, so we will go there and wait, if you wish."

I gave a single nod, and he turned, walking me out to the gardens outside of my bedchambers. I was thankful that he would be buried here for now, until his personal mausoleum was built.

That was a comfort to me. At least he would be close by.

Once the procession had arrived and everyone had attended the grave-side service, everyone had left and I had been left with my husband and our families.

They glanced at one another as I hugged the headstone, refusing to be taken away, whispering amongst themselves...but I didn't care. I didn't intend to leave.

Even after they left, I stayed at the gravestone throughout the entire night.

This...this was where my child was buried. The one person I could hope would love me with their whole heart, who I wouldn't lose...I had lost. You know what...?

Fuck dignity.

My child had been taken from me...and he was never coming back. Dignity was a joke in the face of losing my son.

The next morning, Cinder had come out into the garden, looking upon me sadly, his face gaunt and haggard.

He came and pressed a gentle kiss to my forehead, leaving a tray of food that I couldn't even look at without feeling nauseous beside of me.

He kneeled at the grave for a few minutes, praying and hugging the headstone, and he gave me one last glance before leaving to attend to business.

This routine would continue for several days, until I heard him call Seryn over and whisper something to him. I felt the despair run through Seryn's body as his emotions hit me, and I startled and began to moan and thrash as my body was lifted.

"My lady," I heard Alice whisper even as I saw multiple maids rushing to cleanse the area that I had been occupying.

I saw the filth there, the ground wet and dirty, grimy...

I had been leaving the grave, only leaving to go and to take care of my urination and defecation needs, to use the bathroom...but that was all.

I hadn't bathed since his death.

I had been sweating and stinking all over the grave, and I felt ashamed.

"My lady, let's get you cleaned up. You can go back," she assured me at my panicked expression. "But my lady, you've been...you've..." she hesitated. "You've been neglecting your hygiene. It has even rained on you, your highness. The grave needs to be cleaned, too."

I startled, glancing at her in numbed surprise.

That wasn't supposed to happen...

It had even rained on me?

So, I wasn't simply sweating on the grave, but the rain had been basically bathing the grave with my filth? I felt shame well up in me further. I had been in such a state on top of the grave, so lost in my grief I was.

I had never even realized my state or the mess, and I felt sickened and ashamed by myself.

Alice and a couple of other maids helped me undress and bathed me thoroughly, burning my previous outfit in the fireplace before dressing me in new clothes, and they helped take care of clipping my nails and trimming my hair.

Then, Seryn came in with a truly tragic, pained expression...bags under his eyes and face gaunt from watching over me all of this time during my mourning.

He looked at me with a guilty, morose expression. I got a bad feeling; ominous, almost.

Then, multiple maids held my body down, and Seryn clenched my nostrils shut and shoved a bit of food into my mouth and then covered my mouth.

I struggled, trying to breathe and thrashing, but he shushed me.

"*Eat*, and I will let you breathe," he whispered.

I glared off to the side, seeing my husband standing there with arms crossed, lips pressed into a tight line, eyes full of underlying concern and expression frustrated even as he looked haggard, deep bags under his eyes and his skin more sallow than usual.

"I am sorry," he said, soft. "If I *must* force you to eat, then I shall do so. You've been refusing to do anything other than sit at the grave, so...what else am I to do?" He asked, shrugging before he turned, walking away.

Anger filled my heart, but I didn't know who my anger was at, really. Anger at his sister for killing my child? Anger at Cinder for forcing me to function beyond my grief?

Or anger at myself, for letting myself get in such a sorry state when that surely wasn't what my infant son would have wanted for me?

Seed's Sewn, 316 AR

It was late evening, when we received the news that my sister-in-law's body had been discovered.

"Kyeareth," Cinder called me softly, and I turned to face him. "You know that this isn't your fault."

"I didn't say it was."

"You always clean when you feel ashamed," he laughed. "Asfaloth's podium is perfectly polished, and yet you are here cleaning it as if it's filthy."

I paused. We had come a long way, somehow. I still didn't quite understand it.

We had once hated one another. He had hated me desperately, refused to love me, and I had refused to love him.

Then, we had gotten closer...

I had given myself to him willingly only a few times, but it had been enough to change our relationship a bit.

Then, the pregnancy had brought us closer as we faced the aspect of becoming parents, before the terrible tragedy we had faced.

Somehow, we had grown closer through it all.

"You know me so well...

Chapter 8

Kyeareth...

Folias's Blessing, 316 Ashland Rule

 Prince Cinder's birthday finally arrived, and it was time for the coronation to become the king.
 We had a large celebration, a giant feast, and everything seemed to be going off without a hitch.
 The entire kingdom celebrated.
 I was happy, smiling and actually conversing with my family.

I still felt a bit bitter, seeing my father smiling and lifting my baby sister in the air, laughing and doting on her...the golden child.

The daughter he loved, wanted and accepted.

The daughter he didn't feel any bitterness over having.

Leodore & Laelia

I tried to put it out of my mind, though. It was nice to feel a bit more normal, now. Or, as normal as I could be, being a childless mother in a social setting.

People were a bit awkward toward me, but I could feel their efforts to be kind.

The party helped me feel a bit more busy than usual, and it took my mind off of things.

I wasn't over Asfaloth's death, and it was regularly on my mind, but I was able to function a bit better, now.

I was, at least, returning to some semblance of normal.

I also smiled when I saw that he and I wore matching outfits, our usual color scheme, and I stood tall and proud to be by his side, holding his hand.

He was an extremely handsome young king.

It was at the gift-giving ceremonial part of the celebration that things took a turn for the *worst*.

Year's Fall, 316 AR

"You are almost ready, your majesty!" Alice smiled at me, finishing my makeup. "You look truly magnificent."

I smiled at her softly. "Really?"

She nodded, enthusiastic. "You look like a real queen! I cannot believe that it is already Heaven's Gift Holiday yet again!" She said.

I gave a nod. "Yes," I said, soft. I glanced at her. "Are my gifts for the king prepared?" I asked.

"Yes, your majesty...you did make them, afterall."

"I meant the wrapping," I said, smiling. She gave me a nod. "Good, then. All that is left is to see how he responds."

She glanced at me, nervous. "Are you...sure that you are ready?" She asked, fully aware of the meaning of such a gift. "I am happy for you if you are, but...it is fully alright if you aren't, my queen. Nobody would ever blame you."

I sighed. "I know...but I...I have grown to have quite a fondness for him, even true feelings. I know that I am ready to start belonging to him again."

She smiled, hugging me. "I am happy for you, majesty."

There was a small knock on the door, and I glanced in the mirror before I had Alice let him in.

He stood there, dressed in a brilliant, navy-blue uniform with silver and sky-blue embroidery patterns, and a silver sash with his king's pendants.

He looked amazing, and I matched him.

His eyes gazed upon me fondly. "You look amazing, my queen," he said, giving me a bow and kissing the back of my hand. "What a stunning wife I have."

I smiled at him, looping my arm in his. "Let us get going." I glanced behind me at the maids that were staying behind, giving them a discreet wink.

I had already prepared for the room to be covered in rose petals for when we returned, with a bottle of red wine prepared, and fresh sheets laid on the bed as well as a hot bath prepared.

I had taken care of everything, ready to make this night as special as possible.

We walked through the halls and to the entrance of the ballroom, and upon hearing our names announced, my husband led me through the opened doors.

Whispers and sounds of amazement echoed throughout the room, and everyone—save for my brother's wife—lifted their glasses of champagne, toasting us.

That was...odd.

My father seemed particularly thrilled that evening, having multiple glasses of wine, and my *brother*...to be honest, he looked a bit strained. Almost *queasy*, sick...?

I wondered what was wrong. He was avoiding my gaze, and my brother never did that by choice.

What was wrong?

As we came to the gift exchange, of course the king and queen went first.

My husband gifted me with a new, luxurious cape lined with fur, with gloves and a beautiful pair of boots.

My heart pounded in my chest as I gave Cinder my three gifts; the first, was a new broadsword, made of onyx with a black blade.

It was particularly costly, but it was a beautiful work, and the shiny black of the blade reminded me of his shiny, illustrious black hair.

The second gift was a box of imported chocolates-for that very night. A box of chocolate was often used a symbol of seduction, and I noticed his eyes glance at me, a bit of surprise there.

He wasn't sure, yet, but he was starting to wonder if I was meaning in a sexual way, I could see the look in his bright eyes. I smiled sweetly, and he smiled softly.

He seemed to pass it off as just serving to satiate his sweet-tooth, as I knew that he loved chocolates.

That was a well-known fact in the castle.

The last gift, I handed him the tiny box—*discreetly*, and when he saw the manner of box that it was, a small and delicate thing, he turned away from the crowd and opened the box so that only *he* could see it.

Small boxes of this nature were typically used as private gifts, and only meant for the recipient, after all.

I heard him gasp softly, his entire body going tense, trembling minutely. The third gift was a scrap of red-lace, on a bed of red rose petals. It was the symbol of sex, broadcasting my intentions to him without *subtle* symbolism as I had once done before, back when I was young and innocently trying to gain a closer relationship with him for the sake of being more comfortable around one another.

No, *this* time was bright, clear, and full of intent.

I was a woman reaching out to her man, telling him what I wanted from him in a completely unsubtle way...especially for a *lady*.

He shut the box quickly, whirling around to me with wide, stunned eyes, his mouth slightly hanging open in surprise.

"M-my queen," he whispered, voice thick. I smiled at him, lifting a chocolate out of his box, and slipping it between my lips. "Are you really saying...?"

I gave a nod.

"Yes, I suppose I am..." I admitted softly, and he swallowed thickly.

I heard a throat clear, and we glanced up, out of our own world, as other families exchanged their gifts with one another, to see my brother and his wife standing there with my father and mother, as well as *her* parents.

Both pairs of parents looked proud, my sister-in-law beamed at my brother...and my brother looked guilty, almost green. Positively sick. His face actually held a greenish hue, and I could already start to see the truth.

My stomach sank, as I began to realize what was happening.

There was no other reason for the entire family to be here. I had been piecing it together, but hoping against hope that it wouldn't be brought before me and flung into my face.

I felt Cinder go tense beside of me, seemingly knowing as well.

"Your majesty, newly appointed King Cinder," my father addressed, bowing.

He seemed...almost *tipsy*? It was obvious that *he* had been drinking.

Of course, he had. He wasn't going to consider my feelings, not at a celebratory time like this. Resentment, once again, rose in my belly.

My father had little concern for me, as usual.

"Your majesty, Queen Kyeareth. I would like to ask for your blessing and prayer of goodwill, as we approach you with *wonderful news*! My son, the heir to the Severing duchy, and his wife, are now expecting a child!"

I dropped my glass of wine, unintentionally, and it shattered at my feet.

My father gasped, startled, rushing to help me step back and inspect my foot as I flinched at the shard that had managed to stab me.

"Your majesty, I am sorry for startling you—"

"She isn't *startled*," Seryn said, lifting my foot and delicately plucking out the shard of glass, quickly wrapping the injury. "Did you even *think* to whom you just made that announcement to? Has it been so long that your memory has failed you, or are you just too *inebriated* to consider *her* feelings?" Seryn asked, tone furious.

My father startled, as did her parents, and though my brother looked ashamed and embarrassed, his bride looked...almost smug.

Pain rushed through me, and my eyes locked with my brother's.

He took a step toward me, hand reaching out.

"S-sister—"

I flinched against his voice, speared by my agony, before I turned, bolting out of the ballroom and through the halls.

I rushed out, out, out to the gardens, and made my way to the mausoleum, bursting through the doors and stumbling to the bench by his podium.

How could I take this? How could I suffer through this new circumstance?

My mourning began, renewed.

Not that anyone else would be able to understand.

Didn't this just make the end of us all the more finalized?

I didn't want to face this.

"Asfaloth..." I sobbed, clutching my body to the podium. "I...I can't even..." I sighed. "Your uncle...he is going to be a father." I scoffed, soft. "Of *course*, he is." Tears ran down my face, and I struggled to catch my breath. "I don't even have the right to be upset. It isn't his fault that you died, that he gets to have a child before I do..." I sobbed. "I can't get angry at him for being with his wife...not when I have willingly given myself to your father. How can I fault him for having his wife? I was never his, and he was never mine. I have no place being bothered by such a thing..." I sniffled. "I must be *sick*. Why do I feel so...*betrayed*?"

"*Because he was your first love,*" Cinder spoke, and I startled, whipping to see him as he approached me, a small smile on his face. "Because you are in love with him."

"C-*Cinder*..." I sniffled, composing myself.

"Yes, it is me," he chuckled.

"Cinder, I...I—"

"It is okay," he said.

"...Huh?"

"You don't have to explain," he stopped me before I could say anything. "The night before you moved into the palace, I saw his confession to you in your things. I had remembered, also, how the two of you interacted with one another, and I had always found it a bit peculiar. Not that I was ever worried," he laughed.

"...You weren't?" I asked. "But...how have you known and not been worried?"

"I just...don't see you as an adulterer."

"...Really?"

"The two of you may have had feelings for one another and may even still, and the two of you may have a close bond...but who is to say that is entirely unexpected? You are siblings. You had been together every day for thirteen years, best friends. It is entirely understandable for a romance to have begun to blossom between you. But you are right; you were never his, and he was never yours, nor will you ever be."

"Cinder..."

"How is your foot?" He asked.

He came to me, and lifted my body into his arms.

I grasped my arms around his neck, hugging him as he carried me to our chambers.

When we stepped inside, I suddenly remembered my *intentions* for the evening, and I blushed heavily even as my husband gaped at the room in shock.

Suddenly, he began to laugh.

"W-what?" I asked, blushing.

"You really went *all out*," he chuckled, setting me down on the bed.

He strode over to the night table, setting the box for the lace and rose petals down, before he lifted the scrap of lace to his mouth, kissing it.

"Cinder..."

"You really swing for the fence, don't you, my queen?" He asked, wagging his eyebrows teasingly at me as I covered my face.

"Stop," I whined. "I'm embarrassed enough," I told him.

"Did you...did you *mean* this?" He asked, glancing at me.

I looked away, giving a nod. "Yes...though, I know I've ruined the mood..."

He scoffed. "*Ruined* the mood?" He asked. "I wouldn't say *that*."

"Really?" I asked, surprised.

"What better way to get your mind off of an unfulfilled love than to give yourself over to the man that beckons to fulfil you now? It may not be the same, but...I am here, if you want comfort. If you want someone to hold you...come to me."

I gasped, locking eyes with him, his eyes warm as he gazed at me, already stripping off his clothes, the scrap of lace between his lips. *"I take it that you accept my gift..."*

He gave a tight nod, crawling across the bed and undoing the ties to my gown before he lay me down, draping the scrap of lace over the space between my breasts, and his mouth was on me.

I gasped, losing myself in the sensation of him taking over my body.

The swirls of his tongue against my nipples...

The feel of his smooth face pressing to my tender, sensitive abdomen and thighs...

The delicious, mind-numbing sweeps and dips of his tongue against my bundle of nerves and into my hole.

"Oh, I've missed this," I gasped.

"I've *missed* your tight pussy," he murmured against me. "Now, give me that pretty little hole and I'll have you begging for more of my cock before this night is finished." I felt myself tighten and spasm on the inside even as he crawled up my body.

I felt him tease the head of himself against me, stroking against my nerves until I came with a thrashing gush and crying out his name to the heavens.

"Yes, my queen? What is it?"

"I...I want *more*," I whined.

"More of what?" He said, teasing.

I felt my anger build, frustrated that he insisted on me vocalizing the vulgarity to him directly.

"More of your c-cock...I want it inside me," I whimpered.

My face flamed at my own vulgar words, and I felt tears sting my eyes that he expected this from me.

"Tell me what to do, then," he smirked.

"Give your queen's tight little hole its cock, please..."

I had once tried to be *"lady-like"* about it, like many of the romance novels I had read, but Cinder wouldn't hear of it.

He told me he didn't like dealing with a prudish little lady, but a woman who would make him ravenous in his bed.

If I was honest, the vulgar speech affected me the same way that it did him.

Whereas it made him harder, hard like steel and throbbing and twitching as it hung low in my vision with its heaviness…it made me much, much wetter and slicker, and he seemed to love that response in my body.

"Oh, don't worry, my little queen," he said, gazing down at me with eyes blazing in his lust. "I plan to fuck you and love you until dawn," he said, before slowly giving me his length.

The slowness tortured me, wishing that he would just give it all in one thrust. Though, he was much too slow and too much of a tease to give me that. The rest of the night was full of gasps and moans, touches and caresses, cries and shaking breaths.

He was right, too.

He took my body again and again, even as the sun began to rise outside and light up our chambers.

"I have…a confession," he whispered against my lips. I gazed up at him, giving him my attention. "I have come to realize that I…I don't just not dislike you, nor do I just like you…I love you."

I gaped at him, and he chuckled at my response.

"You…what…?"

He met my eyes, his eyes seeming to gleam in the candlelight. "I love you, Kyeareth. I am in love with you. Truly."

"L...love...?" I asked.

"Yes...it has been a painful realization, with everything that has happened...but it is true. I love you," he admitted.

I gasped, shuddering around him as I fell off the edge of the cliff he'd been leading me up to.

I came against him, ignoring the sopping wetness beneath my rear from gushing all over him again and again throughout the night.

I didn't know if I was ready for that.

I didn't know if I was ready to open my heart to love. *Was that...okay?*

He hesitated. "...You...you don't have to love me back. I know that it is hard for you. I know you're scared of me and I give you anxiety, but—"

"I am not *scared* of you anymore, not really."

"...You aren't...?"

"It is true, you have become a true source of comfort to me. You brought me back to life, after...after what happened. Cinder, I...I care about you. Maybe I love you, too," I said in a sob, clutching my hand over my mouth at the confession, surprising even myself. "But I'm scared...scared to love you. Scared to open my heart to love. Scared...to lose you."

His eyes were wide, but he leaned down to press an urgent kiss to my lips...

He grew desperate in his strides, chasing one last high with me, before I felt him burst inside of me, shuddering against me, and choking on his gasps as he released himself into my waiting body.

When the room became calm and quiet once again, I lay in his arms, tears running down my face.

He lifted my chin up, leaning down to press a kiss to my lips before pulling me into his embrace, lying on his side and hugging me into his body.

"Shh," he shushed me. "It is alright," he smiled sadly at me. "I will protect you. You won't lose me, Kyeareth. Just trust in me."

A sob burst through my lips as I clung to him, crying softly into his chest.

"Kyeareth...?"

"I never...I never expected to be here...not with you."

"I know," he whispered, stroking my hair, but he had me look up at him. "But you are, and I am happy that you are."

"I never thought you would love me..." I whispered.

He chuckled. "I didn't, either. I thought that the best that I could hope for would be to not *hate* you. But as we spent time together, I found things about you that I enjoyed, things that I smiled at...things that I loved. My feelings continued to grow, and it became something more than not disliking you or even liking you."

I smiled against him. "I thought...I thought that my brother would be the only one I held this affection for. I've never trusted anyone the way that I trust him, or Seryn...but you have done nothing but prove to me that you were a soothing, calming force for me. I never...I never could have made it through all of this without you..."

He leaned down again, pressing a kiss to my forehead. "I love you, my queen, and I will wait as for as long as you need me to for you to love me in return."

I smiled. "I love you, too, my king. It may not be the way you want me to, yet, but I do love you," I whispered, before I slowly slipped into a peaceful sleep in his arms.

Chapter 9

Kyeareth...

Nivis's End, 317 Ashland Rule

I was feeling...*strained*. I was always tired, and I could swear I was always hungry and having vivid dreams lately.

I had, in truth, missed a cycle since the end of Year's Fall, but I had no idea if that was because of pregnancy or because of my own problems.

Since the incident with Asfaloth, I had missed a handful of cycles, despite *not* having relations with Cinder at the time.

Since Heaven's Gift Holiday two months ago, we had been together a few more times, but he wasn't available a lot at the moment because one of the countries we had been feuding with was trying to take advantage of their enemy having a new king.

We had already caught multiple spies attempting to infiltrate the palace. They had even attacked part of our navy, and so my husband was strongly considering going to war to finish the feud once and for all.

However, as we sat and ate breakfast, something about the *eggs*...

I just felt sick.

I felt the room spin, and just as I was about to vomit, Seryn rushed over with a pail, letting me empty my stomach into it.

"Darling?" My husband asked, concerned. "Are you alright?"

"I...think that I need to see the physician," I said, nervous.

He heard the tone in my voice, and sent a maid rushing off to call the doctor.

"Do you...do you think you—"

"It is a possibility, of course," I said, soft. "I...I don't *know*. I feel much like I did when I found out I was pregnant before. There is only one way to know."

He picked up an urgent message that one of his Shadow Guardians brought to him just then, and unrolled it, reading the message as we waited for the doctor to arrive.

The doctor arrived quickly, his med-room located close by the imperial bedchambers in case of emergency, and he began his examination of me.

After a few long, agonizing minutes of waiting, he smiled at me, a happy expression but with sad eyes.

"Congratulations, your majesty! You are with child."

Pregnant...I was pregnant again.

My entire world froze, as I grasped my belly and just sat there, openly gaping into space for a moment.

There was a clatter as the scroll fell out of my husband's hand, gaping at us with a horrified expression.

"Y-your majesty...?" I asked, suddenly fearful. "Isn't...isn't this *happy* news? What's...wrong?" I asked, terrified at the stiffness of his posture. "Darling?" I asked again. "*Cinder?*"

This seemed to get his attention. "I...I have to go off to war..." He said, voice cracking. "I am...*needed* at the front," he said, lifting the scroll. "I just got the request...You're pregnant...and I have to *leave*...off to war..."

I gaped at him. "W-what?" I asked, trembling and clutching my abdomen. "N-*now?*" I stammered, horrified.

He rushed to me, taking me into his arms and burying his face into my hair with a sob.

"No!" He cried. "I know I have to go, but I can't leave, not now..."

Seryn stepped over to the discarded scroll on the floor, lifting it and reading it. "This..." He paused. "*This is serious...*"

"What is it?" I asked.

He shook his head. "A civilian city has been attacked by the opposing force. There aren't enough soldiers there to protect the town, and the force's commander is demanding the king to come and negotiate terms to stop hostilities. We cannot put this off. It needs to be taken care of as quickly as possible."

"But—" I started, but stopped when Cinder tensed against me. "Darling..."

He pulled back, looking down at me. "I know it is not ideal," he told me. "But this isn't a situation that I can avoid."

"How...how long is it to get to that town?"

"It is a fortnight each way," he told me. "It is a city on the very edge of the kingdom."

"What?" I asked worried. "But...that's so far! And what...?"

"If the city has already been destroyed and the duke residing there has had to take the citizens into his castle to house them, as it states in this letter, I need to go for more than simply negotiation. I will have to take builders and have new homes constructed, direct action to help rebuild their lives. I am the king...it is my duty to see to it that they are cared for."

A month. A month that my husband would be gone, at the least.

I smiled against him in spite of the situation. "You are such a good king..." I whispered.

He stroked my hair. "I will be back in a month," he promised.

"W-when do you have to leave?" I asked.

"I will need to set out by dawn. I have no time to waste. They know how long it will take for me to reach them, and so they won't stay in a truce-state for very long. If I take longer than a fortnight to get there, they will begin assaulting the duke's estate with all of the citizens who survived...and I can't let that happen."

"But—"

"I know, darling," he said, taking my face in his hands, pressing a kiss to my lips. "I know...but you will be alright. It won't take me long."

Tears filled my eyes, and with a sob, I took him by the hand, leading him quickly to our bedchambers. Feeling a bit sick or not, I wasn't going to let him just leave this way.

"Kyeareth—"

I shut ourselves into our chambers, shutting the door and shoving him into the door, kissing him fervently against the very door.

He sensed the urgency that I seemed to feel, stripping himself and moving us over to the bed without breaking contact with me, before we fell into the bed together...and we didn't move again until the next morning.

When I awoke the next morning, I saw my husband putting on his armor.

"Are you about to leave?" I asked, and he glanced over at me, before giving me a nod. "I see..."

He came and pressed a kiss to my lips, before pressing a kiss to my bare abdomen.

"Please...take care of yourself," he told me. "I have a bad feeling about something, but there is nothing that I can do about it. I need to be sure that I do my duty."

I gave a nod. "I know," I said, before I pulled him in for a kiss.

He smiled at me. "Stay in bed, my queen, and get some rest. I kept you quite busy last night," he chuckled, giving me another kiss before he strode out of the room.

When he was gone, my maid rushed in, helping me get dressed.

"I heard the news," Alice said, sad. "I am so sorry that he has to leave, my queen, but he will return in no time."

"It wasn't *all* bad news," I whispered, resting a hand over my womb. She startled, gazing at me in surprise. I nodded. "That's right...there is a new prince or princess growing inside me," I beamed at her.

She gasped, hugging me into her arms. "Congratulations, my queen!" She laughed in tears, hugging me tightly to her, before I heard footsteps approach me.

I glanced over to see Maxus, my husband's Shadow Guardian. "Hello, again," I smiled. "I am not used to seeing you."

"My queen," he said, kneeling. "I am under command from his majesty to stay behind to protect you, specifically. King Cinder has also ordered that I take you to the Shadow World, to have you choose your own Shadow Guardians to have alongside of your Keeper Knight."

"But, don't you need to be with Cinder?" I asked, suddenly worried.

He chuckled, bowing his head a bit. "Not to worry, my queen. He has several Shadow Guardians, since he is the King. For now, he has assigned me to be at your side and your aid."

"I see," I smiled. "That is just like him. Would you mind doing a favor for me?" I asked.

"Anything, your majesty, please do not feel a need to request, but rather demand it."

I smiled. "Alright. Please, before he departs, go and tell my husband to look up at our window as he departs."

"The window?"

"Yes. He asked me not to leave the room and to rest, but I want to see him off."

He suddenly disappeared, and I startled, not expecting it.

The Shadow Guardians were an elite force of warriors that were trained far more rigorously than even knights, and so it was expected that they had skills that knights didn't...

Within just a few moments, he had returned, startling me again as he returned to my side, kneeling.

"I have carried out your order, my queen," he said, fist over heart.

I stepped over to the window, gazing down at the pavilion where my husband was mounting a horse.

He had never been one for carriages...

There was a large party to accompany him, including several farmers and builders.

I opened our window, letting the cool morning air hit me as I looked down below.

As he finished his speech, he turned, glancing up at our bedchambers.

I smiled, pressing the tips of my fingers to my lips, and then holding my hand, palm up, and "blew" my kiss to him.

He startled slightly, before a bright smile came to his face, and he shot his hand up, "catching" my kiss and pressing the tips of his own fingers to his own lips.

I smiled, giggling softly, and he gave me a small bow, hand over heart, before his procession set out.

I sighed, shutting my window once again, and turning to Maxus and Seryn.

I took a deep breath, and I tried to get my bearings.

There was a lot going on. There was a lot I had to do and think about right now.

This, however, was something that was a good thing for me to take care of, and so I tried to put everything else out of my mind to focus on this.

"I am ready to go to the Shadow World," I told him.

We went through the halls, out of the palace, and through the gardens, through the pavilion, before we reached a set of elaborate doors built into the ground that I had never seen before.

"T-this is..."

"It is the Shadow World," Maxus explained. "The Order of the Shadow Guardians resides here."

"How do I choose one...?" I asked. "Is it like choosing a Keeper Knight?" I asked.

"Is isn't quite like that," he told me. "You will step up to a podium, and the leader of the order will prick your finger and allow it to fall onto the seal on the podium. When the blood soaks into the seal, the Guardians who are meant for you will come forward."

"I-I understand."

"Each one will have a special talent that is designed to help you, specifically. It is driven by the fates."

"Oh..." I whispered.

"You will receive three guardians, but there will be a 'leader' among the three. As I am the leader of the king's guardians, I lead the others, but my orders come directly from the king's mind. He only needs to address me in his mind, and I can hear him. It is a physical, mental, and emotional link. Somewhat like how your Keeper Knight can feel your emotions and feel your physical state, this goes even deeper than that. It is...very invasive."

I gulped. "I-I see..."

He smiled. "You need not be nervous," he told me. "When they become guardians, a part of their soul's essence is actually tapped into with the seal, demanding perfect loyalty. If you should so need it, they would lay their lives on the line for you. You have a set number of guardians, but if one should die, then the next guardian initiated into the order would automatically become bound to you in soul, to replace the one you lost. It is an extremely personal thing." He and Seryn opened the doors for me, and allowed me to step down into the stairway that led beneath the ground.

Telling me not to be nervous didn't help all that much.

I was nervous.

Still, I let them lead me through the darkness, and we finally came to a room lit by torches, a podium there, and a man beside of it.

He kneeled. "My lovely queen," he smiled up at me. "You are finally here to choose," he smiled. "The king has instructed me to have you come here to choose your guardians today. Originally, you would have had them once you had become queen, but you..."

"Lost the prince..." I whispered.

He nodded. "Yes...and you were so lost in your grief that you were in no state to come. We have been anxiously awaiting your recovery and arrival."

"I see..." I glanced at the podium. "Then...shall we?" I asked.

He smiled at me warmly, standing and having me come to stand in front of the podium.

"Once your blood soaks into the podium, the bond will set. The three guardians who are bonded to your soul will step forward out of the darkness, just so you aren't startled. It will sting for just a moment, but it will not grievously hurt you and it isn't dangerous to you in any way."

I heard murmurs whispering in the darkness of what felt like a large space, small shuffling as they moved, waiting.

"Our members are sensed from the moment that they are born, and brought here from all walks of life to train and dedicate themselves to the service of our empire's royalty. The association names them, according to their proficiency or sometimes their appearance. Each guardian that attaches to you was made for you, born for you. Do not fear using them however you might need because I promise...you might just need everything they can offer you. Each one is tied to you for a specific purpose."

"I will keep that in mind."

I held my hand above the seal, and I winced when the leader nicked my pointer finger, allowing the blood to hit the seal and the seal lit up, a bright sky-blue color.

Then, they had me take a seat, as I felt dizzy and disoriented when I felt a sharp pang three times.

I gasped, feeling something pulling in my chest. Alarmed, I looked at the guide, but he just waited and smiled at me.

So, this was normal, I supposed...

I heard three sharp gasps and small groans, waiting a moment, before three men finally came to stand before me.

They all kneeled before my chair, and through my veil, I could hardly see them.

They each wore black, but I could tell that all three of them were strong, well-built, and skilled. Seryn stirred at my side, feeling the intensity of their energy. I was untrained, and even I could practically feel their aura.

Though, one of them was a mage. I didn't know how I knew that, but I could feel it in my own mana, somehow.

I felt the tingling presence there, the kinship.

I hadn't ever been around another person with mana, so how did I know that?

What are their names? I wondered. *What do they look like? I can hardly see anything in this darkness.*

They each stood, bowing with fists over hearts, before they stood straight.

The one on the right stepped forward first, looking at the ground but face where I could actually see him.

He had a small scar over his right eye, but he had light, pale skin, and silvery white hair. His eyes were the palest, dimmest blue I had ever seen.

He looked like a nivis morning, and I was positive that if I saw him out in snow, I wouldn't be able to discern him from the background.

He was about a half-head taller than I was.

"My name is *Winter*, your majesty. I am a *mage*, also skilled at tracking and hunting, and my strength is speed. Though I *am* skilled at sword combat, I prefer sorcery."

I gave a small nod, still feeling a bit dizzy, so I remained seated.

"It is nice to meet you, Winter," I smiled at him, though I didn't figure he could see it through the veil.

I hoped that he could hear it. I already immediately felt pleased with him, knowing that I had a fellow mage by my side.

For people with mana, especially women, being around men with Knight's Aura was intimidating to say the least.

He stepped back, before the guardian on the left came forward, bowing, before he let me see his face.

This guardian was tan-skinned, a beautiful shade of light and creamy brown, with silky black hair and piercing black eyes that seemed to blend with the pupil. He was *frightening*, almost. He was an entire head taller than I was.

"My name is *Eclipse*, your majesty. I am an assassin, skilled at tracking, and my strength is archery, both with a bow and a cross-bow. I am skilled in sword combat, but I am the best at spying and concealment."

I gave another small nod. "It is nice to meet you, Eclipse," I said, though I wondered when in the world I was ever going to need an *assassin*...

He stepped back before the last of them came forward. He was about a head taller than me, and his skin was tanned. His hair was a light, ashy-brown coloring with almost a gray-tinting, and his eyes were a deep, slate-gray color.

He felt *warm*, and I felt peace from him. I didn't know why, but something about him...He felt almost medicinal.

"My queen...my name is *Azoth*."

I startled. I knew that Azoth was a *medical* term, used as a medication and a *solvent*. It was highly sought after by alchemists...and, also...

His name sounded similar to two of my greatest loves.

Chapter 10

Kyeareth...

Astaroth was given his name as a power token, seeing as the real Astaroth was one of the "Great dukes of hell," a high-ranking demon who stood by the devil's side.

It was a name intended to bring about great power and fear, intimidating his enemies.

My father had named him thus as to strike fear into the hearts of the enemies of the duchy, hoping he would derive authority and fearlessness from his name.

Asfaloth, though it may have been similar sounding, held a quite *opposite* meaning. Asfaloth meant "*Sunlit.*" He had been like sunlight to me...a bright, shining light, but quickly stolen away by the darkness of night.

Azoth looked up at me, before standing again. "I am a *doctor* and alchemist, skilled at sword combat and specialize in psychology. My strength is with interrogation. I am skilled in battle, but I am best at analyzing and exploiting weakness and intimidation, and I am also good with alchemy and medicine and potions. And, I already know that my name holds special meaning for you. I am honored."

I gave a nod, and a little smile this time. "It is nice to meet you...Azoth..."

He smiled, and glanced to the head of the association without stepping back from me.

The headmaster stepped forward. "To complete this ceremony, each guardian must turn you away from the others, removing your veil, and you must give him a kiss-seal. This simply means to peck him on the lips, and your energy will *synchronize* with his own, causing him to be highly alert and ready for any thought or feeling you have. It finishes the bond. Then, they will each, one-by-one, replace your veil and turn you back to the rest of us."

I gave a nod, and Azoth went first, helping me to stand and leading me a few feet away so that only one torch would light my face as he turned me away from the others. He gave me a bow, before he lifted my veil, and his eyes widened.

"You are beautiful," he mouthed with a small breath. He smiled; a bit sad. "I see much pain in you."

I startled, but looking into his eyes, I still felt a tugging sensation in my belly. I looked to his lips for an instant, before I pressed a gentle kiss there, and I felt a sudden spark tingle through me. I gasped, and he chuckled, giving me a nod.

"It is done," he said, replacing my veil and turning me back toward the others.

Eclipse was next, striding forward to me and turning me away, lifting my veil. His eyes also showed his surprise. "He was right," he smiled, looking at my face. "You are."

I smiled warmly, and leaned up, pressing a kiss to his lips, and was expecting the spark that ran through me that time.

He replaced my veil, before turning me back to the others, and finally, Winter came up to me. He turned me

• • •
147

away from the others, lifting my veil, and eyes wide, his face flushed and his lips barely parted.

After a moment of silence, I giggled at him. "Nothing to say?" I whispered, and I heard him swallow thickly, nervous.

I laughed out a small laugh, and leaned forward, pressing my lips to his own, but gasped, feeling the tingle once more but only *much* stronger. Why…was it so much stronger? Was it because he was also a mage?

He looked surprised himself, but he gave me a brilliant smile and a bow before he replaced my veil and turned me back to the others. I walked back with Winter to the others, and the three kneeled before me again.

"Now, you may formally introduce yourself so that they may formally pledge their loyalty to you, and you will be all set to go back to the palace," the director said.

I smiled, clearing my throat, before Seryn pulled back my veil. "I am the queen, Kyeareth Renna Severing Ashland, daughter of Duke Leodore Renard Severing, and wife to King Cinder Burn Ashland, mother to prince Asfaloth Blaze Renard Ashland, and…" I cupped my hands around my abdomen, and the three startled, gazing down at my belly.

"Whomever this one may be born to become…" I whispered.

"Our souls are tied to yours; our lives are bound to yours; our honor belongs to you. You are our liege, our master, our lady. We vow ourselves to you, and our lives are forfeit should our vows be forsaken, this so we vow," they all three echoed. "All hail the queen!"

The entire room echoed this, even the many voices of guardians that I could not see.

My three guardians stood, walking with me out of that place as Seryn and Maxus led me, Seryn on one arm and Maxus on the other.

As we came close, I glanced to the mausoleum.

"I would like to stop by," I told them, and they all murmured out agreement as we walked to the building and stepped inside.

I took my place by the podium, resting my hand against it.

"Asfaloth," I whispered, smiling. "I hope that you will forgive me, darling. I had...I wanted you, so desperately," I said, eyes welling with tears and voice going thick. "I feel...so guilty, expecting another baby that isn't *you*...but I hope you know that you aren't any less loved just because I have another child," I whispered, kissing the podium.

The others stood by, silent, looking away from me to give me some manner of privacy, before Azoth came and kneeled by the podium.

"If it isn't too *presumptuous*...I would like to say that we intend to protect your mother well," he said.

"Oh..." I breathed.

"Your mother, and your sibling. We are sad, and heartbroken, that we could not serve you."

The other two guardians of mine murmured agreeing statements, and I gasped, looking at them.

"You...you don't think I'm...*silly*, for coming and speaking to a grave?" I asked, surprised. "I...I know well enough to know that many of the servants think it's...*unhealthy*."

"What?" They asked, surprised.

"Some have even whispered that I am not of sound mind, that I have gone mad. That my mage blood corrupts me."

Azoth stood, taking my hand, and kissing the back of it.

"It would be unhealthy to keep it all bottled *inside*, your majesty. I specialize in psychology, you know, and I think it is quite healthy and proper for you to come here and speak with him. His *soul* may not rest here, in his body, but it is a good place to come to bond with him in your own spirit."

"Really?" I asked.

"I am sure...if it isn't too inappropriate of me to say...that he is happy that you love him enough to come and visit him each day. I think it is beautiful."

Tears ran down my cheeks, and I, hesitantly, took him into an embrace.

I wasn't sure what I was doing, but...

It felt right.

"Thank you, Azoth." I glanced to them all.

"Might you have any orders or requests of us, your majesty?" Winter asked.

I gave a nod. "Please, I urge all of you to become as comfortable around me as Seryn is. He speaks to me without honorifics and pompous, overly polite manner. He is comfortable with me and I am comfortable with him."

"My lady—" They each looked uncomfortable with the request.

"If we are in front of others, of course you should address me formally, but alone, you are each at leave to address me in a friendly and comfortable way."

They each gave a bow, agreeing to my request, before we all left the mausoleum.

"Ah, you've returned!" Alice said, smiling before she glanced to my new guardians. "You three must be the new Shadow Guardians who will join Sir Seryn in protecting our lovely queen," she smiled, before going into a curtsy. "I am Alice Ren Sheeve, named Ren by our queen for Heaven's Gift Holiday. As you may know, she has started her own surname for her people. She has thus named both of her personal maids and four knights with this middle name, in her honor."

They gave a polite bow, before introducing themselves to her.

"I am Seryn Von-Ren Leonhart," Seryn said, giving a bow. "My queen so renamed me, in honor of the three-year anniversary of my having become her Keeper Knight."

"I dub you Winter Ren, Eclipse Ren and Azoth Ren," I told them. "You may add this to your full names and titles, if you wish."

"We actually are not given surnames to keep, in our lives," Winter explained. "When we are born, the mages who run the order sense our presence. When they learn of our existence and our place in their order, the Shadow Guardian Association retrieves us right away."

"Oh..."

"We will simply be as you have so named us," Eclipse said, smiling. "Ren will hold as our last names until you rename us."

I gave a nod. "So," I said, sitting down in my lounge chair. "What are my duties, as your master?" I asked.

"What do you mean?" Winter asked.

"For Seryn, I am charged with providing his uniforms, formal wear, armors, weapons, meals, room, everything. What do I need to provide for you all?" I asked.

They glanced at one another, before Azoth smiled.

"All Shadow Guardians wear the same uniform, which the king changes once he is coronated. However, you will need to provide us with badges that will discern our rank to you specifically, meaning our level of importance to your needs. We will also wear capes in your designated color, to discern ourselves amongst the group of Shadow Guardians inside of the palace. You may have noticed that Lord Maxus wears a navy-blue cape overtop of his uniform, and a golden badge?"

"Oh? Yes, I had noticed that before."

"That is a perfect example to show that he is the king's guardian, and that he is the most important guardian for the king's purposes. The second guardian wears a silver badge, and the third wears a copper badge."

"I see..." I said, contemplating. "What do I do if I need to summon any of you but not all of you at once?"

"Well," Winter spoke up. "Technically, we will all be very attuned to you and we all hear your thoughts—not to worry, we can't focus in or hear them clearly, unless you directly address us, of course, to respect your privacy."

"I see," I said.

"They are very muddled and vague vocalizations in our head, until you actually address one of us. If you think our name directly, we will hear everything you say until you cut off the contact on your own."

"Oh, I see."

"The principle stands that all you need do to summon us is to address in your thoughts, and whomever you think about, we will come to your side immediately."

"I think I understand…"

"This is also important for commands. Our orders need not be vocalized and verbal, so that we are able to fulfill your commands without possibility of being overheard by an enemy. We are also able to answer you in your mind, as well, so there is no dire need to communicate verbally, in case of emergency."

"I see…"

"Seryn can feel your strong emotions and things happening to you physically, but this is how the bonds differ; we can actually hear your thoughts and know your deepest desires. We can locate you anywhere and feel your physical presence even if you are not with us…as long as your bond with us is intact."

I let all of this information sink in, before I decided to try it out myself, thinking over their listed skill-sets and trying to figure out how I wanted to assign them.

Winter was a wizard who could hunt and track, so his skills would be most useful in sorcery and spell casting.

He would be my mage, taking care of my health and potions and remedies, as well as strategic advice, as wizards took high interest in politics and advising rulers…that was why every ruler had a mage nearby.

Also, since I had mana and mage blood, he could help me in that aspect, as well.

Thus, this was an easy choice.

Winter would serve as my golden-badged guardian, and the head of my Shadow Guardians.

Eclipse was an assassin who specialized in archery and hunting, and would serve well as a spy and gathering and giving information, so more of an informant and errand-runner.

He would be my second-ranked, silver-badged guardian.

Azoth was a doctor, alchemist and an interrogator who specialized in mind-break and control, but was also highly skilled in physical combat with a sword.

He would be best as my third-ranked guardian, taking the copper badge.

'Eclipse, I would like for you to find the butler and inform him that I will need three external black, internal sky-blue capes with sky-blue embroidery of my insignia on the outer corners of them. **You** shall be my silver-badge.'

"Right away, my queen," he said aloud, kneeling before he suddenly disappeared into thin air.

"That is so amazing," I whispered.

The other two chuckled, amused, waiting for their orders with their hands locked behind their backs patiently.

'Winter, you will be my personal mage. I am certain that you have noticed, I have mage blood. I think you can help me?'

'That shouldn't be difficult, my queen,' he said.

'I would like for you to begin researching potions and remedies to help me to keep my pregnancy, because I do not wish for any harm to befall this child. I am sure you are aware of what happened to my previous child.'

With a sad expression, he nodded, kneeling. "I will look into it at once, my queen," he spoke aloud.

'You will be my golden-badged guardian, Winter,' I said in my mind, smiling.

He smiled at me, surprised but honored. "I understand, master," he said, before he disappeared.

'Azoth, you will be my copper-badged guardian. I ask that you remain by my side, and I would greatly appreciate your help, healing my mental state, if you can. I would like for you to speak with Seryn, and get all of the information there is to know about me, and come up with a treatment plan to help me recover from these traumas so that I might become a better queen.'

He kneeled. "It would be an honor, my queen," he said, before he asked Seryn to step outside the door with him and I heard their voices softly through the door.

I sighed, relaxing. "I hadn't realized just how much went into the Shadow Guardians. I actually...feel tired," I said. "And all I did was think," I laughed, glancing at Maxus.

"My lady, conversing with the Shadow Guardians telepathically requires emotional and spiritual energy. It will tire you out, physically. It is actually harder for *you* than it is for the king, because you have mage blood and mana."

"Huh? What does that have to do with it?" I asked. "And, I'm sorry for needing so much explained."

"It isn't a problem. And, it is simple, really. It is taking directly from your lifeforce, rather than just spare reserves of energy. Mages handle the Shadow Guardians poorly compared to Knights."

'Winter, I hate to interrupt you, but I just wanted to ensure that I can, in fact, hear you and communicate with you when you are away from me.'

'*I can,*' I heard the immediate response. '*It is no trouble at all. It takes time to get used to it, I am sure. And you are welcome to intrude in my mind anytime, my queen. I am your golden-badged Shadow Guardian; it is my duty to be available to you at all times. Please do not apologize to me for such again. If anything, I welcome you to converse with me anytime, whether it be for business or just for companionship. That is what we are here for. I assure you, all three of us feel the same.*'

'Thank you, Winter. Oh, also...how do I cut off communication?'

'*Just imagine yourself closing a door between you and whomever you are conversing with inside of your mind, your majesty,*' he chuckled. '*Please, do not hesitate to ask any questions.*'

I began to do as he said, imagining myself shutting a door between the two of us...and surely enough, his voice cut out of my head, entirely.

I could still hear the other's vaguely, so I shut the door between them and myself, as well.

I was still a bit overwhelmed.

In fact, I was wholly exhausted, honestly.

When had I gotten so tired? Was this really all because of telepathy?

I slipped into sleep, and after some time, I vaguely felt my body being moved before it was laid into bed, and I felt the bed shift.

I glanced up, and saw Seryn, mask off and room dark, snoozing beside of me.

How long had we been asleep?

Had I not only closed my eyes for a few moments?

"Seryn," I whispered.

He roused a bit, turning his head to me.

"Seryn," I tried again.

I suddenly felt the most horrible instinct hit me, and I became alarmed.

This change in my feelings seemed to do the trick as Seryn finished waking up.

He glanced down at me.

"You had a nightmare again?" He asked. "They have been becoming more frequent," he told me.

"Oh," I whispered, tears filling my eyes. "No, not a nightmare, but I just woke up and I just...I have...the most awful feeling..." I said, getting worked up and starting to tear up.

He scooted down, taking me into his arms. "Shh," he whispered, stroking my hair. "Tell me."

"I feel...something bad...*ominous*."

"Do you have any more specific notions than that?" He asked, concerned.

I considered this. I could see flashes in my mind, but nothing solid.

'*Winter...I am sorry to disturb you, but I was wondering...how **specific** is your magic?*' I asked.

The answer was delayed for a moment, and glancing out the window at the night sky, I felt guilty for most likely waking him, as well.

Finally, his answer came. '*You aren't disturbing me, your majesty; I am happy to be of any service to you. And, that depends; what do you need?*'

'*Do you have the ability to translate dreams?*' I asked.

I could feel him hesitate. '*I **do** have a magic that helps with **premonitions**...do you feel that you've had a premonition, my queen?*' I heard him ask.

'*I think that might be possible that I am fixing to have one. I am usually lucid most of the time throughout, and it is not the first time that I have had this happen, but this is the first time I have felt it coming on.*'

'*I will come to you right away,*' he said, and within just a few moments, he suddenly appeared beside of me, kneeling on the floor.

Seryn startled, surprised, but I patted his shoulder to get him to relax.

Winter stepped to my side, and I felt my head warm as he held a magic circle above my hair like a halo.

"Tell me your vision, my queen," Winter said quietly. "I will review it with you, personally."

I pictured it, even as it took place each night lately, taking a deep breath to steady myself.

I began to get chills, my whole body breaking out into sweat.

"You are entering a vision," he affirmed. "You were right to call for me. This is not just a dream, but a premonition of the magic sort. Please, empty your mind and let it flow. Easy and gentle, stay as lucid as you can and relax so it doesn't hurt you. Breathe."

I took a deep breath, calming myself, and felt my body easing.

"Good. Now, just remain calm, and let your mind's eyes open, my queen. Let the vision come over, peacefully. Do not struggle. As you go through it, tell me what it is that you see, if you can."

I took a few more calming breaths, and I felt myself slip off into a dream-like place. The lights and colors were distorted, and the imagery was a little blurry.

Almost like my vision was covered by stained glass.

"It was just bits and pieces...I continue to have a dream that I am being surrounded by fire and blood, screams...suddenly, I see the previous king, leading me through a dark path..."

I flinched, tensing.

"Shh," I heard Winter soothe. "Go on. Let it flow. Easy..."

"But...before we reached the end, he turned and ran back the other way before he screamed. I was all alone, and then I was outside of the castle, and—"

"Calm, my queen," Seryn reminded as I got worked up again, reminding me to breathe calmly and relax. I felt his hands on my shoulders, grounding me in reality even as my mind was seeing something else.

"What else, your majesty?" Winter asked.

"Then, I was drowning, and bleeding, and everything went black..."

He thought over this for a long, long time. "This is quite alarming, my queen. It looked as if the castle will be attacked, and the previous king will lead you down an escape passage."

"...But he doesn't survive?" I asked, eyes still closed.

"It seems like he was covering for you. You will come out to the outside, all alone, but then you will be cast into a body of water and lose consciousness."

I startled. "Is this going to really happen?!" I asked, alarmed, finally opening my eyes, and looking at him.

He hesitated.

"I am unsure," he said. "Though I may be able to tell you what the dreams mean, I cannot tell you how *accurate* they are, nor if they will come to fruition. I also cannot use magic to find out that information. Mage blood is tricky, and because you have mage blood, only *your* blood itself knows how true it is."

"I see."

"I am sorry, my queen," he whispered.

"No, no!" I smiled. "Your explanation was helpful. I will know what to look out for, at least."

"Unfortunately, if you feel this distressed and alarmed...it is plausible to think that this might actually happen. We need to be careful, and prepare beforehand to be ready and protect the castle...and you."

He gave a nod, before Eclipse suddenly appeared, a box in his arms. "My queen, what you requested of me before has been finished," he told me.

"Ahh, thank you, Eclipse. Azoth, you go ahead and come on out," I told him, and when all three of them kneeled before me, I gave out the capes and badges I'd had Eclipse to get made, and I smiled fondly at them. "Thank you, each of you, for everything that you have done and will do," I whispered.

Fists over hearts, they all bowed to me.

Chapter 11

Kyeareth...

Two weeks passed by, and it was the day of Sun's Falling.

Oh, the irony...

I was eating dinner with my medication to help strengthen my baby, when I heard it; The sound of a cannon.

The palace shook as it come under attack, and the screaming began.

My guardians, as well as Seryn, were all by my side in an instant, even as the former king and his son rushed into the room, ordering the hall to the chamber hall be barricaded off.

"What's happening?" I asked, gasping, and grasping my belly in alarm.

Though I already knew, and my fear spiked dramatically.

My guardians got in defensive stances around me, uneasy with my own emotions coursing through them as if they were their own feelings.

"What is happening?!"

"The castle is under attack!" My father-in-law said, rushed. "We don't have a lot of time before they will breach the gates. They were waiting for this opportunity, since Cinder is away!"

"W-what...I—" I cut myself off, holding my belly, eyes wide and panicked...and he gazed at my belly, shock in his eyes.

"Are...are *you*...?"

I gave a sharp nod. "Yes..." I whispered, tears filling my eyes.

I glanced to Winter. "*My dream!*" I cried, and he gasped, eyes wide. "I had nearly forgotten because it stopped after that night..."

He nodded. "It *was* a premonition, after all..."

"There is an escape passage," my father-in-law said. "I must lead you two to it, right away! You have to escape."

"We can't use *that* passage!" I cried. "I know this sounds absurd, but *please* believe me! I had a premonition that this very thing would happen. In the vision, you lead me through the passage but *you* get killed, and I am left alone...I get hurt and cast into the sea!" I cried, clutching my belly. "Tell me, what else is there? What other way is there to escape?"

He gaped at me. "T-there is none," he whispered, soft. "There was only one escape passage on *this* hall, on *this* floor. It would take you much too long to reach the other passage in your condition."

"*Where is this other passage?*" Seryn asked. "I can take her!"

"On the floor *below* us, behind the throne, in the *floor*."

"In the floor?"

"It is covered by carpet and a table full of jewels, as a *distraction*. Someone would have to stay behind, and put the carpet and table *back*...to hide the passage."

"Where does it lead out?" Azoth asked.

"It leads out to the glass greenhouse by the crystal lake, whereas the other passage on this hall leads out to the back of the palace."

"It is still inside of the palace walls, but it is further away than the back of the palace, at least," the prince said. He glanced to me. "You and I will take that passage, then."

"B-but how are we supposed to get there fast enough?" I asked. "I'm not supposed to be stressed or strained...I am at high risk!" I cried. "I don't want to lose another baby," I sobbed, holding my belly.

They all gave me sad expressions.

"We will do all that we can to protect you; *both* of you...but it is a risk that we have to gamble with," Seryn said. "You are the queen. It is our jobs to protect you and the baby."

"Quickly, your majesty!" Alice whispered, frantic. "They have just breached the palace gates! They will defeat the castle knights and reach the doors to the castle quickly!"

"Come, your majesty. I may not be a warrior, but I have a gift for speed. I can get you there the fastest!"

I nodded, and gave him permission. Lifting me in his arms, Winter ran...and he was right. He was the fastest of my people, so he was the best option that I had for speed.

The halls blurred around us, and he practically floated down the stairwells. The others couldn't even keep up with him.

"H-how are you so fast?" I asked in a whisper.

"Mana and spells help me move more quickly, my queen. Call it cheating, if you wish, but I did train my body for many years to accommodate for it, as well. Magic just gave me a boost."

That was the last that we said until we reached our destination. We all ran out, taking a different hall and rushing through the ball room, quickly, to go through to the throne room.

"The castle is breeched!" We heard maids shouting through the halls, shrieks and cries and death rattles echoing around us.

The hairs on my arms raised, and my blood felt like ice in my veins as I heard the sounds of death assault my ears.

My people were being murdered.

My husband was out at war…and through all of this, even if I lived, it was likely that I would lose my pregnancy.

My hope plummeted.

This was justice for being born the way that I had been, taking that from the duchess, for loving my brother in a sinful way, for taking vengeance on the princess…

As we entered the throne room, we saw several assailants, and as my guardians rushed to defend against them, Alice pulled out a dagger and rushed to block one's path as he approached Winter and I.

"Alice!" I cried, seeing her be struck down.

Other knights rushed to help Seryn and Azoth fight against the assailants, and I felt us moving.

The king tugged us to the table that he'd mentioned before and moved it, getting the carpet pulled back and opening the trap door.

"Go on! You have no time!" He cried, and the prince jumped into the hole, reaching up to let me drop into his arms and we moved so that Winter could enter behind us.

'Winter, what about the others?!' I cried in my mind. 'Seryn, Azoth, Eclipse...they're **all** still **out** there!'

He hesitated, and I could vaguely hear other voices in his head as he communicated with the other two.

'The former king has gotten the table and carpet back in place, and the other guardians, as well as the Keeper Knight, are going to take the other passage to escape. Two of the assailants from the throne room escaped, so it is likely they will tell the others about this route. We have a little time, but not much. We **might** be able to make it if we hurry.'

"R-really?" I asked, relief hitting me.

He gave a nod. "We need to keep going, the others will find a way to join us later."

He sat me on my feet, leading the way as the prince held my hand, tugging me along quietly.

"Are you really pregnant?" The prince asked me in a whisper. I gave a nod, and he beamed a smile at me. "I am so glad that you and my brother have worked past that tragedy," he said, soft. "I am so happy for you."

He gave me a hug from the side, and I smiled at him. "Thank you."

We startled when we heard the trap-door thrown open from the way we had come.

It was a long way through the tunnel, but they would reach us quickly enough.

'Winter, what do we do?' I begged, pleading in my mind for a solution.

'I will carry you, and we will run.'

'What if we don't make it?' I cried in my mind.

He sighed. *'That is the only option left to us. I am a decent fighter, but I cannot protect both of you from multiple attackers at once. My strength is spell-casting.'*

He lifted me in his arms, and I glanced back at my brother-in-law...who stood there, sword drawn, facing behind us.

"B-brother?" I asked, fear striking me.

"Get out of here," he told me, voice quiet but tone firm and serious.

"Flaming—!"

"I will cover you on this end...for my niece or nephew."

"Flaming!" I cried as he bolted toward the way we had entered, and Winter turned, bolting the other direction even as I sobbed against his chest, against his wizard uniform.

"That was brave of him," Winter whispered. "He's a good kid."

I cried out a sob against him, sniffling.

We heard shouting and swords clanging, before a desperate cry screamed out, and Winter ran all the faster.

We *finally* reached the end of the tunnel, and he turned to me.

"***Pretoct tem quehn form tem clutch oh reepah***," he whispered, and as he pressed his lips to my forehead in a small kiss, I saw a shimmering glowing softly around my body, almost like a second skin.

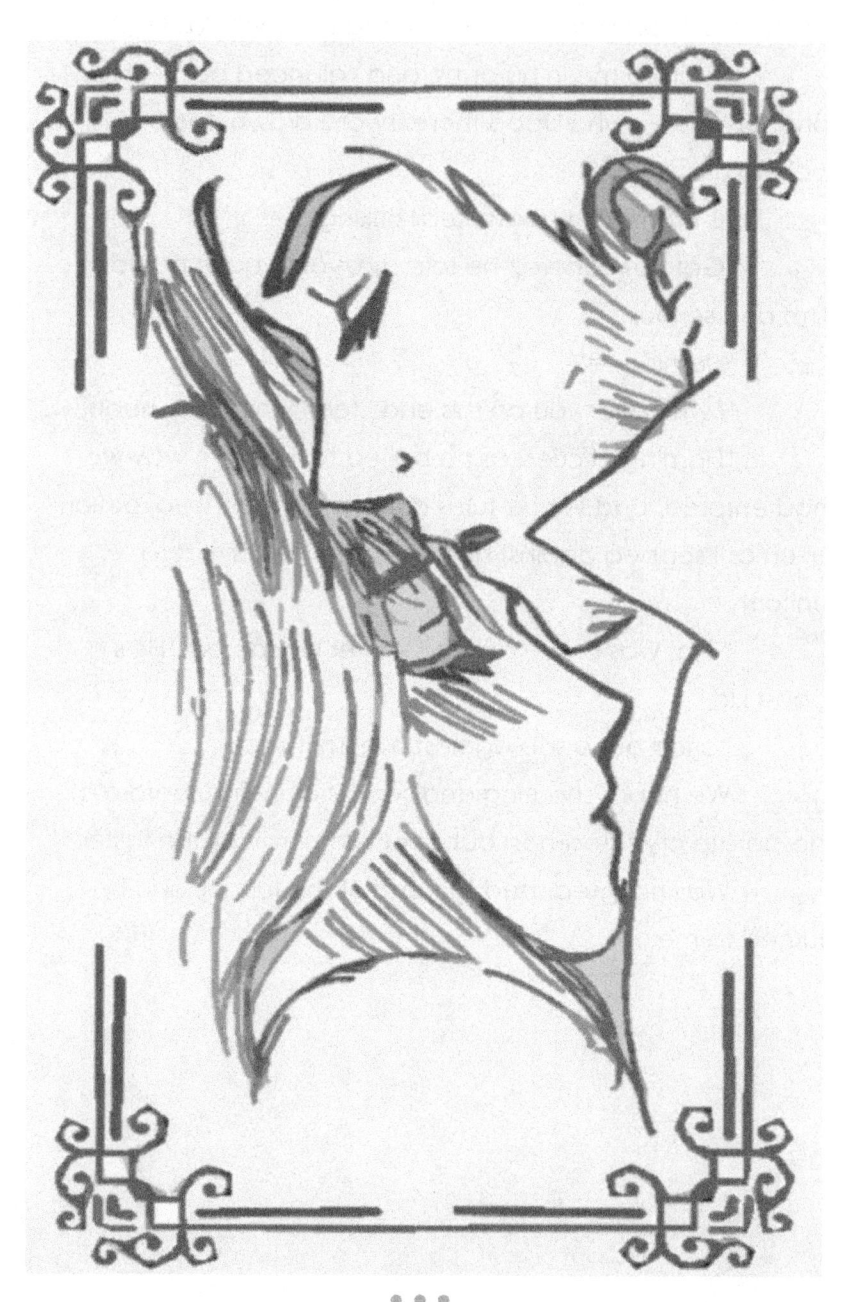

"This is the most that I can do for you, for now," he told me. "It is a protection spell. It will, at the very least, keep you from dying...even if you get captured, stabbed, and thrown into the sea like you saw in the vision...your soul will remain in the body, and as long as you are not cremated or burned at the stake, you will recover."

I gaped at him. "Winter..." I whispered.

He gave me a hug, before he turned, climbing the ladder to the trap-door and opened it, glancing around.

"Nobody is here, but all of the walls are made of glass. We will be able to be easily spotted at this location..." He sighed, and leaned down, grabbing me and helping me up the ladder and out of the tunnel, before he shut the trap-door and barricaded it off so that nobody could follow us.

He glanced around, pulling me over to the door, and glanced out. We could see soldiers rushing into the castle.

I watched, and vaguely heard, voices from Winter's internal dialogue.

"What—" I paused, before I moved to internal voice. *'Winter, what is happening?'* I asked.

'I have managed to contact the others. They have lost the former queen, but the former king is safe. Seryn has driven back a lot of the force, with Azoth's help, and Eclipse has been helping to assassinate intruders from the balconies. The leader of the forces has been identified, however, and they have mentioned a benefactor that is part of our own kingdom.'

I took in all of this information. *'Winter, who is the leader of the intruding force?'*

'It is Duke Steel,' he said, and I startled. *'Yes, as in, your brother's father-in-law.'*

'Astaroth would **never** be a part of a rebellion...'

'We aren't saying for sure that he is involved, but the duke has been overheard as he mentioned to his soldiers that he wanted to deliver **you** to his daughter.'

I flinched. 'What is it with sisters-in-law?' I asked, appalled. '*I don't know what I have done to deserve this! Am I simply cursed?*' I despaired.

'My queen, we don't have time for mourning right now,' he told me, internal voice sad.

'Azoth,' I addressed. 'What is everyone's current status?'

'Seryn and I are defending the second prince, now. We found him at the entrance to the secret exit in the throne room, being forced back by enemies. We have secured the king, and he is safe for **now**, hidden away. Eclipse is on the highest balcony and is taking down enemy soldiers. Winter told us that you two are in the glass greenhouse.'

'Flaming is safe?' I asked.

'He is, for **now**. He is about to join his father. They should be alright, even if the palace is overrun.'

'Has any mention of Astaroth been made?'

He hesitated. '*I **did** hear that he and his wife are at odds at the moment, and that her father decided to start a coup. A separate benefactor was mentioned but not named, though there is an outside source and an internal source. It seems like we have enemies all around us.*'

'Wait...a coup...is the city my husband went to help even **in** trouble?' I asked.

'**That** was true,' Azoth said. 'However, the benefactor of the coup attacked the city so that the king would be called away, and so that you would be left here **alone**.'

'But why me...?'

'It must be something to do with your brother, at least on Duke Steel's end. I would need to know who the benefactor is to know more, though.'

I looked to Winter. 'Winter...is it clear to move?'

'It **isn't**.'

'Eclipse,' I addressed. 'Can you clear it so that Winter and I can get out of the greenhouse safely?'

'I will adjust my position immediately, my queen,' he responded, and we waited for just a moment before we saw multiple enemies start dropping.

"The assassin moved!" We heard voices shouting, rushing to take cover.

'The two of you have a window—a small window, my queen!' Eclipse called in his mind. **'Go!'**

Winter lifted me in his arms, darting out the door and into the woods nearby, going around the lake. Though, it seemed that our momentary good luck and our small head-start wasn't enough to get us out of danger just yet.

"There they are! It's the *queen*!" I heard someone shout, and Winter gasped.

He got me to a gate near the edge of the woods, and he nudged me toward it. 'Get out of here, your majesty,' he told me. 'I will stay behind and cover your escape. I will follow after you as soon as I can!'

'Winter!' I cried.

'**Go**! You won't die!'

I gave him a quick hug. 'Please, all of you...don't die!' I cried. 'I don't want to lose **anyone** else!'

I turned, bolting through the gate, and I heard a flurry of powerful explosions and screams sounding through the forest behind me as I ran.

My stomach began to cramp, but I couldn't stop. Tears ran down my face as I begged and pleaded with my baby to stay with me, to be patient and just let us get through this.

I *had* to keep going, I had to reach safety. I did slow down, but I had to keep going.

"Well, well," I heard a voice from behind me. I startled, whirling around, to see Duke Steel. "If it isn't the woman who *truly* holds my son-in-law's heart."

My blood froze as I startled. "What...?" I asked. "What are you saying?"

"I think you know what I imply."

"You're wrong—"

He scoffed. "Oh, don't even feign ignorance, 'your majesty,'" he said, voice full of malice. "I saw how you reacted when the pregnancy was announced a couple of months ago. That was *not* the reaction of a happy aunt...that was the reaction of a *devastated lover*."

"You don't know what you're talking about."

"*Really?* Then how come there were *multiple* letters found in his chambers from *you*, addressed to *him*? How come there was letter found addressed to *you*, in *your* chambers, *from* him? A *confession*, if I remember correctly. But go ahead, continue to deny it."

"There is nothing between us!" I cried.

"You're really going to keep that story up?"

"I'm telling you the truth! There isn't—"

"Or, perhaps he is your lover in secret? Let us not forget the child you even named for his namesake! Because as soon as *you* reacted that way that night that we announced the pregnancy of my daughter and your brother, he *shoved my daughter away* and attempted to *pursue **you**.*"

I gaped at him. "*What?*" I asked, stunned.

He laughed. "You won't have to contemplate it much longer, I'm afraid. As soon as he finds out that you've been disposed of, he will no longer have an excuse to ignore my daughter, and she will be a true duchess. So long as you live, you will hold too much of his heart."

I startled and groaned, doubling over in pain, when a dagger was shoved through my chest.

I gasped, watching him lift a thick lock of my hair and chopping it off, tucking it into his pocket, before I sent out a final plea to my guardians...and I heard them each crying out to me in my mind.

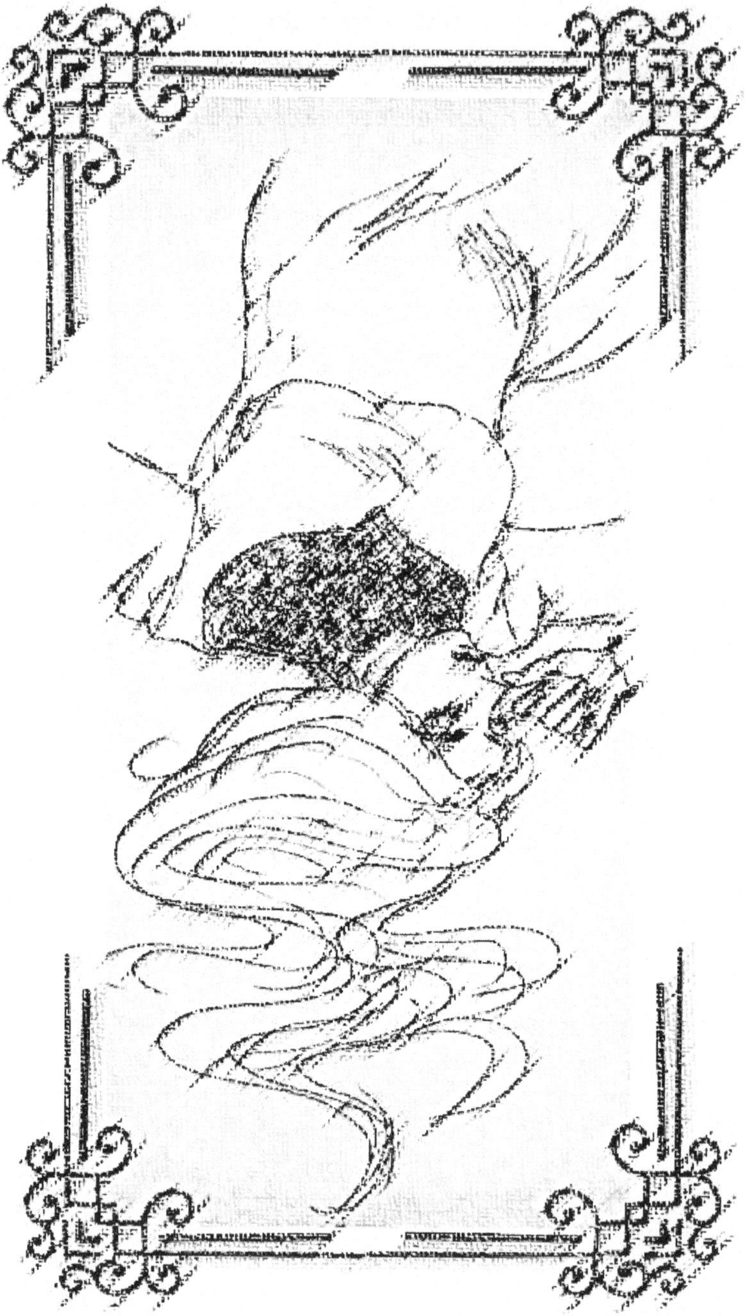

Then, everything went dark, and I felt sharp stabbing pains in my chest as my bonds to my guardians snapped from the strain on my soul.

All I could think as my body was lifted and I drifted into unconsciousness was that my guardians were going to think that I was dead, because—though Winter's magic might save my life and spare me from dying—my bond with my guardians probably wouldn't be so lucky.

All I could think, as my mind emptied and I felt myself being dragged down into the dark...was that my mind might not be so lucky, either.

Chapter 12

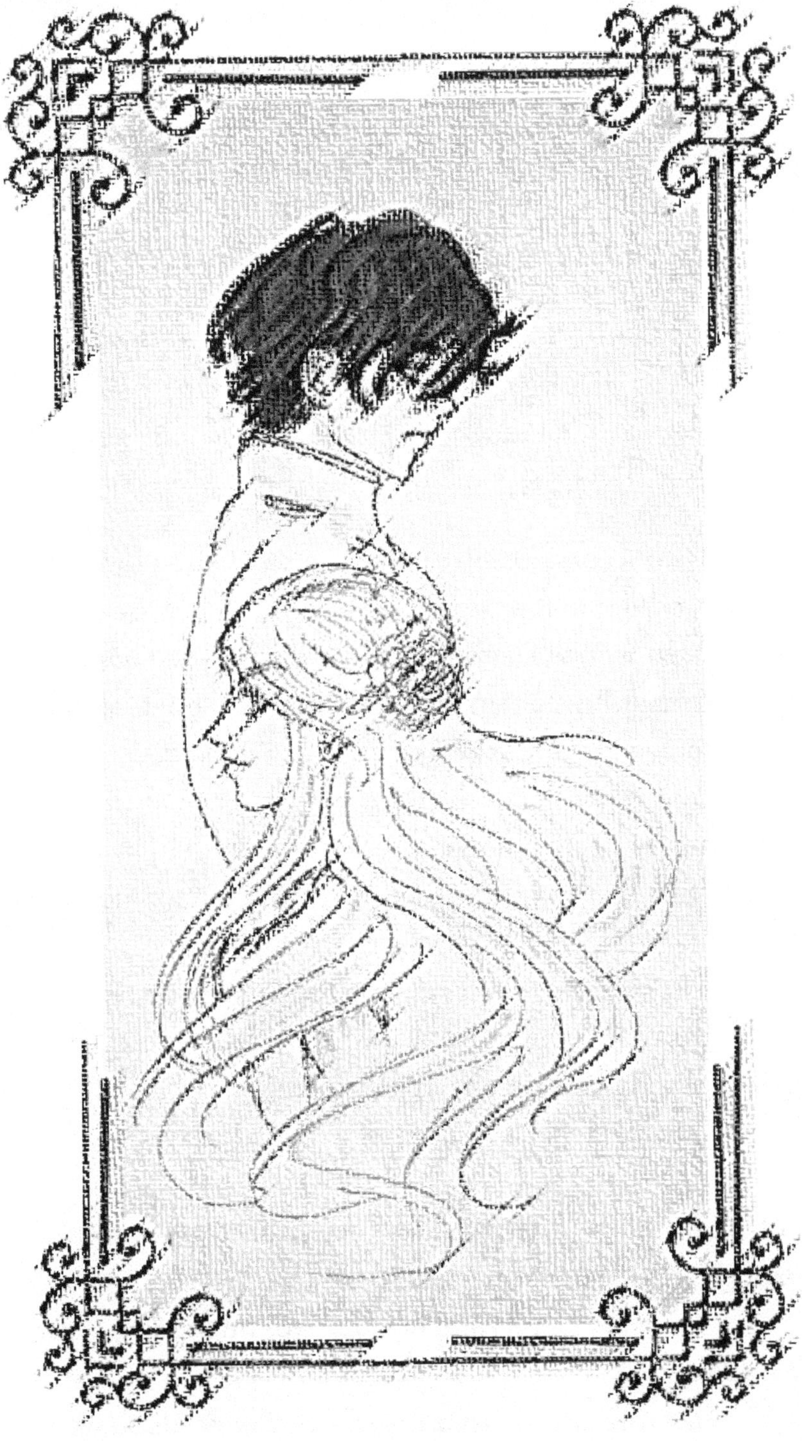

Cinder...

Nivis's End, 317 Ashland Rule

Two weeks passed, and it was only three days after we had arrived to the city I had been requested to help that the messenger hawk arrived, informing us of what had happened. I was startled and horrified at the contents that the letter the hawk had brought to us contained.

My mother, captured and held prisoner. My father, captured and held prisoner.

My younger brother, missing in action from the scene.

My father-in-law—Kyeareth's father—dead.

My mother-in-law and her young child, the child that had been so long-awaited by my cousin and his bride...both captured and held prisoner at the duchy.

My brother-in-law, captured and held prisoner in the capital...?

My brother-in-law's wife, healthy and contentedly progressing in her pregnancy...? Wait, what?

What the fuck? What the fuck was happening in my kingdom!?

My wife...my pregnant wife...confirmed **dead**.

I gaped at the letter, crying out as I threw it away from me, sobbing out an enraged snarl.

"No!" I cried.

Confirmed dead?

*It had been **confirmed**?*

How?

Who had done it?

Why had this happened?

What...was I supposed to do now?

Had I simply not suffered enough, up until this point?

This had to be a joke, right?

I felt at a loss; completely empty as I fought back bile that threatened to spew out from my throat.

My guardians rushed to my side, lifting the letter, and reading it themselves, before they gasped, gaping at me.

"Sire..." they whispered.

"My *queen*," I sobbed. "Who? I didn't even finish reading the damn thing!" I snarled. "Who dared to do this!? Tell me who did it!" I shouted, volatile.

"It was Duke Steel," one whispered, going over the contents again. "From what is stated in this report, the queen was the target of the assault from Duke Steel. It even lists his reason as being, 'because his daughter was threatened with divorce and having the heir to the duchy disinherited over a severe argument with Astaroth over the queen.'"

I knew, immediately, what the cause of the argument was.

There was no way that I wouldn't have known it, immediately.

It was because of Astaroth's feelings for my queen, and her feelings for him.

I roared with my rage, slinging my sword across the room. "All because they had once wanted to be lovers!" I snarled, and my guardians gaped at me in shock.

There was a long, heavy silence.

"**What**...?" They all three asked concurrently.

I imagined that this must have been a big plot twist to them.

"My wife...she and her brother were always particularly close, and they had..." I sighed. "They had genuine romantic feelings for one another, and they *still* do. They've never acted on it, but the feeling *is* there. If ever Kyeareth and I were to have divorced, I honestly would have anticipated that he would have brought her into the duchy to be his bride, morality and public opinions be damned."

It made me think of her reaction to the news of his impending fatherhood.

"Oh, *no*," one whispered as I replayed the scene of the young duke's pregnancy announcement rushed into my mind and I projected it to them.

"She still loved him and he saw her reaction, so, still loving her, he...he couldn't let her go. And then his wife saw his reaction! It was a chain reaction, and it only secured their assurance that Astaroth still loved the queen."

"That's so sad," my other Shadow Guardian whispered.

I nodded. "My wife..." I sobbed, picturing her in my mind. "She...she was pregnant. We had only just found out. We hadn't told anyone about it yet. Now...now, she is reported as being confirmed dead...and I have lost not only *another* child," I sobbed. "But *her*..."

"What?" One of my guardians cried. "Oh, no!" He said, holding his hand over his mouth.

"Yes...she wasn't very far along. Now, they're both dead," I said, clenching my teeth. "I have to get home. I have to make this right, and I have to bring justice upon these evil-doers and coup plotters—"

"But sire, this city still needs aid—"

I glared at him, snarling in my anger. "Do you dare to tell your king that he cannot return home when his *pregnant wife* has been confirmed to be *dead?*" I asked.

They trembled, following me as I announced to the citizens of the town that I had to return home due to an emergency, but that the workers and farmers would remain—well paid, of course—to stay behind and help...before I refurnished my supplies, and got onto my horse, setting off for home.

I rode as hard and as fast as I could manage.

It took only eleven days to arrive.

I was successfully cutting out three days with only having a *single break* during the trip to sleep, as I had been eating while on the way, and we finally reached the capital to find a sight I hadn't ever anticipated seeing in my lifetime.

My heart sank, and fear spiked in me.

There was so much damage. There was so much death. There was a lot happening.

It was jarring, and difficult to process even as I was seeing it.

What was I even seeing...?

The castle was a mess, bodies being buried in the cemetery on the way to the castle. Just how many people had died...?

"The king!" I heard as a voice cried, and frantic rushing took place. I strode into the palace even as enemies aimed their weapons at me, but I made my way to the throne room and faced Duke Steel without so much as looking at them. They didn't shoot.

"Hello, Cinder," he sneered at me as I reached him.

"I am still the Crowned King of this country, Duke Steel. Please, show me the courtesy of at least addressing me as such. Dignity and propriety as a noble, remember? Come, now."

He sighed, giving a nod. "I suppose it is the *least* that I can do, your majesty, for what I have done. I hadn't wanted it to come to this, but I could see no other way to deal with the circumstances at hand."

"Why *have* you done this?"

"Because your 'wife' was the object of my son-in-law's disgusting, twisted, mutated, and morally corrupted affections, and so long as *she* lived...he would continue to ignore and neglect my daughter. I could not allow that. It was my duty as her father to help her secure his attentions to where they rightfully belonged, rather than having her nervous and fearful of him abandoning her."

"*Where* is my wife?" I snarled. "I heard that it was confirmed that she had died...but I want to see the proof. Bring me her body. Above all else, she was my wife! I want her body, at least!"

He looked away, leaning back on the throne, before he stood. "I stabbed her in the heart...before I dumped her body in the river. So, I *am* sorry, but you cannot have her body returned to you."

A strangled, sobbing gasp ripped out of my chest, and I clutched my abdomen. "She was *pregnant!*" I snarled at him.

He startled, and I saw the sadness cross his eyes. "That...*that* is regrettable. I am sorry, your majesty, I know how long you had waited for children, even after the loss of the first prince. Though, I am sure it is better off without a sick, morally corrupt Mage-Born woman like her give birth to more of her kind—"

"You dare to *apologize* to me, even as you stand in front of *my throne* and spew that nonsense from your vile mouth?!"

He looked away. "I cannot give you back this throne," he said. "Nor is it nonsense. It is the truth...and now, I cannot allow you to leave this place."

He began to raise his hand, and I heard the clicking of weapons as they were made ready to fire.

A bolt suddenly speared through his throat, and I startled.

What—?

I was whirling around just in time to see a tall, well-built man in a black and navy uniform, with a black cape with a sky-blue inside, a silver badge on his chest.

I knew, right away, that he was one of my wife's Shadow Guardians.

"Your majesty!" He shouted, rushing to kneel beside me even as the opposing soldiers fled the palace, now that their leader was dead. "Thank heavens, I managed to track you down!"

"Who are you?" I asked.

"I am Eclipse, my king. Your wife's Shadow Guardian. The other two are not here, and neither is Sir Seryn. Seryn left first, searching for the queen. The other two were locked up in the dungeon. I made sure I wasn't captured, as I figured you'd return and need my help with the enemy."

"'Made sure' you weren't captured?" I asked, morbidly amused. "Pray tell, how *are* you free?" I asked, curious.

"I am an assassin," he smirked at me, and I was interested that my wife's soul had chosen an assassin as a guardian.

"How did you know to find me here?"

I noted the silver badge on his chest again as he answered.

"I was busy killing soldiers from the trees, but then I saw the messenger hawk sent out in the direction of the city you had went to help. I tracked the bird, so that I would be able to find you, but then I found your path leading back here, so I came back to wait for you. You were talking, though, so I waited for the right moment to attack him," he said, motioning to Duke Steel.

"Wait...why would Seryn search for the queen?" I asked.

"Why? Your majesty...do you not know?"

"...Know what, exactly?" I asked, getting impatient. "I don't have time for games."

His next words knocked the wind out of me.

Brought me to my knees.

My eyes burned as I gaped up at him in shock.

Reeling. Feeling the pressure of what felt like waves of water covering me, blocking out everything else around me. It was overwhelming.

I was reeling, and I was praying beyond hope that his words were not lies;

.....

"Your majesty...the queen is still alive."

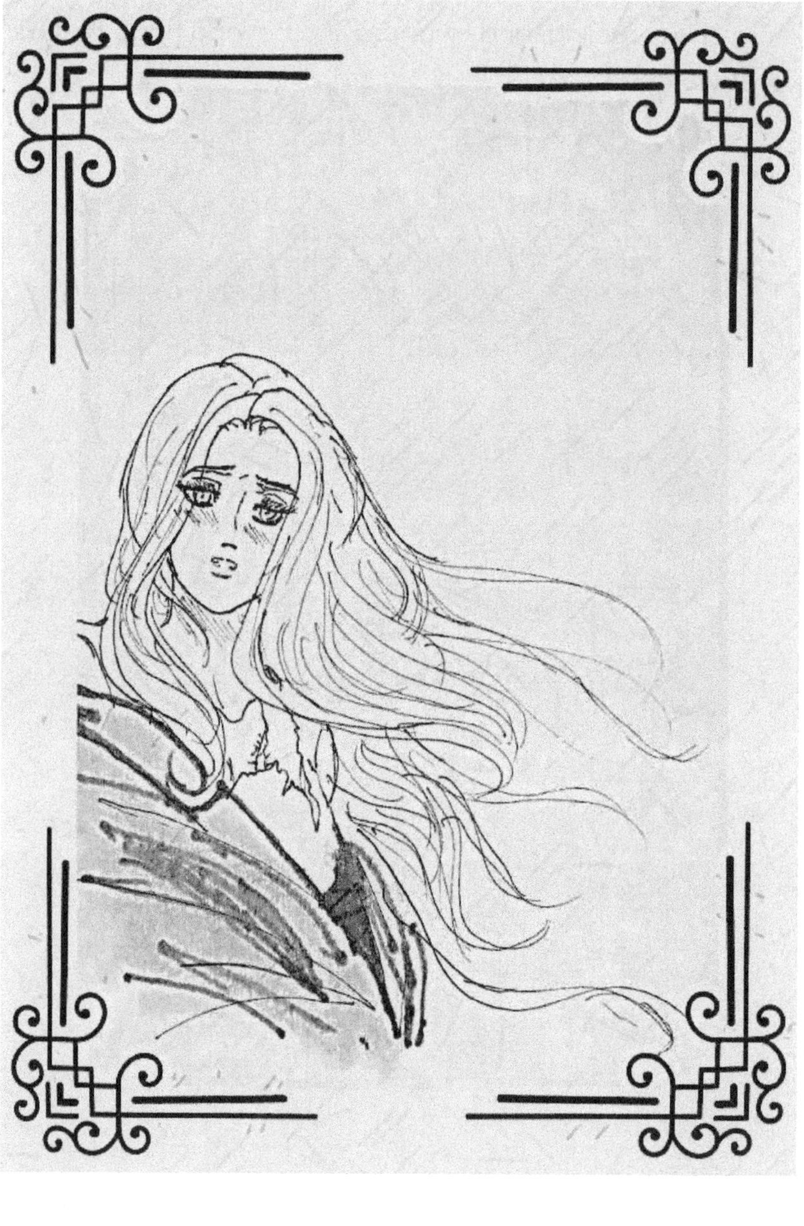

Chapter 13

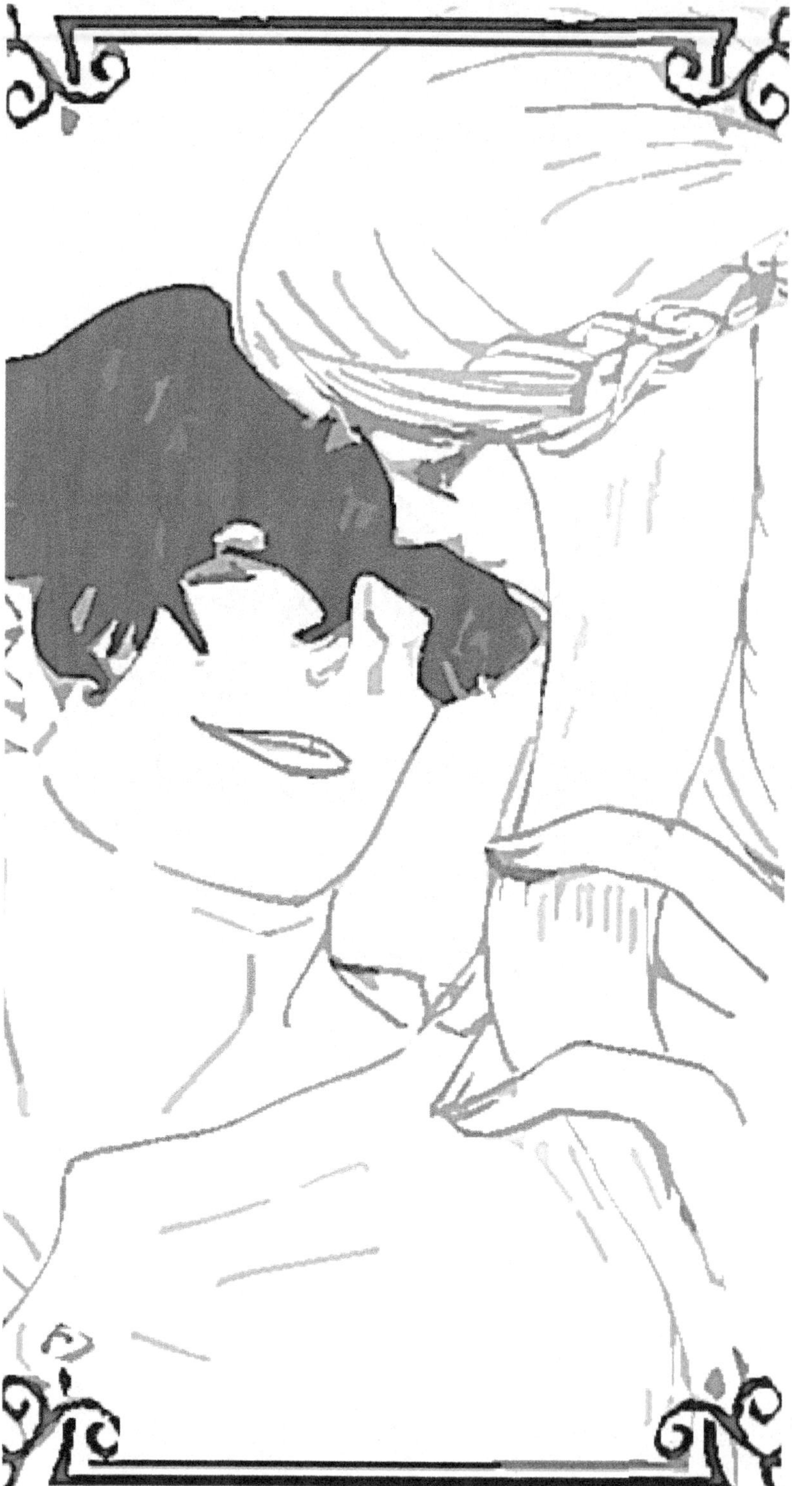

Cinder...

Nivis's End, 317 Ashland Rule

I was lying in our bed, watching the stars and the moons in the sky overhead. I heard my wife shuffle in our bed, and I turned to look at her.

Her stormy eyes were wide, and I watched the lights from the aurora outside dance in her eyes as she looks upward at me.

My heart thumped wildly as I reached so that I tugged her onto me, looking down at me. I reached up, stroking her hair.

"I knew it was a dream," I murmured. "There was no way that you'd be killed and taken away from me."

She gave me a smile. "I was."

I smiled up at her, almost mesmerized by her beauty...until what she said registered.

"What?"

"I was killed. Officially. Now, I'm out there, waiting for you to find me. I'm lost."

"...Lost...?" I asked.

"I don't know where I am. I'm still asleep."

"Kyeareth—"

"I miss you."

"...I miss you," I smiled up at her. "You'll be back in my arms soon, my love," I told her, reaching up and stroking her hair.

"You'd better find me soon, Cinder...or I might just disappear." I felt the ghost of her kiss, even as I shot awake.

I woke up in a panic, startled. "What?" I asked, floored.

I looked around my chambers, before I sighed as I noticed the empty space in my bed.

I just couldn't accept that she was gone.

At least, though, she was still alive, and I could find her. That was all that mattered.

I still remembered finding out that my queen was still alive.

"Your majesty...the queen is still alive."

"What?!" I asked, startled. "But...but how do you know—"

He smiled at me. "Yes, my king. Seryn's seal, while a bit faded over, was still in place on his hand."

Relief poured into me.

If a Keeper Knight's seal disappeared, it meant that their master had passed away, and the same was true if the seal disappeared from the master's hand.

If the seal was still on his hand, then that would mean that she was, indeed, alive.

"But...how?" I asked. "Stabbed through the heart and thrown into a river? How could she live through that...?"

"I haven't been able to talk to the other guardians because our queen is unconscious, and I wasn't able to sneak into the prison."

"Oh, I see."

The guardians could speak to one another telepathically, as long as the master's mind was conscious, both awake conscious and sub-conscious in sleep.

If the master was passed out, knocked unconscious, or the mind was no longer intact and was damaged...then that communication was cut off for them, and they couldn't locate her that way, either.

I strode through the castle, leading him to the castle's prisons.

"King Cinder!" My brother-in-law cried. "I am so sorry!" He sobbed. "My sister...my sister is dead, and it is all because of me," he cried. "My love is gone!"

"She isn't dead, Astaroth," I informed, and he looked at me in dumb shock.

"W-what?" He asked. "Are...are you sure?"

"Seryn's seal is still intact, so he went to search for her."

He stared at me, tears running down his face and hope in his eyes as I opened his cell. "Truly...?" He asked.

I smiled. "Yes," I told him. "Though, the Shadow Guardians are unable to contact her or talk to one another in the mind-space, which means that she is unconscious...she is alive, at the least, as far as we know. We will just have to trust in Seryn, now. He is the one who has the best chances of finding his master."

"Thank the heavens!"

"Yes," I said. "I would rather not lose another child, if I can help it."

He startled, gaping at me. "...What?" He asked.

I smiled softly, warmly. "She and I are expecting another child...or, at least...we were, before all of this."

"Cinder..." he whispered.

I pulled him into a hug as fresh tears ran down his face. "It is okay," I said. "It isn't your fault. You cannot help how you feel."

He froze, pulling back with wide, glassy eyes. "You...you-"

"I knew," I confirmed, and his face showed his horror. "Don't be embarrassed or ashamed, Astaroth. I have told Kyeareth the same. You two were inseparable for many years...it makes sense, in its own strange way. You were best friends, in every sense of the word, and have stayed close. From what I have been told, you and the maid were the only two people she ever got to be close to as a child."

"...That is true," he murmured.

"See? It makes sense if you two...love each other. She may have made room for me inside of her heart, but there will always be a special place for you that I cannot ever fill for her."

"You...you aren't bothered by that?" He asked, incredulous.

I shook my head. "I'm not...because I know that she is loyal. I know that she is faithful...she always has been. She could have had ample opportunity to be with you if she had wished to do so, but she didn't, because she has honor."

He scoffed, soft. "My wife...she found out about my feelings, and...she refused to accept them. She demanded that I cut off all ties to Kyeareth, and I refused."

"Of course."

"So, I threatened that if she tried to make me cut off Kyeareth, I would divorce her and disinherit the child."

I nodded. "Yes, I had heard that."

"Her father...conspired with his vassals, got up funding and an army, and schemed this entire plot to stage a coup, just so that they could kill Kyeareth. When he told me that he'd fulfilled his task...I thought that I would die."

"I know exactly what you mean..." I said.

I strode through the prison to the cell at the end, where I found two men in uniforms that matched Eclipse's uniform.

"Your majesty!" They said, kneeling.

"You heard my conversation with Astaroth, I am sure?" I asked, hoping not to have to fill them in too, and they both nodded. "Who are you?"

"I am Azoth, my king," one said. "I specialize in interrogation and psychology," he said.

"I see," noting the copper badge, and he nodded. "And you?" I asked the other one, who sported a gold badge.

"I am Winter, your majesty. I am a wizard, and the queen named me her personal mage."

"I see," I said. I glanced at the mage. Of course, my Mage-Born wife would choose a mage to be her golden badged Shadow Guardian. "I am not entirely surprised a mage was her top guardian, considering her bloodline...I don't suppose you know how my wife was stabbed in the heart and thrown into a river and somehow managed to live?" I asked, raising my eyebrows.

He smiled at me, a warm, genuine grin.

"I cast a spell on her just before we got out of the secret escape passage, my king. It was a protection spell. It couldn't keep her from getting hurt, but it did keep her from dying. If she is unconscious, we may not be able to locate her, but Seryn still can."

"What does that mean?"

"We have to have the link to her consciousness to be able to communicate with her or locate her with our powers of connection, but he doesn't. The seal for Keeper Knights works differently than the bond and seal of the Shadow Guardians."

"So, what you are saying is that if we can track Seryn, he should be able to lead us to the queen," Azoth said, a contemplative expression on his face.

I glanced at Astaroth, and he gave me a nod. "I will go with them to search for her. You need to stay here, and get things back in order. What is the state of things, anyhow?"

I told him the details, and he sighed. I glanced at Winter. "Are either of you trackers?" I asked.

"Both Eclipse and I are," Winter answered me, and I sighed in relief.

"Winter, can you cast healing magic?" I asked.

"I can, your majesty."

"You will help us track Seryn, then, in case Kyeareth is injured. Eclipse, can you track the second prince?" I asked.

"I can and shall, majesty."

"Set out now, then. I will remain here, and get things back in order. Contact me immediately if there are any developments."

"Sire!" They agreed in unison, and they set out to follow my orders.

All that I could do now...was to wait, and pray. That had been just days ago, the castle was busy being refurnished and remodeled to get rid of the blood and bodies that had been strewn about during the coup de tat. I felt helpless, waiting here for them to do the work for me, but I was only decent with a sword. I couldn't track, nor could I heal.

I just had to wait.

Chapter 14

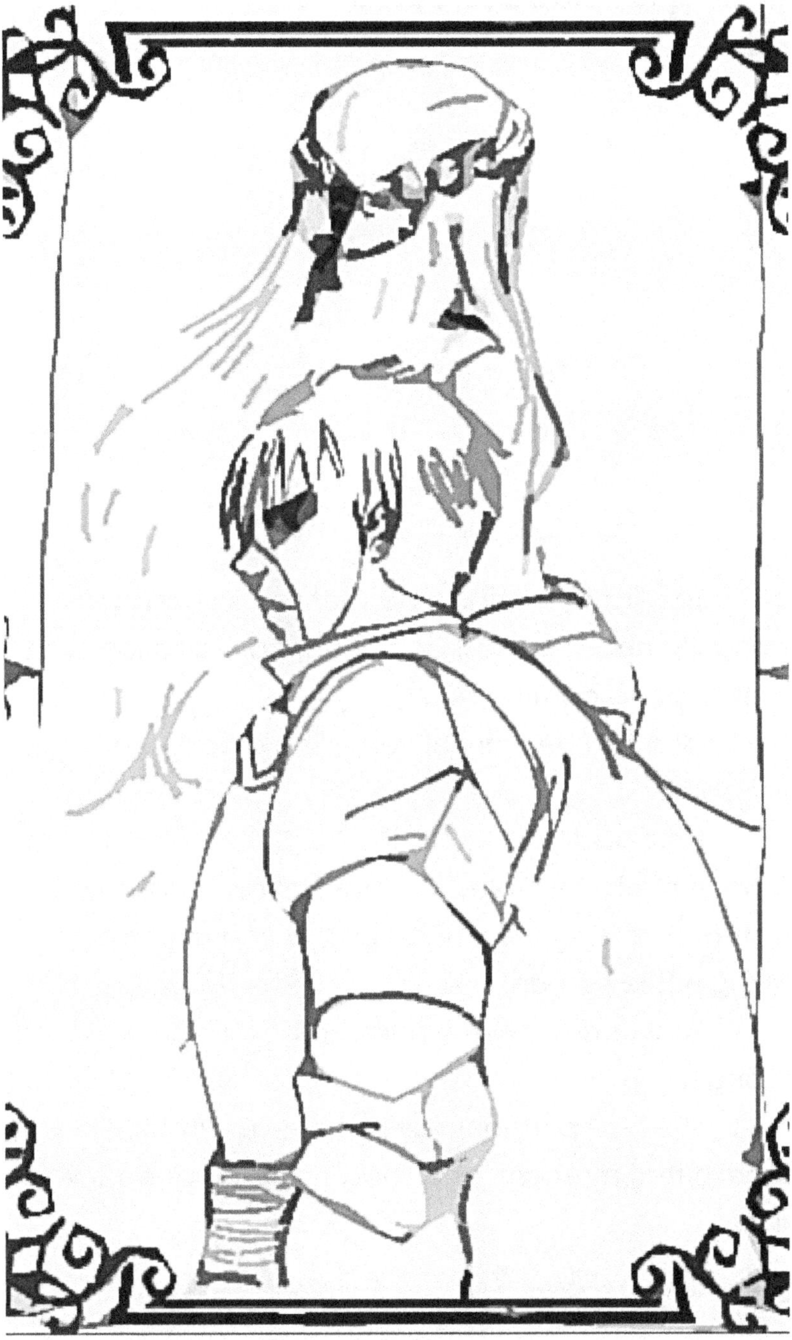

Seryn Leonhart...

Year's Fall, 311 Ashland Rule

The first time I had ever met her, she'd been crying. I'd heard the last part of her conversation, and attempted to comfort her.

"*Should* I be wary of you?" She asked, seemingly unaware.

Little had I known, at the time, that this girl would change me to my core...the base of my mind, my existence, forever influenced by the charm of this young noblewoman.

I never could have guessed how I would change.

She had permanently imprinted her place on my heart in that moment, and I had not even been aware of it.

Solaris's Reign, 313 AR

Time had passed, and now, it was the night of her engagement to the Crowned Prince, Cinder.

It was a lot of pressure on her, at her age, I had to admit.

She was so young, and I sympathized.

I learned that she'd wanted to make me her Keeper Knight, surprising me. She'd been so genuine about it, too.

I could hardly believe that she really sought me out for the position, hadn't even tried to appoint someone else.

The subjugation had taken a bad toll on her, but she had survived.

After the success of the subjugation on me, and Kyeareth losing consciousness, I had time to ask the servants to send someone to the Knight's Order and to my family home, grab my things, and bring them back here to the duchy, and I even had time to get my things set up in my own room that was adjoined to her own chambers.

It felt odd, to be living with this girl now, though I had known to expect it if I was chosen by a noble of high rank.

A Marquess household or a Duke household would often have their Keeper Knight's chambers attached to their master's chambers, to be close by, for safety measures.

Lower households, however, didn't have that.

At least I wouldn't have to take lodging with the knights in the knight's quarters in the barracks.

It was almost an entire day before she would awaken, after a long night and morning of struggling to breathe and sweating badly. She was really having a hard time.

"Are you...alright?" I asked, resting my index and middle fingers above the pulse point on her wrist. "You've been struggling to breathe for a while."

My head pounded, even as her own did, and feeling the state of her body was very disconcerting to me.

She gasped out, groaning as I tried to simply open my mouth, and I looked away.

"I knew that it would be difficult for someone like you, but I hadn't quite anticipated that you would be in this condition..."

"How...how long ago did the party end?" She croaked out.

I chuckled. "It has been almost twenty-four hours, my lady. I've had enough time to send someone to collect my things from my family home, as well as the Knight's Order, and bring all of my things back here...I even had time to get my chamber set up," I said, motioning over to the extra attached room adjoined to her own.

"Is everything to your liking? Have you eaten well?" She asked, and I felt a bolt of surprise run through me.

I glanced at her before turning to face my room. "It is surprising to me that this is your first concern," I said, voice even. I glanced over my shoulder at her. "You seem to be a thoughtful lady."

"You are my knight...It is my job to ensure that you have everything that you need...including food and clothing."

I turned to face her, giving a light sigh. "No, my lady, I haven't eaten since you lost consciousness, and I do have a few outfits, but as my master, it is your responsibility to provide me with a new uniform, armor and weaponry..."

"I...remember," she groaned, and I strode over, resting my hands on her shoulders softly and helping her to sit up. "We...learned our duties...to our knights...a few weeks ago."

"I thought this may happen," I said when she started choking and sputtering when I tried to have her drink a sip of water from a glass. "Your body is still reeling from the subjugation. You put your life on the line to have me as your knight, my lady...why would you go so far for me?"

"Because you are the best," she smiled, and my eyes widened a bit before I gave her a small smirk.

"Indeed," I said, tone cocky. I glanced downward, and my eyes widened further in surprise as I reached forward, grabbing and lifting my handkerchief up into the air.

She gasped, reaching to try to snatch it, but I was too slow, a blush on her cheeks. "You...kept this?" I asked, tone finally showing emotion.

"You...were kind to me."

I shook my head, handing it back to her. "You are the daughter of a duke, my lady. I am sure many people are kind to you."

She scoffed. "You must not know much about me."

Solaris's Reign, 314 AR

"Take the princess to her chambers," the Crowned Prince told the maids. "And bring her a good meal. She needs to get some rest."

I pulled her dress back down to cover the carnage there, before I lifted her into my arms, trying to be as ginger and easy with her as I could. She had already been through enough.

I followed the maids, carrying her away.

My own eyes burn as fresh tears stung her eyes, and she turned her face into my chest plate as I carried her through the palace to her chambers.

She has faced great humiliation, today, and I could only imagine she wanted to bury herself away and hide. I couldn't say that I blamed her.

I could feel the stirring of feeling in my cold, dead heart.

When we got to her chambers, the maids already had a meal and a bath prepared for her, but were surprised when I stepped between them and her after I set her on her feet.

"My lady is...feeling particularly vulnerable and upset at the moment. I would suggest, on her behalf, that you allow me to attend her needs tonight. She has, as you saw, every right to be devastated."

The maids glanced at one another with timid, distressed expressions.

"Of course," one said, bowing. "That was...that was rough," she whispered. "I am sorry, your highness," she said to my lady, bowing.

They all scurried out of the room easily enough, not questioning that I would be taking care of her.

Honestly, they were likely thinking that she had used me for experimenting and oral pleasures before we had come here, since I was a Keeper Knight and now, I was insisting on caring for her myself. However, I couldn't care less what they thought. She was my lady, and I was going to be by her side through this.

When they were gone, I-still holding her hand, even through all this-turned to her. "May I touch you?" I asked, and she flinched, thinking of the pain between her legs. "I don't mean that way, goodness. Calm down," I assured her. "I *mean*, may I change, bathe and feed you?"

She gave permission, and I carefully undid the ties of her gown and corset, letting it slide to the floor, before I unpinned her sweaty hair, undoing the braiding and setting the tiara to the side.

I ignored her naked body—though, I took a mental note that it was nice and pleasing to me, I was more focused on her needs than any desire I may have felt toward her in that moment.

I pushed my mind to ignore my chub in my pants, knowing it wasn't the time or place, my mind letting my actions drift from thought as I pulled her over to the tub and lifted her gently.

I sat her into the warm water, and I took my time soaping up a sponge and wiping down her body, trying to only skitter over the breast area and rear end.

I allowed her to clean her privates herself, and she flinched and groaned at the pain there.

I helped her to wash her hair, before I got her finished and dried, dressed in a fresh nightgown, and I toweled off her hair and brushed it out for her.

Then, I led her to her bed, and she looked around, taking in this new space, her new chambers.

I had her lean back against a mountain of pillows, before I took a bite of each of her food items, checking it for her.

After a few moments of waiting, and feeling assured that it was safe, I lifted a bite up for her.

She let out a shuddering sigh, and I knew that she was not really in the mood to eat, but I hoped that since I had been a saint to her that day by holding her hand the entire time despite how much I hadn't wanted to, she would see fit to reward my dedication by eating at least a little bit of a meal.

I fed her about half of the meal, before she couldn't stand to eat anymore.

"Please, summon someone to bring you a meal and eat something," she asked me. "You haven't eaten today, either."

Well, I had, but only a few bites earlier that morning before she had started getting ready, so I guessed she was mostly right.

I chuckled. "I will shortly," I told her. "You need to stop thinking of others first, and think about yourself. I will wait until you are asleep."

"Do you promise?"

"I promise." I brought her a sip of water and a few other things to help comfort her, including her brother's letter and a bottle of heated water to press against her privates.

She relaxed, feeling the heat take away the tension from the muscles, and sighed as she slipped into a deep, well-earned sleep.

Nivis's End, 317 AR

We had been through so, so much in the last few years.

She was so scared that she would be abandoned, but after an entire childhood of her family's knights ignoring her and neglecting her care, and only having her brother and maid to be close to...it made sense.

After quite some time, she had opened up to me and the Crowned Prince. Not long after that, and then she had become pregnant.

From what had happened when she had gotten pregnant with prince Asfaloth, how excited she had been, how *careful*...

I had spent so many hours with her, helping sooth her morning sickness and her aches, her cravings, feeling the prince kicking and moving inside of her very womb both on the outside of her belly and inside of my own, which had been an intensely intimate experience...

I had been ready to meet the young prince myself. The son of my master. The woman who had, in her own rights, warmed the ice from my soul and burned a place for herself on my heart.

Would the prince do the same?

I had been happy for her, that the Crowned Prince had grown so much closer with her, that they were on good terms.

Then, the child had been murdered while still inside of his mother...

It had been brutal, hard to accept, sickening and heartbreaking.

My lady hadn't been the same since.

She was overly cautious and paranoid after that. She was nervous and tense constantly. Her mana was always agitated, stirring restlessly beneath her skin in her blood.

It was reasonable that she had closed herself off again. Her heart needed a break. It had taken so long for her to open up to me fully, scared that I would abandon her, and then to open up to her husband again.

Then, she had found out she was pregnant again, just before the king had been sent off to help a city in danger. I was so excited for her, but so nervous for her as well, worrying constantly and determined to protect this child.

I would do all in my power to keep her from losing this child, too.

Of course, it would be when the king was a fortnight's journey away from us that the kingdom would come under attack. I could only picture her face in my mind, not knowing where she was or what was happening...I knew that her Shadow Guardians had lost contact with her.

Duke Steel's soldiers surrounded us even in the throne-room, dragging Astaroth in, slinging him to his knees in front of us. We were surprised. Duke Steel entered the room, coming to sit on the throne.

He was cocky, knowing that we had no ability to stop the remainder of his forces in our current conditions, as it was only me and her Shadow Guardians left. We were outmatched and unprepared.

"Well, well, if it isn't the son-in-law who is in love with his own sister?" The duke cackled darkly. "You should be pleased to know that I have seen to it that this *issue* will no longer...be an issue."

"You're sick! I-I'm not with my sister in such a way! She's married, quite happily, to a king! Are you insane? She is a queen! You cannot touch her!"

"You think so?"

"Yes!"

"Really?" The duke asked, looking amused.

"My sister is safe," Astaroth said, confident and certain...but considering the pains that I had been being speared with, I wasn't so certain...

"You naïve little fool," he murmured, chuckling. "You really think that she's still alive?"

"Yes," Astaroth said, though the chuckling from his father-in-law was starting to lower his spirits a bit. "My sister is the queen—"

"Your queen has already met her end!" Duke Steel laughed, shrugging his shoulders as he pulled out a scrap of the gown that she had been wearing that day, and I startled.

The cloth was covered blood.

"Too bad for her, she died painfully even though I *tried* to make it quick."

Astaroth, like myself, had seen her in that pattern enough times.

Enough times to know the material as belonging to his sister...he'd seen her in that very gown many times because it was one of her favorites.

He gaped at the material for a moment...a long, confused moment. It took him a long moment to register what he was seeing, I was sure.

"Kyeareth Renna Severing Ashland is dead," the duke said.

Astaroth shouted out a snarled cry, sobbing and thrashing against the hold of the soldiers who held him.

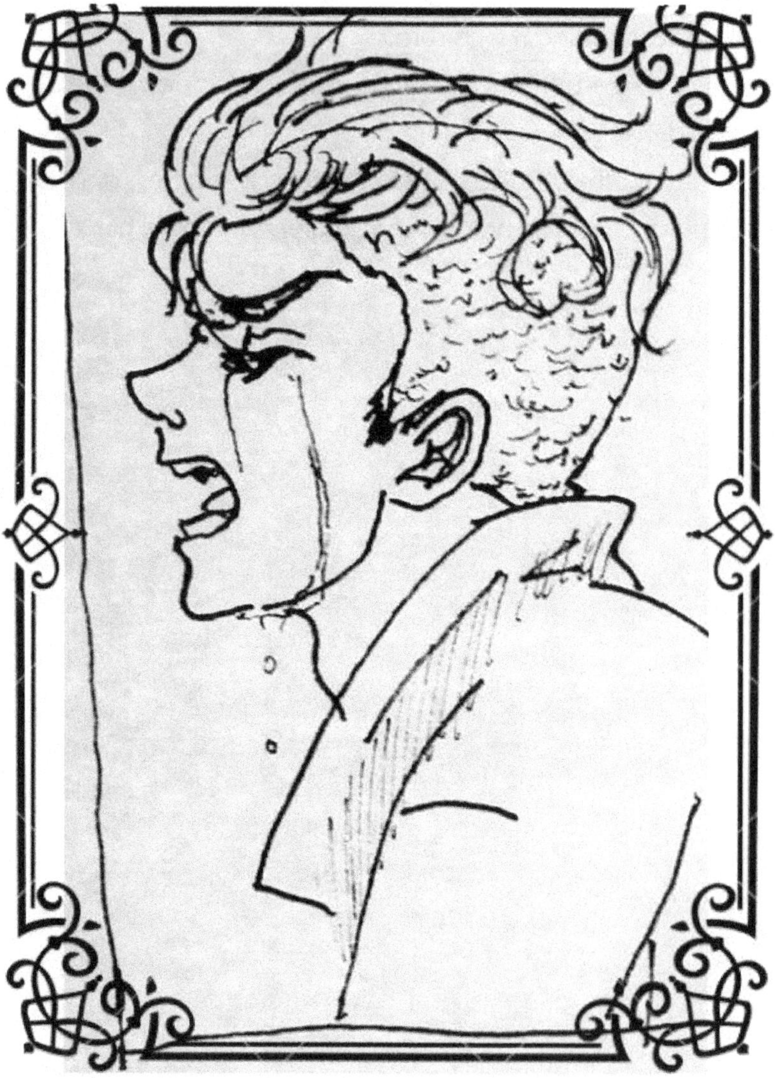

"You *monster!*" He shouted. "You think I will ever love your daughter after what you have done?!"

I turned, rushing out the doors of the castle, and I heard Duke Steel order them to let me go, laughing that there was nothing that I could do, anyway.

I was just a masterless Keeper Knight, now, and as such, it was only a matter of days before I would wither away and die.

That was how the seal worked.

Within twenty-four hours of the death of a master, the Personal Keeper Knight would die as well, unless they had a sorcerer transfer the service seal to someone else at the time of death; for example, if my lady were to die and wanted me to serve her child after she was gone, she could ask a sorcerer to transfer the seal to the child.

That child would not have to re-subjugate me, because I had already been subjugated under that seal, but the magic would transfer.

However, it took a special magic that could only transfer the seal to the next in the bloodline—a child or a sibling, directly.

Astaroth already had a Keeper Knight, and my master's child…was dead.

Most knights didn't get to be transferred in that manner, as this case usually only happened that way when a master knows that they are going to pass away beforehand or the family deeply cares to keep the Keeper Knight in the family.

I had heard that the knight would start to deteriorate rapidly upon the death of their master, but I didn't actually feel any different.

I remembered my chest hurting sharply, being so terrified and alarmed, but...

Did that mean that my lady was dead?

Once I was out of the castle, I took a deep breath and tried to gather my thoughts.

Wait—! Wait, just a moment! I felt like a fool, suddenly, for not thinking of it sooner and allowing myself to panic at all.

I slipped the glove off of my hand, checking my seal.

Still there, I was thankful beyond belief. That meant that she was still alive, after all!

As long as a master was still alive, the seal would remain on my hand.

If it disappeared, that would mean she was dead.

To see it still there in my hand, that meant that she was still alive.

I ran, picking up the faint scent of my lady's perfume, following it to where I had last heard that she was so that I could try to track her from there…

CHAPTER 15

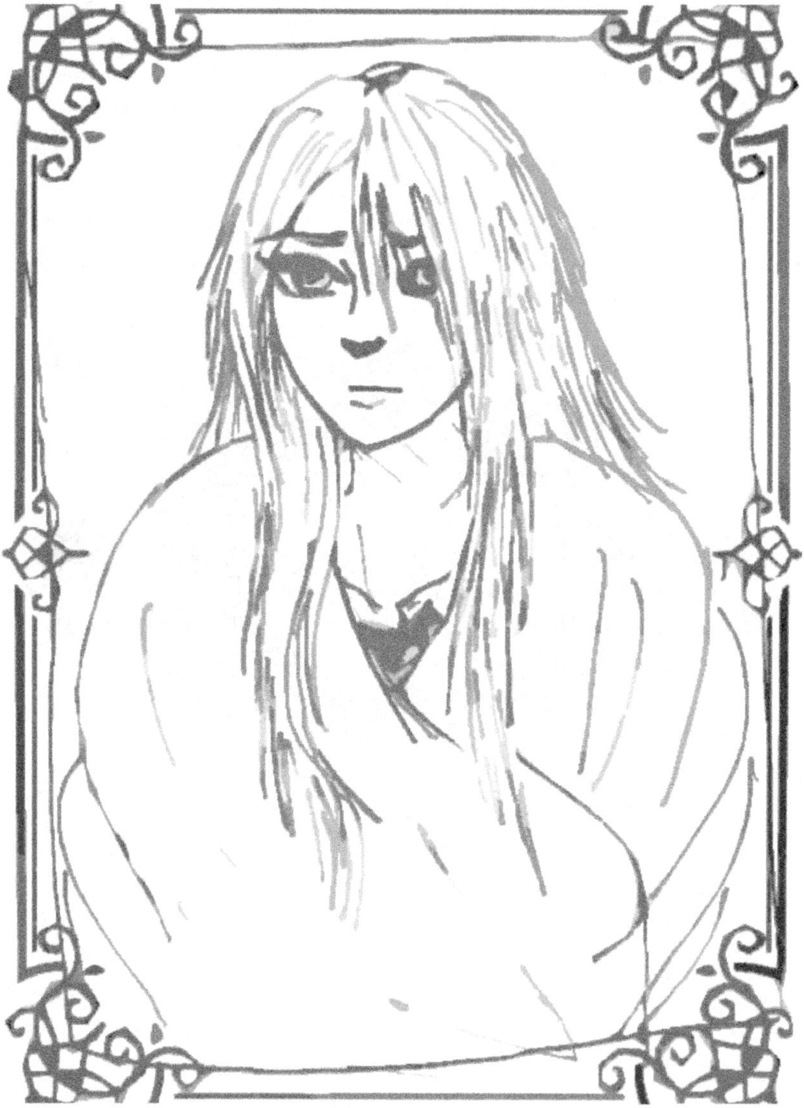

Kyeareth...

Seed's Sewn, 317 Ashland Rule

    I heard voices around me, but I couldn't make out the language they spoke in.

    It didn't sound like my mother tongue...but then again, I wasn't even positive if I would recognize my mother tongue when everything that I heard was jumbled. All that I could really hear was my heartbeat roaring in my ears.

    Where was I?

    What had I been doing?

    For that matter...who was I, exactly?

    Oh, no.

    This was alarming...

    I opened my eyes, groaning and groggy, and I startled when a couple of people rushed over to me, trying to...

    Apparently trying to, from their body language, get me to quiet down...?

They were shushing me and desperately motioning for me to be quiet. No matter what the language, a lot of body language was simply universal.

I realized then that I was shouting, and I cut my voice, quieting. I hadn't even realized I was screaming...

Oops.

I glanced around, taking in my surroundings.

There was a man and a manly-looking woman, both with tan, olive-toned skin, and dark hair. The woman had short brown hair and brown eyes, and the man had shoulder-length black hair with olive-colored eyes.

They looked to be related, with similar facial structures and features.

The man, though, he seemed...familiar to me...something about the hair and eye color that felt soothing to me, in that moment, though I wasn't sure why.

That black hair and those green eyes struck me for some reason, but why?

Stil wrapped in a blanket, I tried to sit up, but I groaned softly, clutching my chest as I fell back to my back. They rushed to motion for me to stay still, and they spoke in hurried voices in a language that I couldn't understand.

The man seemed to think of something, bringing over a hand-held mirror, and lifted it to show my chest...

There was a gnarled, deep stab wound there, stitched sloppily, and looking like it was starting to fester a bit as it was purple and green and nasty looking.

I startled, heartbeat going wild in my chest.

Good heavens!

How on earth had I survived something like *that*?

More importantly...how had it happened?

...On a positive sidenote, I was beautiful otherwise. I had light, silvery ash-blonde hair and light, beautiful blue eyes with swirls of grey...like storm clouds, almost.

I had serious bags under my eyes, and I looked malnourished, but I was obviously beautiful when cared for.

The woman brought me a chipped clay cup filled with water, and I glanced around my surroundings again.

It looked like I was...in a *barn*...?

Or rather a stable, probably, from the sound of the horses in the background.

How had I gotten here? Was I supposed to be here?

I held out my hand, motioning my head in a nodding motion to show that I wanted my head up, and they helped me sit up.

"Where am I?" I tried, and they startled.

They glanced at one another, before the man attempted to speak to me.

No, I couldn't understand the language, even now that I could fully hear him speaking. "I'm sorry...I don't understand."

They seemed to understand this with my sad, disheartened body language, at least, even if they couldn't understand my words.

The woman spoke to the man, and he suddenly seemed alarmed, standing, and going to glance out of the window of the barn. Meanwhile, the woman brought me a plate of beans and a steamed potato, offering it to me.

I took it, gladly, because I didn't care what it looked like or what it was...if it was edible, I was starving.

I winced at the bland flavors, and she looked a bit embarrassed as I ate the food, but when her own belly growled, I stopped, glancing at them.

From my clothing, it looked like I had been a noble of some sort, just...seemingly lost?

The woman wore ragged clothing, dirty and unkempt...she had thick gloves on her hands, and galoshes on her feet. She looked like a stable-hand.

The man looked a little better, wearing a pair of decent pants, somewhat nicer boots, a button-down olive-green shirt and a simple but decent-looking grey and black plaid vest over it. His hair was tussled and windblown, almost curly but wavier. I figured with his more kept-up looks, he was likely a carriage-driver or something of that nature that required him to be seen more.

I ate about half of the meal on the plate that the girl had handed to me, before I offered it back to her.

She startled, and shook her head, but I gestured it toward her again.

I saw the man glance at us, giving her a smile and a nod, and she reluctantly took the plate and ate a little bit of the food before she offered me the rest.

I ate it with no complaint, since I had given her the chance to finish the rest but she had still shared the rest of it with me.

I felt safe here, at least. They didn't seem to mean me any harm.

We heard a sudden harsh voice shout, and we startled.

The man helped the woman lift me, having me hide behind a stack of hay near the back of the stables, before he rushed out and she joined him outside for a few moments.

What was going on...?

I cautiously listened to a door open, and raised voices.

The man who had been helping me spoke calmly, and then the door shut again as the men's voices left.

The woman waited some time before she made her way back to me, looking a bit nervous.

"What's wrong?" I asked.

She glanced at me, looking a bit worried, before she sighed, speaking to me again in a tongue I didn't know.

We heard what sounded like a cart leaving, horses whinnying, and I could see out of a nearby window that the man who had been helping me with this woman was driving a wagon away, a hat now on his head.

So, he *was* a carriage-driver...that was why his clothes were a bit neater and tidier than the woman's.

I could guess, from the bed set up nearby in the back corner of this stable, that she was either a slave or a servant of low birth to a lord somewhere.

I didn't know how I knew this information, when I didn't even know who I was or where I came from.

If I was of low birth, I wouldn't be able to discern their jobs so easily, I wouldn't think.

Finally, the woman came to me, and motioned to my chest, to my wound, and it seemed from her expression that she was asking me about what had happened.

I gave my most sincerely-lost expression and shrugged my shoulders, saying "I don't know" in a sad, confused tone.

She gaped at me, before pointing at herself.

"Gaia!" She said. Then, pointed at me, before pointing to herself again. "Gaia. Hm?" She asked, pointing to me again.

I thought for a long, long moment, before I shook my head, shrugging and looking away, embarrassed as my cheeks flamed.

She gasped, seeming to understand.

She tried one last time, pointing to herself. "Gaia!" She pointed after where the wagon had left, imitating holding the reins of a horse and tipping an imaginary hat—like the hat the driver had been wearing before. "Cassian!" She said. Then, she pointed to me. "Hm?"

She seemed to hope that I just didn't understand what she was asking, but unfortunately, I did...and I just didn't know the answer.

I shook my head, clutching my hand over my heart. "I don't know..." I said, tears filling my eyes, before soft sobs came out of my throat, and I slid to my knees. "I don't know." I whispered.

She sighed, plopping to her knees, and giving me a hug, attempting to soothe me as she patted my back roughly.

During the time that Cassian was gone, she spent the entire time chatting to me, wild gestures and expressions, and I couldn't help but be a bit charmed by her behavior.

Not in a romantic way, of course, but in an awed kind of way.

I wasn't sure if I had ever met someone like her before, but I enjoyed the reverie from thinking about my predicament.

I was happy that I had someone so...perky to spend time with, and I vaguely wondered how I had grown up to be so thrilled by such erratic tendencies.

Was I a very sheltered child?

Were my parents... missing me?

It was almost dark when the carriage returned, and she gasped, rushing me back into my hiding spot before she rushed out of the barn.

I glanced out of the window to watch as she unlatched the horses from the wagon, bringing them back into the barn and brushing them, getting their feed and water ready even as the apparent head-of-the-house tossed a couple of coins to Cassian, and then stepped back into a very nice-looking manor.

Cassian stepped into an off-building attached to the stables for a few moments, before he re-emerged, dressed in a loose black shirt tucked into tight black pants and boots, glancing toward the manor before he trotted into the stables quickly, and I came out from behind the hay.

I was wobbly, but I was able to walk if I was assisted to a standing position, now, and I was thankful to be on my feet.

I heard Gaia quickly relay to him about the day, and he seemed taken-aback, alarmed, glancing at me with a concerned expression before he walked over to me.

He was about a head-and-a-half taller than me, and in this lantern light, his striking features were even more handsome.

He glanced back at Gaia, saying something with a frustrated voice, before he led me to a blanket laying on the pile of hay behind the stack, where I had been to begin with that morning, having me sit with his help and sounding like he was scolding me a bit.

Acting like a worried older brother or something, I smiled endearingly at the behavior.

Did I have any brothers? I wondered about myself.

He kneeled in front of me, eyes a bit warily-confused. He then touched his own chest.

"Cassian," he said, soft. Then he pointed back toward the stable. "Gaia." Then, he held his hand out, palm up, almost as if asking for my hand, a curious expression on his face. "Hm?"

Tears stung my eyes again, and I cried softly as he panicked, looking around, alarmed, before he pulled out a handkerchief, muttering what sounded like an apology.

In the universal tone of the phrase, "I told you so," Gaia approached us, saying what I assumed was that very phrase.

He asked her something, before she shrugged.

"How did I come to be here?" I asked, and they startled, glancing at me.

I sighed, frustrated, trying desperately to think of a way to ask the question in a way that they could understand.

I pointed to myself a few times, before I pointed to my chest at the wound, then I shrugged my shoulders very overtly, then gestured to the makeshift bed I'd been laying on.

"How?" I asked.

It seemed to dawn on the woman, and she rushed over to her bed and grabbed a book of parchment and a pencil, drawing.

After a few moments, she showed me a picture of a river, with a woman face-up resting against the bank. She then turned the page, drawing again for a moment before she showed a quick sketch of her and Cassian coming across me, finding me, and bringing me back to the barn.

She drew a picture, then, of them nursing me back to health and helping me.

Tears filled my eyes yet again, only this time, it was out of thankfulness.

They were obviously struggling servants, and they had come across an unconscious, wounded woman in the edge of a river and had brought me back here, helping me get back my strength.

Sobbing softly, I reached out, startling them, before I pulled them both into a hug.

"Thank you!" I cried softly. I leaned back, clasping my hands together in almost-prayer, bowing to them. "Thank you!"

They glanced at one another, surprised, before they both smiled at me warmly.

No matter how thankful I was, though, there was a question that I needed answered...how had I even *lived*?

I had, quite obviously, been *stabbed* in the *chest*.

How was I living?

How had I even come to be stabbed and thrown in a river, anyway? If I was a noble woman, how on earth had it come to happen like this?

I sighed, frustrated, before I thought of something. There was a symbol that was used for medicine in almost every continent, as well as a symbol for a sorcerer. I gestured for the sketch-pad, and she let me see it as I drew out the symbols, followed by a poor drawing of myself, and a question mark.

They took a look at the drawing, and Cassian immediately understood.

He spoke to Gaia, and she sketched for a moment before she showed me a picture of a sun with an arrow pointing up above it.

I guessed that they meant they would help me with that in the morning.

My stomach growled loudly, and they both chuckled at me before Cassian left for a bit.

When he returned, he held three plates of beans and potatoes, and we all sat down and ate before Gaia brought me a cup of water again, and then I got settled into my makeshift bed, letting my fatigue settle in as I fell into sleep even as they continued eating their meal together.

I had only been asleep for a short time, when I began to dream about some man that I vaguely recognized, stabbing me through the heart.

I dreamed about being drug to a river, thrown in, clutching my belly desperately as I tried to keep my head above water.

I startled awake to Cassian shaking me by the shoulders, Gaia sitting up in her own bed, alarmed and staring at me with wide eyes.

I gazed around, clutching my chest, gasping.

"Shh," Cassian whispered, gently reaching a hand to brush the sweaty strands of my hair out of my face.

He checked my temperature, and sighed.

He took the drawing nearby, of the medical and sorcerer symbols, and pointed at them, before pointing to the drawing of the sun rising, seemingly reiterating that they would take care of this with me in the morning.

The rest of the night was uneventful, and when I awoke next, Gaia was eating a plate of scrambled eggs. She offered me a plate when she noticed I was awake.

"Cassian?" I asked.

She nodded, pointing toward the window, and I saw the wagon driver at the door to the manor, seemingly explaining something to him.

Was he...telling the master of the home about me?

Wouldn't they be punished if the lord found out that they were hiding someone in his barn?

I was immediately concerned, before Gaia started coughing and hacking, very over exaggerated, and I startled.

The lord glanced toward the stables, before he sighed, giving a nod and gesturing toward the road, before he gave Cassian a small bag of what must be coins, and then went back inside.

It seemed that they were trying to make him think that Gaia was sick and needed medical attention, and were getting leave to take her to a doctor!

Smart thinking, and I was thankful they had a lord who seemed to be at least humane enough to care about the health of the staff.

Cassian came to the stables to grab the horses and got them hitched up to an open wagon rather than the nice carriage the manor's master had ridden in the evening before, before he noted that I was awake. He gave me a nod and a small smile, before he brought me a burlap cloth.

He suddenly wrapped it around Gaia, lifting her much like a sack, and then set her back on her feet and gestured the burlap to me, so that I would understand what he intended.

I gave a nod and a small giggle, before he wrapped me up. He got Gaia set up in the front where he would sit, and put several other burlap-wrapped items in the back.

It seemed he would have to also run some errands while we were out, and he needed that to help disguise me in the back.

When we were all set, he clicked at the horses and we were off.

After a while of riding, Gaia reached into the back and tapped my shoulder, and I sat up, unwrapping myself, and I gasped.

We had reached a town, and I gaped.

With the burlap still wrapped around most of me, most people weren't paying attention, but from most of the townspeople, I could guess that I would be...quite a shock around here...

• • •

Most of them had darker, more olive-toned or tanned skin, and dark hair. I didn't see even a single person with blonde hair.

Just how far *had* I drifted from my home, exactly...?

I couldn't fathom how far I must be from there, to be in a place where nobody looked like me. If anyone was, by chance, looking for me, I figured it would probably take a long time...if they were able to find me at all.

It wasn't looking like a positive outcome, frankly.

We came to a building with the symbols we were looking for, as most physicians' offices also had wizards present—I knew that, somehow—and Cassian made sure I kept my head covered by a hood he had me put over my head quickly, before he led us inside.

A physician glanced up, noticing us, before he saw the wound in my chest and gaped at me openly, speaking quickly to my care-takers.

They glanced at me, giving a rough-explanation, and the doctor came up to me, looking at me with worried eyes.

He began to ask something, waiting a moment, before the language would change.

Oh!

He was asking me the same question, in multiple languages, before I finally, *finally* understood something!

"Can you understand me?" He asked.

Finally! Finally, a language I understood! Thank heavens that this man knew so many languages!

I finally had someone I could speak to!

"Yes!" I cried, and he gave a sigh of relief, having went through multiple languages before finding my tongue.

He wrote out several questions in what I assumed was their language and handed it to them, and they looked over the sheet as the doctor then began talking to me.

"I wrote out the questions that I would ask you, so they would be able to know what I was asking you and I wouldn't have to interpret so much to them." He gave them a nod, before he looked to me and asked me. "Do you know where you are?"

I shook my head. "No."

"Do you know where you come from?" I shook my head to this question, as well, and he sighed. "Do you know *who* you are?" He asked me, and I shook my head. "I see. So, I guess you don't know, how you got that wound?" He asked, pointing to my chest. "It is starting to get infected, so first things first," he said, applying salve to it and fixing up the stitching. I winced as he worked, but he finally finished. He met my eyes again. "You really don't know?" He asked.

I shook my head, and he scratched his head, and turned to them. They glanced at me worriedly before speaking to him, and he sighed.

"Can I give you a physical examination?" He asked.

I gave my permission, and he had me lay on the table.

He began checking me over, before he paused, grabbing an instrument, and going over my abdomen again, eyes wide.

"You are pregnant!" He cried, and I startled, sitting up with Cassian and Gaia's help.

"W-what...?" I asked, surprised.

Pregnant...?

He quickly relayed this to the others, and they gasped, glancing at my belly quickly, alarmed.

Tears filled my eyes, and I began to cry, sobbing brokenly into the air.

Pregnant? Who was the father?

Where was the father? For that matter...

Was I even married?

I looked to my hand, and there was no ring. I didn't know how I knew to look for one, since that wasn't a tradition in all cultures, but for some reason...I knew that I was supposed to have a ring if I were married.

The lack of a ring could only mean that I wasn't married, right? Or had I gotten divorced? Had my ring been stolen?

There were so many possibilities, and my brain was overwhelmed at all of the possible scenarios.

This was too much. This was just, simply, too much.

Wails came up out of me, covering my face.

"Am I married? Do I have a husband searching for me somewhere? Did he...do this to me because I was pregnant?" I asked, and he sadly relayed my questions to the other two.

They gave me sympathetic looks, glancing at one another.

"Wait a second...I am wearing what seems like a noble's clothing...are there any nobles missing in this country?" I asked.

He looked away. "I would have heard about that," he said. "Not to mention, miss, that your hair color and skin color...are quite uncommon here. Almost unheard of. I can't imagine how far you must have drifted down river."

"Is there any way to track where I came from?" I asked. "If we go up river, we would eventually find out where I came from...wouldn't we?"

He shook his head. "There is a place up the river about twenty miles that splits...one goes through to a different kingdom, and this branch brought you this way, and there are several connectors to one another before the place where the siblings found you."

Oh, so they *were* siblings, I confirmed.

That explained why they seemed so close, but didn't seem to be a couple. It also explained why they looked similar to one another.

I sighed. "There is a wizard here, right?" I asked, and he nodded. "May I speak to the wizard?"

He gave a nod, calling out a wizard. "Gradian!" He called, and I watched a tall, lean man with silver, tussled hair and pale skin stepped out, his dark golden eyes studying us.

"What is it, doc?" He asked. The doctor motioned toward me, and he startled. "That hair!" He said.

"M-my hair...?"

"You are from the Ashland Kingdom!" He informed me.

"Huh?" I asked, confused.

"I heard this tongue, and I was wondering how someone with this language was here, but I hadn't paid it much mind until I saw you. You definitely have the tongue and the look." Then, he saw my chest. "Oh, man! You are lucky that you had such a powerful spell on you!"

Chapter 16

Kyeareth...

"*Spell?*" The doctor asked, before relaying to the others what was happening.

Gradian nodded. "There was an extremely potent, powerful protection spell placed on her. That level of skill is difficult to achieve. As long as her body wasn't cremated or she wasn't burned alive, she would live through whatever happened to her. That explains...*that*," he said, gesturing to my gnarly chest wound.

"...What does that mean?" I asked him.

He smiled at me. "I doubt you went through that without having someone, *somewhere*, who cares about you searching for you, miss. A sorcerer of *very strong*, powerful magic was determined to protect you, at the very least. That is no simple magic; you must be strongly favored by a powerful sorcerer indeed."

"But, then...how do I figure out where I came from?" I asked.

He scratched the back of his head. "Chances are, you likely have someone tracking you already...whether that be a pursuer to hurt you, or to help you."

"You mean...they might find me just to hurt me again?" I asked, holding a hand over my wound.

He looked away for a moment before looking back to me. "Hurting you seems unlikely, if you were stabbed and then cast into the river. That means that they weren't worried about keeping your body. If the spell was cast on you *before* you were stabbed, the person who stabbed you must not even be aware of it, because if they really wanted you *dead*, they would have burned your body so that you couldn't live through it. Though this is very powerful magic, I do actually recognize it. It is just startling to actually see it here. In this case, if they had known about it, they would have known that stabbing you would do no good, so I doubt that you have that kind of pursuer. The only way to kill someone under this protection spell is to burn them."

"What should I do, then?" I asked.

He glanced at my caretakers, speaking to them in their tongue, before he looked to me. "You can possibly continue to hide there at the manor, until someone comes looking for you. The Ashland Kingdom is about a two-months' journey from here, so it'll take a little time. According to these two, they found you a week ago and have been hiding you in their lord's stables without any incident."

I glanced at them. "I wish that I could communicate with them," I said.

He smiled, before he turned to them, talking to them for a moment, before Gaia shoved Cassian forward, pointing to him and looking like she was nervous.

Cassian relented after a moment, nodding, and the wizard glanced at me again.

"Stick out your tongue," he said.

I did, and I cried out when it suddenly stung when he touched his fingertip to it, before he did the same to Cassian as he stuck out his tongue.

After a few moments of letting our tongues stop hurting, the wizard pointed at me.

"Try speaking to her."

Cassian looked at me, giving Gradian one last glance, before he gave me his attention again.

"Can you...understand me, now?"

I gasped, smiling and clapping, nodding, and he smiled warmly at me.

"I am so glad to finally *understand* someone," I said, relieved. "It is scary to be lost in an unknown country, with people that I can't understand trying to help me. Thank you so much for your help," I said.

He smiled. "I can only imagine," he said. "We will try to keep helping you. I am Cassian, and this is my sister, Gaia. We were fishing when we found you, and we couldn't believe it! I was shocked you survived at all, but survive you did," he smiled. "We were scared to bring you back to the manor for various reasons, but we couldn't just leave you there."

"...Scared...?"

He glanced at the doctor and magician. "Well, honestly...he isn't exactly hospitable, nor does he have a good reputation with women. He is widowed, you know, and he...is a bit of a cad."

"Ah..."

"He isn't someone who you would want to be around. If you don't believe me, you can try it, but I would suggest against it."

"Oh, yes," the doctor murmured. "He is known to frequent the red district each night."

"The *red district*?" I asked.

"The whore houses," Gradian said, scoffing.

"That was because there was often a ruckus over the servant women in his manor, which is why so many of them quit their jobs and most of his servants are male or overtly masculine." The doctor said, and sighed.

I glanced down at my torn, tattered gown, before I glanced to the wizard. "I would rather not risk them getting in trouble for hiding me, and if their boss is someone with less than honorable intentions, it might not be safe for me there. Is there anywhere else that I can stay? Somewhere that might not mind me staying for a while, for free…? That sounds terrible, I know, but…but I could get a job!"

Gradian thought about this. "We have an extra room *here*, at the health clinic, actually. The doctor and I live here together, in the upstairs apartment. There is an extra room and bathroom with amenities. Would you like to stay here? The siblings can continue coming to visit you and help you when they can?"

I looked to the doctor, and he smiled. "Would that work for you, miss?"

I glanced at them. "That's really alright?"

"Absolutely. You have quite a high amount of mana, too, in case you weren't aware. You are Mage-Born, yourself," Gradian said, contemplating.

"Yes…"

"I could, perhaps, work on figuring out your abilities and affinities until you have the baby. Then, we could work on teaching you to harness it. That would help you in determining what you are able to do, in any case, until someone comes."

"But...what about the father? What if he comes and tries to take me back?"

"Miss," Cassian started, looking away. "Are you...sure you even *want* to go back?" He asked.

"What do you mean...?"

He shrugged. "Maybe the sorcerer put a protection spell on you so that you would survive, so you could start a better life...because he knew what would happen?"

"That is a possibility," Gradian said, stroking his chin. "Many sorcerers, especially powerful ones, can get glimpses of the future. Perhaps he knew how you would come to be injured, and that's why he cast the protection spell upon you. I suppose it would depend upon whether or not someone really does come to find you."

I gasped as I got a light cramp in my belly, and I was suddenly reminded of another important detail.

"Also, I am concerned about this, too. I'm...I'm carrying a child," I said, whispering. "I don't have a ring, so it would seem that I'm not married," I said. "But what if I am married, and I just lost the ring? What if I lose the baby? If someone comes to find me, would they be mad that I'm pregnant? Or mad that I lost the baby, if I lose the baby? Or—"

The wizard rushed to my side. "Whoa, easy, easy! Calm down. You are over thinking things."

"But—"

"Listen to me," he told me. "Can you do that?"

I sighed, nodding. "Yes."

"Good. Now, listen to me. Getting over stressed will only make things worse. Shh," he said, working me through some deep breaths.

When I finally calmed down, he spoke again.

"Alright...now, to the concerns about the baby. I can prescribe you some medication to help strengthen the baby and the pregnancy, if you wish," the wizard said. "That is very easily done, and should give you assurance that your baby will be alright. And if you choose to do so, I can cast a spell with a bit of your saliva and your blood, to try to discern where you may be from."

"You can really do that?" The doctor asked, impressed.

"If I can get permission to cast a spell upon the womb, I could possibly even determine more information about the child."

I glanced to Cassian, before I looked to the doctor. "Wait, wait. I am concerned about something else, too. Isn't *this* visit costing *money*?" I asked, concerned. "I don't have anything I can offer, and I have no idea where I'm from, who I am, or if I have a family who can give compensation—"

They all gaped at me, before the doctor shook his head as they all rushed to calm me down again.

"No. This is a serious set of circumstances. We aren't charging you for this. You were found in the river, gravely injured. Of course, we aren't charging you for any of this, and we aren't making them pay for anything either," the doctor said, pointing to Gaia and Cassian. "Besides," he said, a smirk on his aging face.

"Besides...?"

"If a noble really *does* come to find you, and they care for you and are a good person, they will likely offer a reward for us helping you."

I laughed. "Oh, so I'm a found purse, basically."

"Exactly," he smiled.

The wizard nodded, before he had me lay on the table again, and he got a vial of my saliva and a few drops of my blood before he drew out a magic seal, chanting words in the ancient tongue, and I startled when my hand burned badly.

He gasped, glancing at my hand. "You have a Personal Keeper Knight seal, miss. You *must* come from a high-ranking house, for you to have such a thing. Only Marquess households and higher-ranking households have Keeper Knights, as far as I'm aware." Then, he turned his attention back to my belly, and he began chanting again. After a moment, he looked at me again. "How much do you want to know?" He asked.

"Anything and everything that you can tell me," I confirmed, and he nodded.

"Alright, then." He took in and let out a deep breath, slowly. "You carry a *second* child," he told me. "I do not mean two children, I mean...you have had a child occupy your womb once before...the womb is already used, although..."

"Although...?" I asked, fearful.

He sighed. "It looks like you must have miscarried in the past, because I cannot sense a living soul-link to you."

"...What is that? A soul-link?"

"A soul-link is something in which I *would* be able to feel, in the case that you had a living child," he said, eyes moving beneath closed eye-lids, as if he were looking inside my womb personally. "Your baby is too early in development to tell gender, or any detail, for that matter, but the bloodline itself is very *old*. I know that there aren't many households that go back this far."

"What does that mean?"

"It means that your child is a child of a strong house, and the bloodlines are mixed of the Knight's Faction and Mage's Faction almost equally. The infant feels...happy, but nervous, which leads me to the knowledge that it was *not* conceived with fear or pain or anguish, but rather with...giddy anticipation."

"...Is that a good thing?"

He sighed, finally, taking a gasp and backing away from me. "It is. It means that the child was not from a forced union, and that the father meant you no harm during conception. That much, at least, is a good thing. But the child is nervous, too, worried about making it to the world."

I hesitated. "Is that...because of my previous child?" I asked.

He gave a nod. "That is more than likely. If you miscarried before, that would explain why the infant's energy is so nervous but so *hopeful*; because your unconscious mind is terrified to lose the baby, but you are so happy to have the baby at the same time." He smiled at me.

"So, one more time so that I understand, what does that mean?" I asked.

"That means, at the very least, that you are not in danger."

"I see."

"It also means that you are more than likely from a high-ranked noble house of the Ashland kingdom, in a political marriage, and feel stressed and pressured to conceive a child for the union. That is a very common scenario among the kingdom, in any case. You may or not be searched for, depending on if the husband was happy about the conception or not."

I looked away, saddened by this news. "I just...wish that I knew what was what, so I could know what to do from here. Do I need to get a job and just start living a new life? Should I just wait for someone to find me without really doing anything? Or, should I be running and hiding?" I shrugged. "I feel at a loss."

The doctor sighed. "I don't know what to tell you...it is hard to get information about other kingdoms here."

"What is the last thing that you heard?" I asked.

"Last we heard, Ashland's king was called to war before someone tried to stage a coup, and their second prince is missing. Half of the royal family is dead. Their entire country is in uproar. I can't get information about specific noble houses, though." He held up a newspaper. "If I get news that seems to pertain to you, I will let you know."

Cassian glanced to the doctor. "Alright, well...her treatment is decided, yes? To be honest, my sister and I need to get going, lest our lord start getting angry at us for taking so long. We weren't supposed to be gone for very long."

"Yes, we will treat her properly, of course," the doctor assured. "You did great, considering...and yes, I imagine his temper isn't easy to deal with. You'd better go on back."

After promising to return to visit me as much as they could, the carriage driver and his sister left, and Gradian looked at me.

"Would it be alright if I get you a few outfits? You need to get out of those dirty rags," he told me. I nodded, and he smiled. "Alright, let me get your measurements."

So, he took my measurements with some tape before leaving the clinic to go and get me a few outfits from the town's clothing shop while the doctor showed me to the spare room in the clinic.

It was nice, and inside was a small woodstove in one corner, a couple of racks with ingredients and a pan and a big pot.

There was a bed in the other corner of the room, and a small door that led to a toilet room with a bathtub as well. There was a dresser by the bed.

It was a nice room, and though I suspected that I was a noblewoman, I was surprised that they were actually offering a room this nice to a stranger that they didn't know.

"We have a bedroom each here in the clinic," he explained. "Occasionally, we rent out a room to people traveling through because the inn of the town is small. So," he said. "Are you hungry?"

I nodded, and so he went to the stove, getting it fired up and grabbing the pan, making quick work of some peppers, tomatoes, and onions, tossing in some mushrooms.

Then he was grabbing out some pre-prepped pasta and filling the pot with water, getting the water boiling and putting the pasta in once it started boiling.

He went to the side I hadn't seen, grabbing a smaller pot.

Then, he started throwing a bunch of tomatoes into the pot with some spices and herbs, and it began to smell amazing as the dish came together.

My stomach was all too eager for this meal...

Soon enough, he was dishing out three plates of pasta with tomato sauce and sauteed vegetables at just the time that Gradian returned with some bags of clothes and shoes for me.

It was a delicious meal, and I sighed and rubbed my belly, full, when I was finished.

I went over to the washing basin, and attempted to help him wash the dishes—that is, until Gradian motioned me out of the way, shushing me when I tried to protest, and he led me over to the bed, having me sit down.

I began to unbraid my hair, stroking my fingers through it to brush it out, before I stepped into the water closet and changed into my nightgown.

As I stepped out, Gradian was stepping out to smoke a cigarette, and the doctor was finishing the dishes.

"I hope you have a good rest, my lady. Please, alert me right away if you need anything."

I smiled, giving another curtsy. "Thank you, doctor, I will."

He smiled, before he turned to the door and left my room.

I sighed, letting myself sit on the bed, and I tried to relax.

Veras's Height, 317 AR

A second and a third week, then a fourth and a fifth week passed by similarly, and though things were still uncertain and nerve-wracking, I had to admit that I had very much enjoyed my time, so far.

A few days after I had arrived, I had met the Count's daughter out in the town while I had been out with Gradian, and we had started talking.

The count was the lord of the manor where Cassian and Gaia worked, it turned out, and despite her father's horrible reputation, his daughter seemed to be rather nice and kind. She had a hard time making friends because no women around the area wanted to be targeted by her father.

I enjoyed talking to her. She was a sweet girl.

Well...Gradian had been translating, anyway.

She quickly decided that she liked me, and insisted on inviting me to have morning tea-times at the manor.

Cassian and Gaia were, of course, surprised to see me at the estate, but it was quickly decided that Cassian— much more useful than the Count had originally thought him to be—would start translating for me, and teaching the Count's daughter my language so that we could communicate.

As a bonus, Cassian's pay was increased.

Most of the ladies in town did not like to be around the Count, and so, the Count's daughter didn't have any friends, despite that she was my age, so her father was only all-too-happy to accommodate for her to make a friend.

Everyone avoided coming here, but honestly...

I never had understood the reluctance to be around the Count.

He was an odd fellow, and not the most attractive, but he hadn't been particularly rude to me or done anything out of the way. At least, he hadn't yet.

It would turn out to be a few weeks that had passed by without much incident, until one morning that I was inside the manor, using the bathroom and cleaning up before going to return to tea...when the count finally showed his true colors, and scared me as he made a pass at me.

Of course, being the only one who could translate what I was saying, the count began relying *heavily* on Cassian to spend all of his time at my side, wherever I may be on the estate, so that anyone could speak with me.

Which meant that he was always *close by*, even when I went inside the estate. Especially when I went inside, really.

I had been on my way back out to the garden from using the toilet, having been enjoying my conversation with Arian—the count's daughter—but needing to take a pause to do my business, when the count had caught me, alone, in the hallway...trying to find my way back to Cassian and back out.

I heard him muttering, somewhat frustrated, and I thought that it must be because I had turned down his offer to stay in the manor with his daughter a few days ago.

He'd made the offer to me at the last tea-time, and I had turned it down, since I was so comfortable at the medical clinic.

I was on my way back out to his daughter when he had stridden close to me, and I backed against the wall, overwhelmed by how close he was all of a sudden.

What was—

His face was heated, eyes heady, and I could practically *feel* him salivating.

I felt my blood run out of my face, making me a bit lightheaded, and just as he was about to press his lips into mine, I heard Cassian's voice call my name.

I slipped under the arm of the count, bolting for Cassian's presence, and he glanced back at the count, who was walking away rather quickly, caught.

I gulped, clinging to Cassian's shirt.

"Are you alright?" He asked, steadying me as I swayed. He patted my back soothingly, glaring after the Count.

I shook my head. "That was...so scary," I whispered. "I thought...I thought he was going to kiss me."

He hesitated, hands trembling a bit. It was clear he was also rattled, angry on my behalf. "It *looked* that way, too. This...this was why we advised you not to stay here, my lady," he whispered. "This is why we advised you to stay away. You need to get back, now."

"I-I think that I'm ready to get some rest," I said, soft.

He led me back outside, and I gave a polite curtsy and quick goodbyes to a shocked Arian before I turned, walking toward my temporary home.

Cassian told her that I suddenly wasn't feeling very well and asked for me to be excused, before he followed after me.

We began back toward the clinic, and he got to talking to me as he often did lately.

"I am so sorry you had to experience something so...unsavory. He is a lonely widower, yes, but there was no excuse for him to treat you that way. Especially considering your condition. Perhaps he thought your present state might make you more...welcoming of his advances?" He mused, shuddering. "Ugh. Although, I too have to wonder who the father of your baby is, what he was like...what he looked like," Cassian said, voice a bit distant as he watched me. "Your pregnancy is coming along quickly."

We arrived back to the clinic, and I led him through to my room, where we sat down.

I gasped as I felt the baby kick me.

The baby had started moving, fluttering and kicking in my belly, and from what the doctor had told me upon his visit that very morning, it seemed that I had conceived sometime around Heaven's Gift Holiday, so I was already five months along in my pregnancy.

"He looked a lot like you," I whispered, and he startled.

"...What?" He asked, a bit choked.

I "hm'd," trying to think of a way to explain it.

How could I put this?

I felt a little awkward, but I told the truth.

"I see this face in my mind every night; a man with beautiful black hair and piercing, golden-green eyes above me, his eyes and face full of love as he touches me..."

He stayed silent, hesitating and not knowing how to respond.

I shuddered. "He has a cocky countenance, and a confident stride, exuding this powerful, radiant beauty in every action...almost...*kingly*."

He chuckled, a bit nervous, running a hand through his own black hair. "That's awfully *specific*..."

"I've also had dreams of a knight who wears a mask covering half his face at my side a lot, and a man who looks startlingly like me, growing up with me...a twin, it looks like."

He took in this information, considering it.

"Do you...*want* to go back?" He asked, and I looked at him. He came over to me, sitting at my side. "I..." he sighed, looking at me with a somber look. "You have been here going on five weeks, my lady, and we still don't know your name or where exactly you came from, though you continue to remember small details like those," he chuckled. "I...I would be willing, if you *wish*, to claim responsibility for you and for the baby," he said. "I make ends meet, and I..."

"You..." I said, waiting for him to continue after a moment of silence. "You...*want* to take responsibility for us? But...why?"

He blushed, looking at me. "I know this is forward, and you probably don't reciprocate, but I feel that I should at least inform you, because I don't want you to feel blindsided. To tell you the truth, I fancy you, my lady. I would...I would love for you to consider me, possibly..."

I gasped, surprised, taking him in. I had somewhat thought that, guessed it, but I hadn't expected the sudden confession.

"Cassian..."

He was quick to start nervous chatter, feeling awkward. "And what if no one shows up for you...?" He asked, looking away into the distance.

"Please, don't say that! I don't want to think about the idea of someone not looking for me, Cassian. I need to have hope that I can look forward to someone wanting me to return home, and that I actually have a home to return to..."

"But my lady...you have been here for quite a while...and we haven't heard any word. I don't want for you to have to give birth and raise the baby alone," he said. "Your baby will need a father. What if you give birth alone and people shame you both? We don't even know your situation, and I don't want for people to treat you badly or for you two to struggle. I would be happy to take care of you. I've been saving up money, I could provide you with a safe home and comfort. We could have a life together."

I smiled, resting my hand against his cheek. "Thank you, Cassian. You are so kind, and so considerate. You have helped us more than any other passerby would, with no guarantees or promise of reward...but I wish to wait just a little longer. I don't want to agree to be with you, only for some husband and *you* end up getting hurt."

He blushed, but gave me a nod, and I pressed a small, gentle kiss to his cheek.

"Thank you, Cassian. I truly appreciate your kindness to us."

Chapter 17

Kyeareth...

Three more weeks passed by, and it was almost Veras's End, when I woke up gasping, choking, and crying.

Cassian was by my side, pressing a cool wet cloth to my forehead.

"C-Cassian...?" I asked.

"Shh," he said. "You had another nightmare."

I wasn't perturbed.

It happened become often now, that Cassian came by often with the count's daughter and Gaia to visit me in the early mornings and the evenings.

Gradian and the doctor wanted me to be looked after because I started struggling, with cramps and random sharp pains in my chest and in my hand, with cramping in my belly as well.

They didn't think it was safe to leave me unattended.

He brought me a glass of water, helping me sit up to take a sip in my bed.

"Where is he?" I sobbed, covering my face. "Why hasn't he come for me?" I cried. "He seemed to have loved me so much in my faded memories, so where is he now?"

He looked at me with a pained expression, before he took my lips in a kiss.

I gasped, pulling back and looking up at him with wide eyes.

"C-Cassian?"

"My lady," he whispered against my lips, his face sad. "Please...it has been *eight weeks*. Choose me, please...your baby will arrive before you know it."

"Cassian..."

He kissed me again, before resting his forehead against my own. "Please...let us come up with a temporary name for you, and let me marry you and claim you both. I can help you," He urged, his tone thick with emotion. "It would protect you and I could take care of you."

I closed my eyes, letting tears fall. "How can I be so unfair?" I whispered. "How could I do that, when someone may show up? What if our affections grow for one another, Cassian, and then someone comes for me and I'm suddenly married to them, or obligated to go with them? I'm not even from this country, and I wouldn't be able to stand up in a court and say, 'Oh, I didn't know I was married,' and be able to stay with you. I can't do that to you."

"And what if they don't? Don't you wish to marry before the child arrives?"

"But Cassian, I need to know for *sure*, first," I said, sudden determination forming in my heart. "I need to know if there is someone. *Then*, I will make my decision."

He sighed, before he nodded. "Yes, my lady."

He let me get back to my rest, leaving me alone to my thoughts and to rest.

• • •

Although I was lost in my thoughts, I didn't get much sleep before morning arrived.

I got out of bed, and dressed before I left my room. I saw the doctor sitting at a nearby table, drinking tea.

"Good morning," he said. "Did you sleep well?"

I shook my head. "I need to see Gradian, urgently."

Gradian was stepping out as I said that, and he stretched, giving me a contemplative look. "You're finally ready," he said. "You've been waiting and waiting, but now, you want to actually seek it out yourself, and move on your own."

I gave a nod. "Yes..."

"Lie down," he said, motioning to the table, and I did so. "New memories?" He asked.

There was suddenly a knock on the door of the clinic, and the doctor let in Cassian, who slowly came into the health clinic as he saw me lying on the examination table, his focus moving to me.

I looked to Gradian. "I have been seeing a man with black hair and golden-green eyes, a very...confident stride and air; cocky almost, and a knight with a mask covering half his face...oh, and a twin brother who looks exactly like me."

He startled, glancing at me. "Are you *positive* that those are your memories?" He asked. "Because if so, then I already have a feeling I might...actually already know, as that is so specific..."

"*Really?*" I asked, surprised, and Cassian gaped at him, sadness and surprise on his face.

"You mean...you know someone with those descriptions?" Cassian asked him.

Gradian nodded, before he closed his eyes, chanting softly. His hand rested over my belly.

"Your *son*..." He whispered. "You shall have a son, and he has black hair. His father's blood is running strong in him, now, and I can feel the strength in it. Both of your bloodlines are powerful, elder lineages, going back hundreds of years..."

"A son," I whispered. "I'm having a son..."

I smiled, happy tears burning my eyes, and Cassian stirred at my side.

Then, my hand burned, and I cried out, a sudden image of the knight in my mind's eye.

"*I know this knight*," Gradian said through a strained voice, eyes moving beneath the lids. "This knight is Seryn Von-Ren Leonhart," he grated out, and his eyes opened, suddenly, solid white, glowing as the air around the room picked up.

We gasped, watching his power increase even as a line of blood flowed from his nose. I felt the mana in my blood rising, too. He groaned, but managed to rush and get the information out quickly even as he struggled.

The words were slurred, almost. Garbled...just barely distinguishable. "Seryn is the Keeper Knight of her majesty the Queen, Kyeareth Renna Severing Ashland, wife of his majesty the King, Cinder Burn Ashland, daughter of Duke Leodore Renard Severing, twin sister of young Duke, Astaroth Renard Severing, mother to the deceased Prince Asfaloth Blaze Renard Ashland!" He cried, before he gasped, collapsing to the floor as his eyes went back to normal.

Cassian helped Gradian up, but the wizard quickly began to wipe his nosebleed while gazing up at me in astonishment, getting up on shaky legs and gaping at me the entire time.

"The *queen!*" The doctor cried, falling to his knee in a kneel. "Your majesty!"

"You..." Cassian gasped, looking at me with stricken astonishment. "You're...a *queen*...?" He asked, barely above a whisper.

"Cassian..." I whispered, reaching out for him.

He fell to his knees. "I *beg* you for forgiveness!" He cried. "I...I *kissed* you, without direct permission. I kissed you first...Oh, *heavens*..."

"Cassian," I said, teary-eyed. "I...I care for you, you're my dear friend, so please...don't act this way. I never told you not to—"

He shuddered, tears in his eyes as he gazed up at me. "You never initiated or reciprocated, though! You say that you care for me...but what could I ever hope for? To be your *concubine?* A...a male mistress? A whore? You are a queen, of a large kingdom. The Ashland Kingdom doesn't allow such things..."

I bit my bottom lip, sighing and wiping my tears before I glanced to the wizard. Cassian was right.

I was a queen, to a large and powerful nation.

I didn't know the circumstances around my accident, how I had been injured, but I knew that I had to go back eventually. As scary as that was, they had all assured me that there was no way that a sorcerer would place a protection spell on me if I didn't have someone who cared for me somewhere.

That was both scary and comforting.

I needed to find out.

"How can I return home?" I asked Gradian.

"Concentrate on your knight, *truly focus*. Since he is bound to you by the subjugation spell, if you actually forcefully summon him with all your heart, he will be able to locate you. That is likely what he has been waiting for all of this time."

I closed my eyes, picturing the knight in my mind and screaming his name in my heart with all that I had, ready to go home.

I felt a sharp snap on my body, and I gasped, my hand stinging badly, before I could picture him in my mind.

He stood, crying out in the middle of the forest by the river, before his body stood to attention, gazing directly at me, pointing at me and shouting my name, a crowd of people behind him, and they began to run in my direction.

I didn't know how, but I recognized him. I felt the connection, even though it was only minutely.

I startled, stumbling back a bit.

"*Did you see him?*" Gradian asked.

"Yes," I nodded.

He closed his eyes, a hand coming to my forehead, and he chanted.

He gasped. "I know where that is! That's only about an hour away!"

"Really?" I asked, startled. "But…that would mean…!"

"So…they really *were* searching for you," the doctor said, soft. "But because it is so far from here to your own country, your trail had gone cold by the time they reached this place."

"It seems so…"

"I am amazed they managed to track you this far, considering how much time has passed. If your memories had been intact, you likely would have been found much sooner."

I smiled softly, in spite of myself, as I stroked my growing belly.

"Soon, my son," I whispered. "We will go home." I turned, facing Cassian. "Cassian...as the queen of the Ashland Kingdom, I formally invite you to join me, with your sister, at the royal palace. I cannot think of two better friends to have."

He startled. "W...what?" He asked, stunned.

"I want you two to come with me...please. I want to give you guys a good life, in thanks for helping me. I am a queen," I laughed, still taking it in and reeling.

We sat there, waiting, for another hour, before there was a huge commotion outside...

"They're here..." I whispered, still surprised.

Gradian glanced out the window, and startled. "Oh, wow..." He whispered.

"Huh?" I asked.

"So, this has to be the sorcerer who cast the protection spell on you!" He said, pointing out the window. "I've never seen him in person, but I've heard stories! Lord Winter is one of the most renowned sorcerers of the age," he said. "I can't believe you had someone like *him* under your employ! You really *must* be a queen," he said. "His bloodline is the top of sorcery; he is a master. I can't believe I'm even getting to see *him* in person. This is such an extraordinary honor for someone like me!"

I hadn't realized that Winter was such an important and high-classed sorcerer, but Gradian made it seem almost as if he were the creator of magic, with the way that he was acting...

There was a knock on the door, and the doctor came and had me stand behind a thin curtain, and he even came to stand in front of me, blocking me from sight for certain, before the door clicked open.

Light beamed into the room, and I heard rich, rich sounding boots hit the stone floor.

I peeked around the doctor and the curtain for just an instant, startling when the man from my dream glanced around the room, and I quickly hid behind the curtain and doctor again.

"Excuse me," he said in a rich, luxurious voice, and I felt my body tremble as a blush filled my cheeks.

I hadn't heard his voice in my dreams, but I couldn't imagine a better sound.

"This may sound a bit odd," he said, hesitating.

"Go ahead," they encouraged.

He cleared his throat. "It may be an odd question, I admit."

"Go on."

"Yes...an odd inquiry, but have you seen a young, blonde-headed woman with blue eyes in this area? Her Keeper Knight sensed her around here, and this is the first building you come to when coming out of the forest. I've been searching for *months*," he said, his voice cracking, tone exhausted.

"May I ask your relation to the lady?" Gradian asked, arms folding across his chest.

"I—"

"Your language and appearance are obviously from the Ashland Kingdom, months away. How do you know this lady you search for?"

"I am her husband," he said.

"And how is it, *pray tell*, that a wife managed to get months away from her husband?" Cassian practically snarled the question, full of underlying bitterness.

The man hesitated.

He shifted on his feet, looking like he felt guilty.

"I was called away from home, to help a town in my kingdom that was in desperate need...while I was away, our home was attacked. My brother-in-law's father-in-law staged a coup, and attempted to kill my wife. Thankfully, we have a powerful sorcerer who is a dear friend of my wife's, and before she was attacked, he cast a protection spell over her in secret. The coup-plotter took her from home, stabbed her, and threw her into the river, where she drifted for quite some time to come to be in this place."

"If she has a Keeper Knight, how did it take so long to locate her?" The doctor asked.

We already knew the answer, but we wanted to see what the man would say.

"The link was cut off, for some reason. The same is true with her Shadow Guardians. It wasn't until this morning that her Keeper Knight began to feel the bond reconnecting with her, before he was able to give an exact location. It was hard to track her, being in the river for so long, and her traces had all but disappeared, so tracking her the usual way was almost impossible."

Gradian unfolded his arms. "Can you tell us her name?"

The man had a smile in his voice. "She is my queen, her majesty, Queen Kyeareth Renna Severing Ashland."

The doctor, Cassian, and Gradian all glanced at one another.

"I just have one last question," Cassian said. "Do you *love* her? Or do you simple seek her out of obligation?"

I peeked around the curtain, and I saw the warmest, but most heart-broken expression I'd ever seen on this man's handsome face. Tears filled his eyes, but didn't fall, making his eyes look like lime-tinted, liquid gold.

"I *love* her, more than I've ever loved anything or anyone else." Finally, his tears fell.

Gradian glanced back at me, and I smiled, giving a nod.

He turned his attention to my husband.

"Then...you have come to the right place, King Cinder Burn Ashland," he said.

Cinder startled. "You...know me?"

Gradian nodded. "Yes...and we have someone anxious to return to you." He smiled and he gave a small bow as the doctor moved out of the way and pulled the curtain aside.

I gasped, gazing at my husband, as he gaped at me, shock on his face.

"Kyeareth..." He breathed, before he strode over to me, his gait timid and nervous, afraid that I might disappear. "Is it...*truly* you?" He asked, voice cracking.

He collapsed to his knees, hugging my thighs as he openly sobbed and cried into the skirt of my gown against my legs.

"I thought...I'd never...see you again!" He sobbed out. He glanced up, and gasped, taking in my belly. "The...the baby...!" He choked, face surprised. "The baby survived?" He laughed out the question, standing and taking me into his arms, burying his face in my shoulder. "Our child survived! Oh, love, I've been so worried!" He cried.

I patted his shoulder awkwardly with one hand, smiling and laughing nervously as I rubbed the back of my head with my other hand.

He froze, backing up and looking at me in delayed horror.

"W...what...what's wrong?" He asked.

"Your majesty...when she was found, the lady had absolutely *no* memories...she has regained *some visual* memory since then, but still didn't even know her name until she remembered yours and Seryn's appearance, as well as her twin brother," the doctor explained. "She still doesn't actually...*remember*, yet."

"What?" He asked, stricken by this information. He turned around to take me in, his eyes full of sadness. "Then...you don't remember me at all...do you?"

I looked away. "I have...memories of you and I...during the nights," I whispered, blushing, and he blushed heavily.

"Oh...oh!" He said, blushing and covering his face, laughing. "How awkward," he chuckled. "You remember nothing but *that*," he said, looking away.

"Precisely," I murmured.

His pink cheeks and ears were adorable to me, and he chuckled under his breath. "An awkward first-meeting for you, I imagine..."

I glanced at Cassian, who was looking on wordlessly, and I walked over to him, taking his hand.

I could practically feel the tension hitting the air as my apparent husband watched me initiate contact with another man.

"I would like to get my few things, and we need to pick up Gaia and your things," I smiled. "And I simply *must* pay my last regards to the lord of the manor," I laughed, before I turned, facing the room again even as the king gaped at me. "...What...?" I asked.

"Who...is *this* man?" He asked, keeping his tone as even as he could manage, looking at the hand I still held. I released Cassian's hand, rubbing the back of my head in an awkward fashion.

"This?" I asked, looking at Cassian. "This is Cassian. It was he and his sister who had found me on the river bank. They brought me back here to this health clinic, and they all nursed me back to health."

"Oh, my!" They gaped at Cassian, surprised.

"Cassian even learned our language, to communicate with me. They were perfect to me, and if it weren't for them, I would probably still be in that river somewhere."

He flinched, and turned to Cassian, extending his hand quickly, rushed and desperate.

Cassian took it, shaking his hand, before my husband even gave him a bow. I startled, as did Cassian.

"I formally thank you, sir, for helping my wife when she needed it the most. I owe you the greatest debt, and I will see to it that you are repaid for your act of kindness. Please, name anything, and I will see to it that it is done if it is within my power."

"*I* would like to figure out a reward myself," I said, and Cinder paused, glancing at me.

"As you will it, then," he smiled, and then he opened the door.

I glanced back to the doctor and his wizard, and I tugged on my husband's sleeve.

"Um...excuse me," I said, and he startled, turning to face me.

"Please, call me 'Cinder,' 'darling,' 'dear,' anything..."

"Oh, okay...um, then, excuse me, Cinder, but...this doctor and this wizard have helped me so much, the wizard is the one who taught me how to call the knight here even if the bond was tampered with...I would appreciate it, very much, if you could donate some funds to them to help them continue to be able to help others the way that they have helped me."

Cinder's eyes widened, and he beamed at me and gave me a bow. "As my queen wishes it," he said, and a servant came in with a case that he opened, showing that it was full of gold and jewels.

The doctor and mage both gaped at it, surprised, in shack and awe.

"*Wow...*" The wizard said, shocked. "We might need to save royalty more often," He joked.

"Thank you both," I gushed, pulling them both into a tight hug.

They patted my back awkwardly, laughing, before we went to go get Cassian and Gaia's home...and perhaps make that creepy count face some justice.

Chapter 18

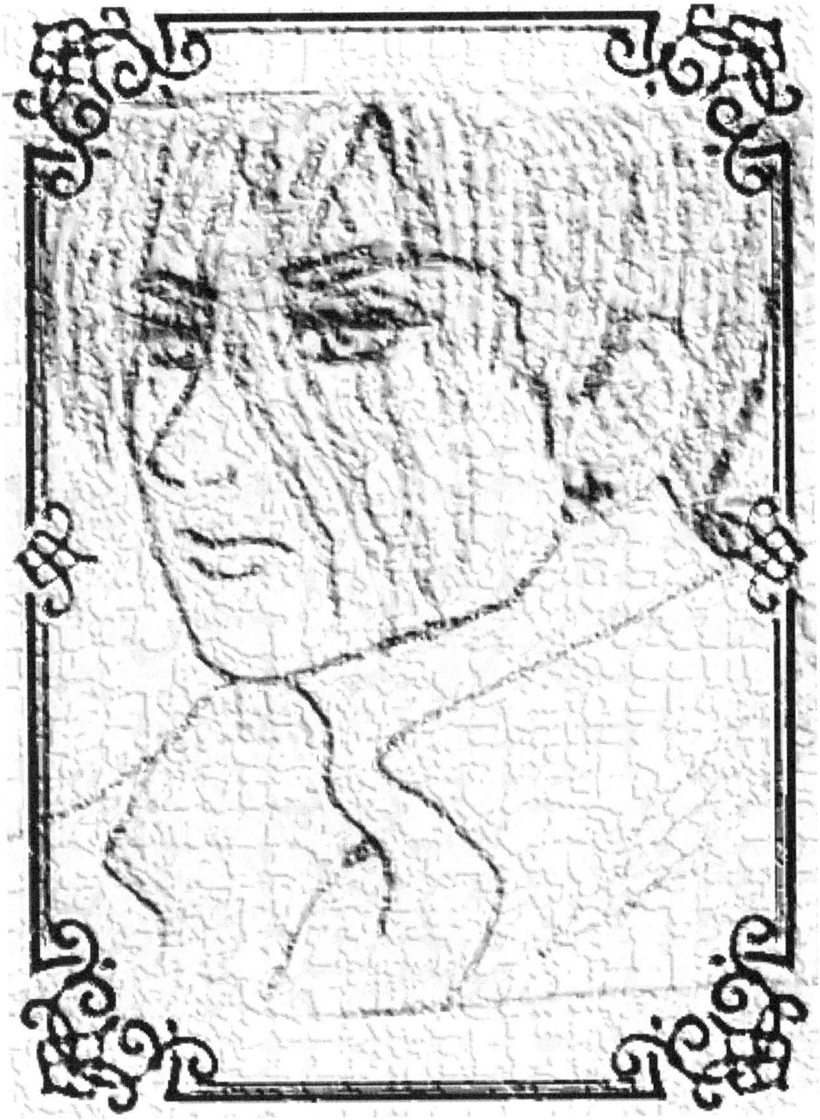

Seryn...

Veras's Height, 317 Ashland Rule

It had been a rough few weeks, to be sure.

I had actually managed to track my lady quite a good way, before the group of knights and my lady's Shadow Guardians had found me.

Lord Winter had a summoning spell prepared, for whenever we managed to find her, so that I could summon him to wherever we were immediately.

Queen Kyeareth had drifted what was almost a two-months' journey on foot in the river, which had only taken a couple of weeks due to the fast current, and I was thankful that she was still alive.

Winter let me know that he had cast the protection spell on her, so as long as she wasn't burned to ashes, she would live, at least.

I could only hope that she would recover and that the baby would be safe.

Meanwhile, Eclipse was still searching for the second prince, who was *still* missing. The former king was mourning the death of his wife, the current king's mother.

It was a difficult time, but I found out that, thankfully, Duke Steel had already been executed, the coup had been foiled, and the prisoners released, thanks to King Cinder and Eclipse.

I got vague aches and pains around my chest occasionally, and after a few weeks, I began to feel powerful emotions, though they were muddled and seemed so far away...

Our bond was strained, on the verge of being erased, and I couldn't understand why.

The only thing that I could think was that her mind was severely incapacitated, somehow, because if she were in a normal state, then I wouldn't be having such a hard time locating her.

Many weeks later, my hand had begun searing badly one morning. Suddenly, I saw my lady in my mind's eye, calling for me with all of her heart, hands clasped over her heart.

I looked directly at her, meeting her gaze, and I shouted her name, pointing to her and rushing off in the direction that I spotted her.

As we ran, Winter summoned the king with a tagging summon spell, and as he arrived on the scene almost as if he'd been teleported to us, he rushed with us.

Soon, a city began to come into our view.

"Are you *sure* that you have found her?" The king asked, bags under his eyes and obviously exhausted, devastated, sleep deprived...and terrified.

He looked like an absolute wreck...

"I am sure. She is in this town, somewhere around the entrance of the city."

He gave a nod, following me with the group as we ran.

Finally, we reached the first building that you come as you come out of the forest's edge, and the king hesitated...

Timidly, almost, he stepped into this building that had a sign indicating that it was a medical facility.

Thankfully, it was a widely known universal symbol used on our continent, and could be found in every individual kingdom in this land, so we were able to recognize it for what it was.

I heard some conversation, before I heard a shouted voice speaking what sounded like a question—

I stepped up to the door, and I saw a physician, a young wizard, and someone who looked like a young commoner man...but I certainly...

Most of all, I certainly felt my lady's presence from this place! I knew that she was here, likely hiding and listening...

Though...why would she hide...? That didn't make sense...

I felt my heart clench painfully when she was finally revealed, so happy and relieved to see my lady but so terrified as to why I couldn't feel her emotions, why I couldn't feel out her physical condition...

It was truly a relief, though, when it was revealed that she was, indeed, heavily pregnant at this point, the young prince or princess safe in her womb, and I felt that burden ease off of my weary heart.

Then, the *reason* that my bond felt to be incomplete with my lady...was because she had no memory of herself, of her life or who she was.

We startled at this information, unprecedented.

How did we proceed from here?

I had been so afraid that something like this might happen; that she may become *mentally damaged*...but to lose *all* of her memory to this degree?

I hadn't anticipated such a severe thing, and fear and doubt crept up in my heart. How could a Keeper Knight even truly serve a master who no longer knew him?

I could protect her if I was physically by her side, of course, but my ability for her was severely cut by this revelation, as it was with her Shadow Guardians, as well.

They couldn't speak to her telepathically or communicate with themselves in the telepathic mind space if her mind was incomplete this way...

This was truly frightening...

My queen made it clear that she wished to reward the doctor and the wizard, so the other knights passed up a chest of jewels and gold, and I passed it to the king, before he presented it to the men.

Then, the queen made it known that she wished to go to the residence of her companion, to get his things and retrieve someone else to join us for the journey home, and I heard her mention that she wished for this man, this Cassian, and his sister to come back to the *palace* with us...

Who was this Cassian?

He looked remarkably similar to the king, honestly, though his skin was a bit darker and the shade of green that his eyes was, indeed, was also darker...

His hair fell around his shoulders with a gentle wave, but his facial features, eye-shape and the like favored the king's.

He wasn't quite as muscular, having a lean and average physical body that was not trained in combat skill.

He dressed like a—

I paused that very thought when I saw him help us load into the wagon, and he sat up front, taking the reins to the horses.

So, he was, indeed, the carriage driver.

I wasn't sure how I felt about this development. The queen was already married and getting on much better terms with Cinder before the coup happened, so I felt defensive over their relationship, oddly. That was strange, considering everything that they had been through, but before the coup, Kyeareth had finally been coming to peace with Cinder. I didn't want anything that could damage that to come into her life.

Sadly, it seemed to be too late for that notion...

We rode for a little while, before we arrived to a large manor for the area, and as this Cassian got off of the driver's seat, he held out his hand for my liege, helping her off of the wagon, before helping the rest of us unload.

She rushed over to the stables nearby, calling for someone, before she returned with a somewhat masculine-looking woman who looked similar to Cassian, with short, dark brown hair.

"This is Cassian's younger sister, Gaia," she told us, and the girl bowed repeatedly to us. "She and her brother saved me from the river, and they have both welcomed me with open arms. Please, be good to both of them."

Wait...they had been the ones to find her?

They had saved her?

Now, things made more sense to me and I could understand why she wanted to reward them!

We all murmured greetings, but the girl looked at us with a confused expression before speaking in a different language to her brother, and he gave her a brief explanation...before her face lit up, and she gaped at the king, coming and falling on her knees and crying out excitedly at his feet, pressing her face to the ground.

The king startled, glancing to Cassian and then to Kyeareth.

"Excuse me, your majesty, my sister is expressing her thankfulness that you have come for the queen and that the queen isn't...*abandoned*," Cassian said, looking away and rubbing the back of his head sheepish...

It was made known that he had obviously been guilty of being convinced of that, himself. It was quiet as the king glanced sadly down at the girl. I knew what he was thinking; I was thinking it too. It had taken us entirely too long to locate the queen, when we should never have lost her to begin with. Of *course*, it would appear to an outsider that the poor girl had been abandoned, pregnant, destitute.

The king leaned down, patting the girl on the shoulder, and smiling at her, motioning for her to stand up, and he shook her hand, thanking her for helping his queen as Cassian translated between the two.

I glanced at the king, and we seemed to be wondering the same thing;

Why had Kyeareth been staying at the clinic, when there had been an inn or even this nobleman's manor to stay in?

Surely, if she was friends with this Cassian and his sister, they could have found her better accommodations, yes?

It was a bit confusing. She obviously *looked* like a noble.

"Your majesty..." Cassian started, trembling, seeming to have caught on to our thought processes. "Please forgive the humble accommodations of the clinic. She could have stayed *here*, and it was offered to her. It was offered, but she was...a bit *uncomfortable* around the Count, as he is a widower who made it a bit...*overly* obvious that he was smitten with her, thus the meager accommodations she had to suffer. I know that as a queen, she deserves much better...I am sorry."

The king froze in his place, gaping at Cassian, before he glanced at Kyeareth, and she laughed nervously, looking away, giving a single nod...confirming.

The king glared out of the open doorway, hearing a new voice speak up even at that moment, and Cassian gasped, standing, and turning to the voice.

"Oh! Oh, no. That is the count, your majesty—"

King Cinder scoffed. *"And?"*

"Well—"

"Like I'm worried," he said, smug, and we watched as he then grabbed Kyeareth's hand before he turned, striding with his cocky, strong, confident gait toward the count.

We all followed him like magnets, drawn to see what he was going to do.

We watched as the count paused, a horrified expression on his face as he looked between our king and queen, seemingly realizing what we were here for.

The count, you see, looked to be in his late thirties, and was a thin, lean man. He wasn't particularly *unattractive*, but he was obviously not remarried for a reason. Let's just say, he most likely had to *buy* nightly attentions, and I wouldn't have been surprised in the least to learn that he was someone who was unclean and held disease. His looks paled in comparison to everyone else here, to top it off. He spoke in a nervous, fast-paced voice in his native tongue, glancing nervously at the king, before Cassian quickly translated the situation for him, and the man backed up, glancing at the king's sword.

Cassian turned, giving a small bow. "Please forgive us, but I tried to help her make a friend in the count's daughter. He, unfortunately, took a fancy to her and got a bit too...invested in pursuit. He attempted to kiss the queen not long ago, and the queen hasn't been very comfortable even coming here since—"

The king's eyes widened as he pulled out his sword.

The count squawked out, an unattractive noise, stumbling further back and falling to his knees, hands clasped and begging.

"Translate *this*," the king said, glancing at Cassian before he looked back to the count. "I am the husband of this woman. She is the *Queen* of the Ashland Kingdom, Queen Kyeareth Renna Severing Ashland, and I am King Cinder Burn Ashland."

We waited for that to be translated before Cinder continued.

"I have returned from overruling the coup plot and saving our country, and I have come to retrieve my queen."

Cassian quickly translated all of this, and the count gaped at them both, shrieking out what must have been apologies, bowing and pressing his face into the ground, sobbing.

The king stepped forward and pressed the tip of his sword's blade to the back of the neck of the count, who began to plead louder into the dirt.

"Tell him that, in recompense for the audacity of flirting with my wife, I will spare his *life*...but I will be taking the carriage driver, the stable woman, and the horses and wagon."

Cassian relayed this, and the count began to urinate on himself, quaking in is spot, bowing further and muttering out thanks before the king glanced to the brother and sister again. They nodded; and the knights helped them to get their belongings loaded into the wagon.

Cinder turned to the queen.

"Are you ready to go?" He asked.

Chapter 19

Seryn...

When night fell and we sat up camp, Kyeareth sat awkwardly around the large fire with us, looking around at us.

"So..." She said, glancing at the king. "Can we...*introduce* ourselves? I mean, I know *your* name, but can we introduce all of ourselves to one another? Aside from you, I don't know anyone...I barely know who you are," she said, feeling a bit nervous and awkward.

"Oh, of course," the king said. He looked at me, first. "This is—"

"Seryn Von-Ren Leonhart," Kyeareth said, and I startled.

"Do you recognize me?" I asked, hopeful.

"When the wizard Gradian was helping me locate you, you flashed across my mind as he told me your name, so I at least did know that."

"I am your Keeper Knight, my lady," I introduced. "Yes, I have been with you since you turned thirteen."

"Oh!" She said. "How old *am* I, *exactly*? I know that I was born in 300 AR, but I didn't know what month..."

"You will be seventeen in Solaris's Reign of this year," I told her, and she gasped. "Yes, you are only sixteen."

Cassian fidgeted nervously at this information, and I had the feeling...especially, from the glances he kept giving her...that he was rather smitten with her himself. That would likely explain why he had thought to take her into his home and let her move in, basically, were it not for the count who had run the manor and put her in a difficult position.

I was sure that if it hadn't been for that sleazy count, Kyeareth certainly would have been staying with this man in his own dwelling.

It was a hunch.

He seemed like a good, decent man, at least, with no particularly devious motives fueling the action...just fancying her.

Which, to be honest, wasn't *wrong*, nor any fault of his own.

Many men, I was sure, fancied Kyeareth initially.

"I am Winter, my queen," Winter spoke up, and I realized I'd been missing conversation due to my internal thoughts.

"I am your personal sorcerer. You may have guessed this already, but I am the one who cast the protection spell upon you. We were under attack during the coup at the royal palace, and I knew that you could very well face a life-or-death situation, so I made the decision to cast that spell before you got away from me."

"...Why?" I asked.

"Unfortunately, it did come down to that, but you had actually...had a premonition about the coup, not long before it took place, so I had anticipated that your 'death' might happen just as you had predicted, and it did. I am just glad I thought to cast the spell beforehand. It seems your *own* latent magic ability is nothing to scoff at; premonition is a powerful tool. You are quite remarkable, your majesty," Winter complimented.

"Thank you," she smiled, bowing her head. "It is thanks to *you* that I am alive."

He blushed, looking away. "It is my duty as your Shadow Guardian and personal sorcerer, your majesty."

"I am Azoth, my queen," he spoke up. "I am one of your Shadow Guardians as well, though I specialize in interrogation and intelligence, mental health and capacity...I am quite skilled in battle, but I prefer the mind. I am your copper badged guardian."

She seemed to contemplate this. "Do you...think that you can help me remember everything?" She asked, voice sad. "I don't remember anything, only bits of memory flashes that cross my mind here in there, but those don't help me."

"I am certainly willing to do my best to assist you, my queen," Azoth said.

The rest of the knights introduced themselves, until it came down to the king. She glanced at him expectantly, and I remembered her asking us to introduce ourselves. Seriously, I was out of it. Having been tired and stressed for so long, I needed a break...and badly. She looked at the king, asking him to give her a piece of their history to her, at least, so that she could feel more comfortable. She had, after all, just found out she was actually a wife.

He sighed, and looked away. "Well...when we were first arranged, we didn't like each other for quite a while. In fact, we kind of, uh...*hated* each other. It took a good while for us to overcome those feelings. However, we grew close over the few years we've been together, and we came to genuinely love one another. We've...been through a *lot* together."

"Is it...true that I lost a child?" She asked, and the king startled, gaping at her in pained surprise.

"How did you—?"

"The wizard, Gradian, he said that my womb looked pre-used on the inside...he could actually see it with magic. He told me that he couldn't sense a soul-tie, though, no link to a child, and that must mean that the baby...isn't alive. Is that true?"

He looked away, eyes brimming with tears, giving a nod. "It is," he said, voice thick. "Though I am not comfortable telling you the details at this time, however...I am sorry."

"Then can you at least tell me one thing? Can you tell me...when did that happen?" She asked.

"...That was almost two years ago, now," he told her. "We have come a very long way, and now...we have a new life to look forward to," he smiled at her belly. "I am so hopeful for things to work out this time."

She glanced at her belly. "...I still don't know how to feel about you. I mean, you are handsome and seem kind, but...I just learned that I'm married, that I've already miscarried a child and I'm *only sixteen*. A fresh new start, and I learn right away that my life is nothing like I would have even thought. This is just...so *much* to take in," she said.

"I completely validate how things must seem from your point of view, and I am sorry that you are going through all of this. I know it must be overwhelming for you. I suppose, until you regain your memories, we will just...start things from the beginning again, if you aren't opposed to that?"

"I think you mean *'if'* I regain my memories."

"Well...if you don't, then perhaps that would be a blessing in disguise. Our past is...filled with painful memories for you."

"Oh..."

"Perhaps, it would be most healing for you, in any case, for those memories to remain lost. Though, we will need to reinstate your bonds to your Shadow Guardians and your Keeper Knight in your new mind."

"Reinstate the bonds?" She asked, and I considered this.

"I hadn't even thought about that. Surely, there has been at least one other case where something like this has happen, right? Having Keeper Knights bonded to their masters is a long-standing tradition, so I am sure that at some point, needing to have a wizard reinstate the bond has been necessary at some point...right?" I asked.

"I will speak to any sorcerers that I need to in order to find out for certain," the king said. He met my eyes. "We will help to fix these cracked bonds, I assure you. I know how dangerous it could be for you if it isn't taken care of."

"How so?" Kyeareth asked, immediately concerned, glancing at me.

How could I explain this in a way that she could understand it?

She didn't have her memories, after all.

"An incomplete bond will slowly deteriorate the knight and guardians over prolonged periods of time," Winter answered her. "I remember reading about a prince of old who had a serious injury, and his head was damaged...severely enough that his mental capacity was permanently affected, and he could no longer even speak. His guardians and Keeper Knight ended up deteriorating, rotting away, before they died. If a master dies, the bonded Shadow Guardians simply get released from bond-hood and go to train other members at the organization they hail from. But the deterioration of the mind, while the master is alive? A death sentence to the guardians who serve that master."

She gaped at him, before looking to me, a frightened look on her face.

I stood, going to her and kneeling in front of her. "It will be alright, your majesty. We will surely be able to reinstate the bonds with your new mind, I am sure. Try not to worry."

Though I said this in an effort to comfort her, I was nervous about whether or not it would be true.

Solaris's Gifts, 317 AR

We were about a week away from the capital, now.

We had been travelling for about seven weeks, and now, the queen was even closer to her due date, as she was about seven to seven and a half months pregnant.

She was showing well, now, and was glowing.

We had learned, through her recounting, that the wizard from the physician's office where we had found her had told her that she was carrying a son.

A prince who *would* have been the second prince, but would now be the Crowned Prince as soon as he came of age, when he turned thirteen.

She and the king sat and talked a lot in the wagon together, slowly learning about one another...well, more like, the queen learning about herself and the king.

We told her all about her family, a bit about her background and circumstances so that she would be a bit more prepared for that...

We knew that, just because her memories were gone, everyone else's wouldn't be. She would still be treated as she always had been, and if she weren't prepared for that, it would hurt her even more. We wanted to at least let her know it was likely.

There was even more to it than just how she was treated, though, however.

Things had changed drastically since she had been gone.

Her father had been killed in the coup, after all.

Her brother was now the reigning Duke Severing.

Their mother and youngest sibling were alright, but still shaken up from the ordeal.

There was also...something even bigger. I wasn't sure how she would react when she met Astaroth again, but...there was something that had happened, and it might just change everything.

We told her about her interests and hobbies, how she enjoyed drawing and reading romance novels, gossiping with her recently deceased maid about the characters and enjoying discussions about it with me, as well.

We told her that she was very interested in tournaments and watching the knights sparring, knowing that she loved the sword, was interested in weaponry and archery, as well as sorcery.

We told her about the king's family dynamics, how he and she had met originally, and about how they had grown much closer over their time together.

We enjoyed feeding her during the trip, as she had been severely malnourished from the long journey down river, unconscious and unable to take care of herself but—thankfully—unable to die.

I noticed, during this time, that Cassian watched her very forlornly.

I knew, now, from the look in his eyes; he'd had romantic affection for my queen.

I finally decided, one day, to ask her about this when she went off to the river to get a sip of drink.

"Excuse me, your majesty," I said quietly, and she glanced at me.

"Oh, um...Seryn..." She said, soft. "What is it?"

"I wanted to ask about the nature of your relationship to the man that you invited to come with us, your majesty. I know it isn't my place, but I have seen the two of you watch each other often, and you two regularly glance at one another..."

She gasped, gaping at me for a moment with a heavy blush on her face, before she looked quickly away. "I...hadn't realized that I'd been being so obvious..."

I smiled, going and squatting beside of her. "...So?" I asked, smiling at her warmly.

"You...won't get mad?"

I scoffed. "I am your knight, my queen. My job is not to get mad at you, judge you, spy on you or otherwise pry into your business. My sole duty is to *protect* you in every possible way and to be here for you. So...in other words, you can talk to me about anything, and you can even forbid me to speak of it ever again, and I will obey you... You always have talked to me about everything, just so you know."

She smiled. "I am glad that I had such a handsome knight to rely on," she laughed softly. "It *is* true, he fancies me. And honestly, I had started to consider accepting him. He was so kind to me, and we grew close in the time that I stayed with them. He...he offered to claim me and the baby, if nobody came for me."

I gaped at her, before throwing a new-perspective glance over at the man.

That was a huge responsibility to take on, and it was a very honorable thing to do.

I smiled. "I am thankful that you had such an honorable man helping you, your majesty. That is no small measure of honor." I wasn't lying, I really was impressed by his courage and honor.

She nodded. "I know. He didn't have to offer such a thing. They could have taken me to a doctor and left me there to fend for myself, but they didn't. They took me into their own lives, taking care of me until I was well enough to stand and move on my own."

I thought on this for some time.

What would she do, now that he was joining us at the palace?

Would she offer him a title?

Land?

He was a carriage driver, and though I was sure he could be trained, at this age, it would take him years to become proficient in any weapon, so he wouldn't be good to have knighted.

Days continued to pass, and we finally arrived at the imperial city.

When we reached the city, we didn't hold a large welcoming ceremony...though, there was someone at the doors of the palace that I *hadn't* anticipated to see, and I was thrilled to see him alive and safe.

He looked a bit roughed up and a little underfed, but he was safe, now.

"*Sister!*" Flaming cried, rushing over to the wagon, and practically leaping into the back. He was grabbing her hands and pulling the queen into a tight embrace, beaming a smile at her. "Were you terribly worried? I know that we got separated there, and I was actually taken captive for a while!"

"Flaming—" Cinder started, trying to cut him off. "I am glad you are safe, but Kyeareth—"

Flaming wasn't paying attention, looking ecstatic to see Kyeareth, and bypassed his brother altogether. "I was starved and beaten a bit, but eventually my Shadow Guardians located me and rescued me. It took quite a while, but I'm back! I've been worried sick about you, sister. I heard from my captors that you had died!" He pulled her into another tight hug, rocking and bouncing and tearfully overjoyed to see her...but when she didn't respond in kind, he pulled away, a devastated look on his face. "S-sister? Why do you look at me with such a face? You act like we're *strangers*! I know it's been a while, but it's *me*! Flaming, your most favorite brother-in-law who adores you!"

She glanced at us, before she gave him an awkward smile. "Oh, uh, yes..."

He gaped at her for a moment, before he looked to the king. "What on earth—"

"We will discuss it in detail later, Flaming," Cinder sighed. "The queen is tired and hungry, and has been away from home for a long time. It is past due time to get inside and get bathed and fed, wouldn't you agree? Though, I am happy to see you safe, and I am thankful for the warm welcome."

The prince looked devastated even as he got back off of the wagon, and we all unloaded and went into the palace.

He kept throwing worried glances to Kyeareth, as did Cinder, and it seemed to be the general consensus that this...might not go as smoothly as we'd hoped.

There was going to be a lot of changing and adjusting to be done around here in the next days...

I glanced at the king, and he gave me a nod. "Take the queen to our chambers," he said. "I shall send someone with a meal and someone to help her bathe, and a physician later. I am sure there are reports that I need to catch up on, since I have been absent for so long." He glanced up, then, noticing his father coming down the stairs to receive us.

The former king wore a happy look on his face to see the queen. "Welcome back! I am so happy to see you safe, your majesty!" He spoke. When she clammed up again, his eyes widened, concerned. "My queen...?"

"I...I just want to get this out of the way," she said, suddenly. "I've lost all my memories, alright? I don't know *any* of you! I'm sorry, but I'm having a hard enough time with taking in who everyone is and that I have lost connections to you all, but to see these heartbroken looks over and over is tearing me apart!" She cried, grasping the sides of her head.

The king and prince startled, looking at us with hundreds of unanswered questions...even as Cassian leapt from his position in line, and she sobbed as she embraced him, giving us all a wary, tired expression.

My heart shattered in that instant, because I knew that she truly was not my queen.

It was just an empty shell, this girl who sought comfort from an outsider. Albeit an outsider who'd saved her life, but an outsider all the same...

An outsider who wasn't her husband.

I went to her, gently placing my hands on her shoulders, and directing her to the King and Queen's chambers, even as we left all of the others standing there, silent, and awkward.

When we got to her chambers, she stepped inside, hesitating before she walked around the room, looking around at everything.

"Do you...feel anything familiar about this place?" I asked her.

She glanced around. "*Sort* of...I definitely feel like I've been here...but there isn't anything that I actually recognize."

"This is your shared chambers with the King," I told her. "He has already selected a new personal maid for you, since..."

"Since mine *died*..." She filled in, and I gave her a nod. "Was I there to witness her death?" When I nodded again, she shuddered. "I guess I am grateful that I don't remember that."

I smiled. "Alice was a very good woman. She died protecting you, and helped you escape. She bought you time."

"I feel like her effort was in vain, if I was stabbed and thrown into the river anyway."

"Not *necessarily*," I said. "Try to think of it like this; She died protecting you from someone who was going to take you to that fate immediately, but because she got in the way and bought you more time, you were able to get to a place where Lord Winter was able to cast the protection spell on you in secret, and in turn, really *did* save your life. That spell was not cast upon you until after she had already died."

"...I see..."

"In other words, it was her sacrifice which gave the wizard enough time to get you somewhere safe long enough to take that measure. Without that sacrifice, you could have been killed sooner."

She smiled. "That does make it seem a bit better, then. Since I don't remember, I thought she just...died for no reason."

"I was there, and I do remember, my queen. Believe me, though her sacrifice is heartbreaking...she would be so proud to know that she was able to aid in saving your life. There would have been no time to cast the spell on you without that sacrifice."

"Oh..."

"The same goes for the second prince; he entered the escape passage with the two of you, and he stayed behind, risking his life to protect you as Lord Winter took you and ran, trying to get you to safety."

"But why?" She asked. "What am *I* to these people?"

"My queen...you are our *queen*. You are kind, and gentle, and compassionate. You are warm, and modest. You are not someone who abuses their authority. You are considerate to the servants, and even gift them things for their birthdays, you bring them fruits and vegetables when you come back from market...you give to the less fortunate...My queen, you are beloved by this entire kingdom. They were devastated when they thought that you were dead."

"I just...I don't see how someone like me could be such an important person."

• • •

There was a sudden knock on the door, and a maid stepped in, letting us know that Kyeareth's bath had been prepared, and she took her off to bathe as I stood on the other side of the partition, keeping a respectful behavior but close enough to protect her.

When that was finished and she was dressed, she startled to see the King sitting at the small dining table in their chambers as the meal was delivered.

"Your majesty," she said softly, giving a curtsy.

He looked away, a slightly disappointed look on his face, but he didn't say anything about the overtly polite and formal way she spoke to him.

"What is the matter?" She asked. "Do we...often eat together?"

"We usually eat *every* meal together," he said. "Unless something truly urgent comes up, I take all of my meals with you, my *wife*."

She blushed, looking away and stroking her damp hair. "I-is that so...?" She asked, voice small.

"Are you...*displeased* by this...?" He asked, nervous.

"No, no!" She cried quickly, waving her hands in front of her before she cleared her throat, reining herself back in. "No, your majesty, I am not displeased...just, um, surprised."

He smiled warmly at her, and she blushed again, looking away once more.

I chuckled silently.

He had been able to win her heart once...perhaps he could do so again, and even easier this time, since there was no bad history between them in her mind.

The slate was wiped clean.

"I have arranged for the director of the Sorcerer's order to arrive by tomorrow afternoon," the king informed, looking at me. "I have given a brief summary of the situation, and he sent word back immediately that he would bring all of his material on the subject to find a solution."

"Good, then," I said, hopeful.

Kyeareth suddenly gasped, grasping her belly, and the king leapt to his feet, alarmed. Kyeareth startled, gaping up at him, before she looked down at her belly.

Then, she grabbed his hand, and lay it upon her abdomen.

I watched as his face, concerned, lit up into a bright smile and a small laugh came out of his chest.

"Oh, oh I see!" He said. "I am sorry for startling you, I thought something might be wrong, but it is just that the baby is a strong kicker."

"So, your majesty—"

"*Cinder*, please...you are my wife. It causes me to cringe to hear you address me so formally."

"Cinder, then...um, what will we name the child?" She asked.

He paused. "Well...your brother was the reason you named our late son what you did." He pondered for a moment. "No matter what we name the child, I figure that you will likely make it an honorary name, named for someone close to you, as you did with your brother and our late son."

"What is my brother's name again...?" She asked, fidgeting. "I...I don't remember the child's name, either. I'm sorry...but, when I try to remember, my head hurts a bit with all of the information."

Cinder and I both startled at this, and I grabbed a notebook and wrote it down for her, handing it to her when I finished.

She gasped, stroking the names.

"These...names...they *feel* familiar to me. I don't know why, but something about them strikes something in me."

He hesitated, before leaning forward, pressing a gentle kiss to her forehead. "I thought that they might."

"Astaroth, Asfaloth...you are right, they are similar. Do they...mean anything? I feel like they each mean something."

I smiled. "Astaroth is the name of one of the grand dukes of Hell, a mighty demon at the right-hand of the devil himself. It is meant to be an intimidation tactic to cause his enemies fear. On quite the opposite end, Asfaloth means 'sunlight.'"

"Oh...so, why did I name him that?"

"He was named something similar in sound to your brother, because many people know of your strangely...close relationship with him. It was meant to be a bit of a *joke*, in case the child looked like you, to name him after your brother, but also to honor your brother. The child did, indeed, look like you. You wanted to imagine him as the sun itself."

"I see," she whispered, considering this. "I will wait until we see the baby, then, before I name him."

"A good decision," he smiled.

She glanced up at the portrait on the wall. "I've...been wondering..." She motioned to the portrait. "Is that—?"

The king nodded. "It is. It is a vision of what our son would have likely looked like, had he lived past infancy. We didn't know what eye-color he had, but we at least knew what you and I looked like as children thanks to portraits from the past, and the painter did a phenomenal job combining the faces together to blend into this beautiful angel."

Tears filled her eyes as she gazed upon the painting. "It is...beautiful," she said. "He is beautiful. I wish I could remember—" She cut herself off. "Well...maybe *not*..."

"I can tell you, honestly, that you don't wish to remember. I would love to forget it, sometimes. Truthfully, it was...a quite *gruesome* affair," I said, soft. "It may be best if you never remember it. It would hurt you deeply...especially to be reminded of how you reacted to the grief."

"Oh..." She said, voice barely audible. "Did I...not take it well...?"

"That would be an understatement," the king said. "It took a very long time for you to come out of that."

"But I did come out of that...?"

"Well...yes, sort of. You were still fighting to stay above water, trying not to drown in your own mind, when you were...*hurt*."

"Oh, I see..." She looked to the king. "When did that...happen?"

"It was Solaris's Gifts, of 315 AR," he told her. "It was about a month before he was due to arrive."

She gave a solemn nod. "May I...see his resting place?"

He nodded, standing and taking her by the hand. "Of course, you may."

"It won't hurt you to take me there?"

"...It may," he admitted. "But he was your child. You deserve to go, and I go there often, myself. So, come. Let us go."

We both led her out to the mausoleum.

Chapter 20

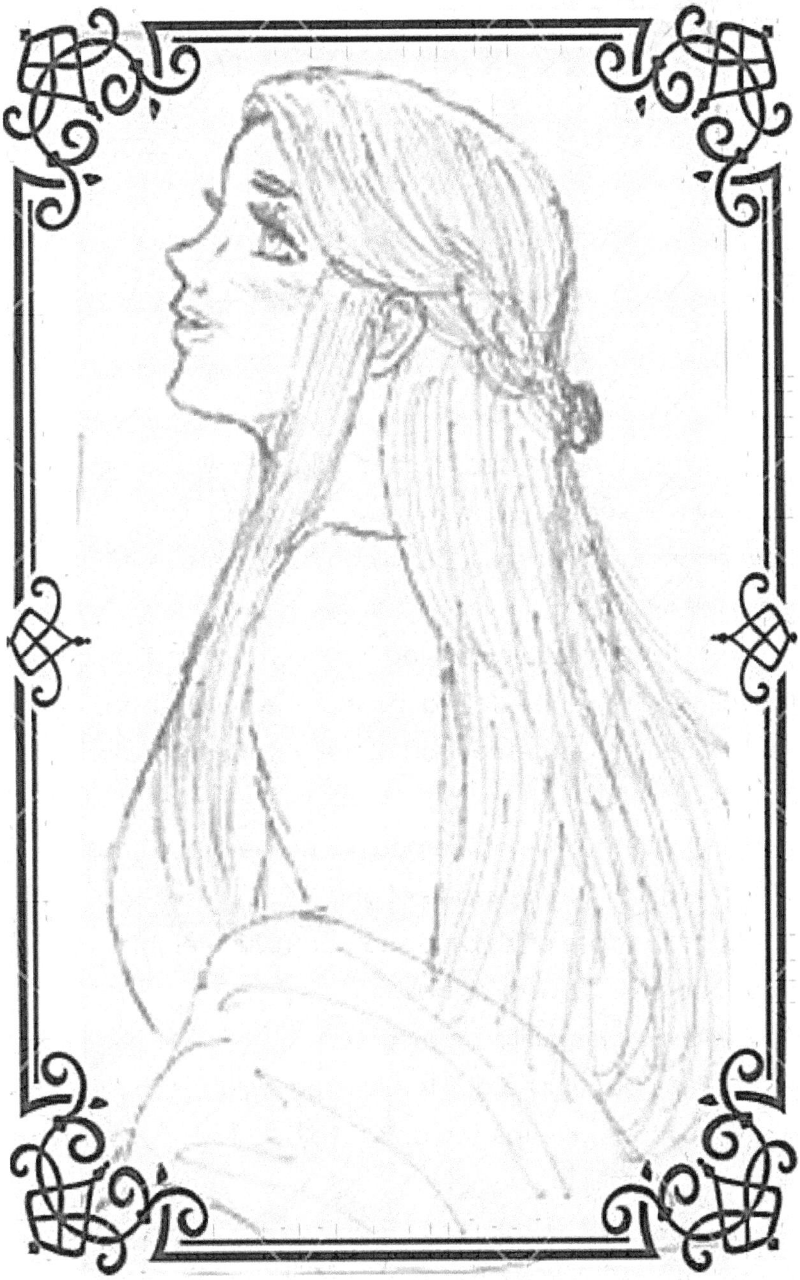

Kyeareth...

When we reached the mausoleum, I was surprised to see how well-kept it was, how decorated and high-maintenance it seemed. It certainly was the gravesite of a royal, to be sure.

My stranger-husband led me over to a podium about the height of my chest, telling me that the baby's body had been buried into its center, sort of like a standing grave of stone.

On the outside of the podium made of the finest, shiniest marble, was a plaque of gold with his name inscribed, the date of his birth and death, his weight and height, and the color of his hair.

It was a beautiful memorial.

"It is beautiful here..." I whispered. I glanced to the king. "You must have the servants take good care of this place."

"Actually," he said. "You and I, we take care of this place ourselves, personally."

I startled at that. "What?" I asked, surprised.

"You truly loved Asfaloth. You would never leave the care of his mausoleum to the servants...and neither would I."

I blushed a bit when he bowed, reaching for my hand, and kissing the back of it, holding my eyes with his own.

He smirked at me. "At least I know that I can still make you *blush*...even if you don't remember me."

"G-goodness," I said, blushing harder and looking away.

He looked so much like Cassian, because when he flirted with me...his eyes darkened a shade, closer in shade to Cassian's.

I wondered if I had ever truly been attracted to *Cassian*, or if my soul was just attracted to the similarity to my own husband. Cassian was a good-looking man, but the similarity to Cinder was striking and surprising.

They could have been brothers.

Being separated from my husband would surely be devastating to my heart, so it would make sense for that to be the case, wouldn't it? Was that why Cassian had caught my heart so quickly?

I knew that I couldn't be with Cassian...I was married.

Happily, so, if what I was being told was to be true.

After all, I wouldn't be in my currently heavily pregnant state if that were not the case, would I?

Cinder didn't seem to be the type of person to force me...

He seemed to genuinely care for me, in any case.

My detachment seemed to deeply hurt him, and that hurt me somewhere deep in my heart somewhere, for some reason that I couldn't fathom, lest it be that I truly did love him, in my heart of hearts.

As we stepped out of the mausoleum, I startled to hear a beautiful violin playing nearby.

It was a beautiful melody, with a sad tone, almost.

Suddenly, I glanced in surprise as Cinder reached his hand out for mine, offering me a dance even as he bowed slightly at the waist, his eyes looking up at me...almost nervous.

I gently took his hand, and he pulled me into his hold, into the position that I needed to be in, and we began to step and sway to the music.

The song seemed familiar, but it was foreign feeling, as well. I didn't know why.

"It played the first time we ever danced. I actually didn't plan this," he said, chuckling. He glanced over to the player, who bowed even as they continued playing. "I hope you don't feel overwhelmed. I wouldn't want for you to feel pressured or anything..."

I shook my head. "I don't," I told him.

He smiled. "Good."

After we finished our dance, we gave each other a bow and curtsy, before he led me by the arm, back to our room.

We sat there awkwardly for a bit, before I cleared my throat and lay down, staring at the skies outside of the window. He pressed a gentle, light kiss to my forehead, before he told me that he had some work to do. So, I fell into a light, restless sleep as he left to go handle office work, and Seryn sat at the nearby table, quietly sipping on some tea. I still wasn't sure what to make of all of this. It was overwhelming.

After months of thinking I had been an abandoned, perhaps even abused, pregnant woman...I had learned, in a rapid time frame, that I was married and loved and cared for. A queen. The wife of a king.

It was a lot to take in, with a short time span in which to take it in.

I had to wonder how the king, himself, was really taking all of this. He didn't seem to let on that he was stressed, but it couldn't be as simple as he was making it out to be, either. I was crucially aware just how awkward this must be for him, too.

His pregnant wife was missing for months, after she had been supposedly killed, and then he finds her...only for her to have lost all of her memory?

I was sympathetic to him, knowing how difficult and strenuous this situation truly was.

I couldn't say that I got any real, true rest that night, and the following morning arrived too soon, it seemed.

I had been left without much sleep that night, so truly, I was exhausted.

There was a knock on the door, and I glanced to see my husband stride confidently into the room.

I had to admit...his confident manner and posture, his confident striding and gait...it was highly attractive to me.

He held this powerful air about him.

It drew me in.

"It is time to re-secure the bonds," he said, glancing at Seryn, giving a nod.

Seryn wordlessly helped me up and they let the maids help me get ready. With as tired as I was, I didn't really have the energy to protest, and I didn't even try to do so.

I appreciated the assistance, no matter how strange it felt for me to get help with something as simple as dressing myself.

It couldn't be helped, though. I needed to have help.

When I was dressed, I was led to a chamber where there were several wizards, hooded and cloaked—all but one, who wore a special crown-like headpiece...and I knew from his energy and his air that he was the head wizard in charge.

His garb was different, as well.

"I greet your majesties, the King and Queen," he said, bowing. "I have heard of the situation, and I have managed to find a way to re-establish the lost knight and guardian bonds, at least. I cannot restore the queen's memories, but I can use the lingering bonds in her body to form new bonds to this new mind."

"What happens if she regains her old memories?" The king asked, concerned.

Seryn and my Shadow Guardians all murmured in agreement.

"Then the original bond will still be in place and awaken once more. This will actually help to strengthen that bond, if that becomes the case. However, I can tell you that using my magic to help re-establish these bonds...can affect the baby."

"What?" I cried, alarmed. "But we can't let the baby get hurt—"

"Oh, no, your majesty! Not in a harmful way, my queen. Rather...it could imbue the child with magical properties, give him abilities that he would otherwise not have. The Royal Bloodline is, technically, a house that is made up of Paladin Knights, though there aren't many."

"What does that mean?" I asked.

"Paladins are special-classed Knights who also possess traces of mana. When they marry, they can choose a bride from either faction; mage or knight. The current king's grandfather was from the Knight's Faction, and his wife was a Mage-Born."

"Oh..."

"Then, their children had mixed blood, but no mana. However, though she didn't have much active mana, the king's grandmother happened to be the daughter of someone whom was very important in the Sorcerer's Sect in another kingdom. As a powerful knight with mixed blood—no matter how little it is—he is technically in the paladin section."

"Oh, I see. That makes sense."

"You, however, your majesty...you are from a Knight's Faction family where the duke of your household is a hero knight, yes, but your *birth mother* was a noble woman from a mage family in another nation. Your blood is much more potent with mana than his. You are also Mage-Born, and have strong and powerful mana."

"Then—"

"That means that the child could have taken more after the Knight blood, getting Knight Aura rather than Mage Mana, like his father, but...it is honestly much more likely that the child could have the opposite thing happen."

"But what does that mean for ruling—"

He sighed, seemingly tired of explaining.

Thankfully, not tired enough to deter him from actually doing so, it seemed.

"Being part of the Royal family in a country ruled mostly by the Knight's Faction, it could be potentially risky if your son were to develop Mana ruled blood. The Knight's Faction and Mage's Faction are barely keeping peace as it is."

I hesitated. I didn't want to ask another question, but since I had lost my memory, I didn't know what all of this meant.

I needed more information.

He seemed to sense this from my lack of response. "Forgive me, your majesty, if I seem irritated. I am not used to having to explain so much. I understand that you lost your memories, so you don't remember any of this, but it is exhausting to go through all of this information."

"I...I'm sorry, I—"

"No, please, don't apologize. It isn't your fault." He took a deep breath. "We currently live in a kingdom that is ruled by the Knight's Faction, and we have an unsteady but relatively intact peace agreement with the Mage's Faction. It was a political move to marry you to the Crowned Prince in the first place, being that you are Mage-Born despite being part of a Mage Faction family. However, this situation involves the future rule of the nation. *This prince* will become the Crowned Prince; the next in line for the throne of the kingdom."

"Right," I said, nodding and showing that I was paying attention.

"The problem is, If I perform this magic upon you, it could possibly alter the child. I cannot currently tell which would lead in his blood—the Mana or Aura. He could, currently, become a master Knight with high levels of Knight Aura, like his father."

"I see," I said.

The head-wizard continued on. "Filling you with magic to help you re-connect these lost bonds, however, may possibly give the child stronger *magic*...in which, rather than becoming a knight, as all of the former Crowned Princes have been, he would become a *mage*. The Knight's Faction would strongly contest such a thing."

"...What is so bad about that...?"

"A *mage* has never been the Crowned Prince...mainly because most of those in the Knight's Faction frown upon sorcery in general. Their principles are firmly against many magics that are practiced. Only Paladins, who have ability to use both aura and mana, accept both of them together in harmony...but there aren't many Paladins currently in our kingdom. Your child would face higher danger if it were found out that he was a sorcerer. He would have to hide it. The Imperial family is supposed to only have limited magic if any at all, so as not to hold too much authority over either faction. It is meant to make it fair. The Mage's Faction would be thrilled by this, but the Knight's Faction would not accept it."

"Oh..." I whispered, worried.

I glanced at my knight and my guardians, who I knew needed to be connected to me mentally in order to live.

I could, potentially, never recover my memory, but if I *didn't*, and I didn't establish these new bonds...

It could kill them.

I couldn't let that happen.

I might not know them that well, but I didn't want them to die.

So, I made my decision, and I sighed. "It won't...actually *hurt* my baby?" I asked.

He shook his head. "It will not, I promise. It will not hurt you, either, as the formal bonds have already been established. This magic will simply reinforce the bond perimeters and structure, and reassemble it so that it holds to your new mind."

"Alright..."

"So, that is your decision?" He asked.

I nodded. "Yes. I understand the risks, and I understand the consequences of those risks...but I can't let them die, on the chance that I don't happen to get my memory back."

He nodded. "I understand," he said with a smile.

He had me sit on a chair nearby, and had all of my guardians and my knight lay their hands upon my hands.

As the sorcerer began to chant, I began to feel strange.

I felt a sense of familiarity, a strong pulling and tugging, almost dizzyingly powerful. I felt nauseated, like the room was suddenly spinning around me.

Finally, just as it was becoming unbearable for me, the pressure ended, and I could suddenly hear voices in my mind, even though no one spoke.

I gasped, looking at my guardians.

"I can hear you," I whispered, and they all smiled, kneeling.

"Yes, my queen," the dark skinned, black-haired one said. "It is good to feel at home again," he smiled.

I remembered him as being "Eclipse," my silver badged guardian.

"There is something familiar about it," I said.

There was suddenly a quickening in my belly, a tightening, and I gasped.

Azoth gasped, reaching out to catch me as my legs gave way. "My queen!" He called me. He glanced to the head-wizard.

"The baby is...*responding*..." Winter whispered.

The wizard nodded. "I was afraid so. As soon as I felt the spike in energy, I had thought as much. It is, of course, possible that the child already had mana rather than aura, but now, it is certain; The child will hold magic."

The knights in the room glanced nervously at one another, and I looked to them.

"We'll be okay, though, won't we?" I asked.

"It is just...we will have to lie about his abilities," Seryn said. "In order to protect him. We cannot ever let him be who he truly is, and we will have to teach him not to show his mana. It is as it was said earlier, a full-fledged sorcerer has never held rule over this kingdom. The knight families may even try to start a war over this. We may not have to worry about it if there comes to be a second prince, but the nobles and Knight's Faction won't accept it if their Crowned Prince is a sorcerer."

"But—" I cried, clenching my gown. "What if we train him as a knight, too? What if he just...became a powerful paladin who has advanced magic? Would that be so terrible?"

"*True* sorcerers can't become full-fledged knights," my husband said. "It interferes with their mana. He would have to have an almost equal amount of both mana *and* aura for that to be the case."

"...I don't understand."

"I know that you aren't aware of this, but in our bodies is one of two streams—an 'aura' stream, and a 'mana' stream. Those in the Knight's Faction only have aura, and the same is true in reverse for the Mage's Faction."

"But the royal paladins—"

"Paladins are exceedingly *rare*, and again, the aura and mana have to be almost completely even in amount. Such a thing almost never happens naturally in the factions, and takes a lot of breeding between knights and mages. Sometimes, it happens by chance, but that isn't common at all."

"So...our son will spend his days in hiding?"

"Well...yes, if he is to be the Crowned Prince..."

"Nothing can ever be done about it? There is no changing the people, and no way that we can even train him as a knight?" I asked, sad.

He looked away. "Not a proper knight with aura, no. And, if it is discovered that he *is* a sorcerer, it is likely that the people will revolt. War could break out..."

"Can the energy be leveled out?" I asked my personal sorcerer.

Winter shook his head. "His body has now been imbued with magic, forcefully, in order to help you. Unfortunately, that means that we cannot change it. This is considered holy restoration magic, which means that it is permanent. That is another reason that the Knight's Faction frowns upon sorcery...anything done, intentionally or unintentionally, with magic...is usually *permanent*. Extensive spells are required to change anything, and even then, it may not be reversible."

I gasped. "Does that mean...that the protection spell on me was also permanent?" I asked.

He nodded. "Yes. Unless you are burned alive, or die of natural causes—say, a disease or old age—you will survive. The only exception would be a curse, which only hag-witches can perform in black magic, which is also very extremely rare. Even finding hag-witches is very unlikely, and most of them are heathens who refuse to even hold a conversation with people, let alone work with someone to cast curses over people."

"I see," I said.

"So...be careful who you share that information with, my queen."

"Why...?" I asked, getting more and more frightened.

"If it were discovered that you had that spell upon you, it wouldn't take much for someone to know exactly how to dispose of you. Only the people in this very room can be completely trusted. None of here, who are all sworn by blood oaths to protect the royal family lest we die...none of us would ever do anything that could put either of you at risk. You have nothing to fear as long as you keep that secret."

I gulped, grasping my chest. "I will take your warning to heart." I felt a bit woozy. "Is there...any way that I could lie down? I feel dizzy."

Cinder almost immediately had me in his arms, carrying me to a nearby bench and having me lay down easily.

"I am sorry, I wasn't thinking. All of this is so much to take in, and with so much happening and going on, you must be very stressed. Please forgive me for being so inconsiderate."

"How much longer does she have before the child is due?" The head wizard asked.

Cinder calculated in his mind for a moment. "She conceived in Year's Fall, so she is due in the next couple of weeks or so."

"Do not be alarmed if the child is born a little prematurely," the wizard said, giving a bow. "The magic will help to strengthen him and develop him faster, so he may arrive a little sooner than anticipated. That doesn't mean that anything is wrong."

My husband nodded. "I will keep this in mind. Thank you or the warning. After what happened last time…" He drifted off. The wizard nodded, knowing what he meant by it.

With that, Cinder lifted me again, and together, we all went back to the king's chambers...my chambers.

We spent the rest of the night talking, until I finally managed to fall into a listless, light slumber.

I had to say…that I couldn't see things going too horribly, if it kept up this way.

Cinder had done his utmost to make sure that I was comfortable. He was considerate, caring, and warm. He was also very dutiful in his work, but he still made time for me.

Living here, with this man…might not be so bad.

I felt loved. I felt cared for and valued.

So, why was it that they insisted so much that I might not wish to recover my memories?

Everything seemed to be fine enough.

I couldn't understand what could be so terrible about my life for them to insist that I didn't want my memories to return, even the worst of them...

Solaris's Reign, 317 AR

It was in the middle of Solaris's Reign, when I awoke to whispers and movement around the room.

I peeked open my eyes, to see the maids and my guardians, my knight, and my husband gathered around me, my husband smiling brightly at me and holding a tray of pastries.

...*What was happening?*

Why were they all here, gathered around me?

"W...what is going on?" I asked sleepily, yawning, and moving to sit up against my pillows.

"*Happy birthday*, my queen," Cinder said, bowing slightly before he leaned forward and gave me a kiss on the forehead. "You are seventeen today! So, I wanted to bring you this tray of your favorite treats, and I have a surprise for you when you are finished getting ready," he said, smiling.

I felt my heart tug. "It's my *birthday*?" I asked.

He nodded. "Yes. I didn't want to overwhelm you with a big celebration or startle you with a surprise, so I thought that *this* surprise would be a bit better. Nice and calm and quiet. Your next surprise will probably be a bit more exciting; or, at least, that is what I hope. I have a feeling that it will be a good thing for you."

I smiled. "Yes, I am sure that I will like it," I said softly.

"I sure hope that you will."

"Thank you, your majes—Cinder," I corrected myself quickly. It still felt weird in my mind, calling a king by his first name.

Had it been awkward before the incident and my memory loss, too?

I couldn't imagine that it had been, but I also couldn't imagine it not being awkward, either. I couldn't feel this awkward about it if I hadn't felt that way before, could I? I wasn't entirely sure.

Husband or not, it seemed disrespectful in my noble-classed mind, but I had to remind myself of my position, as well. I was the queen, wasn't I?

I knew that I didn't remember anything from my life, but the teachings were so engrained in my mind and body that I just automatically responded in kind.

He stood, leaving and going to bathe, while I sat chatting and laughing with my guardians and knight, sharing the sweets that my husband had brought me.

They enjoyed feeling the baby kick inside of me through my belly, and we all discussed possible names for the child.

When we had finished eating and getting ready, he escorted me out to the drawing room, where I was met by someone.

"*Sister,*" I heard a voice say.

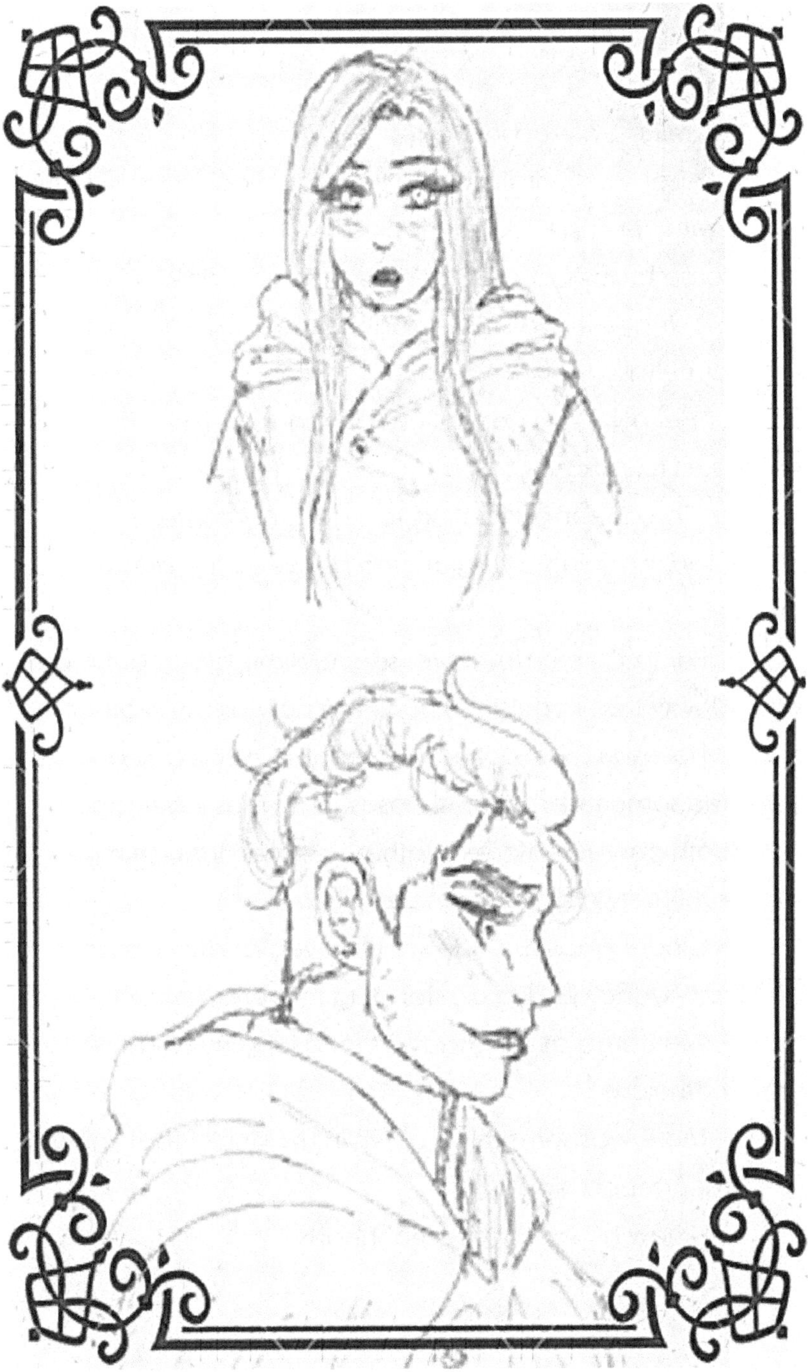

I almost felt a pulse quicken in me, my heart thumping wildly.

I felt paralyzed in place.

All of my guardians and Seryn startled, restless, turning to me with varying looks of shock and awe on their handsome faces...and Cinder glanced at them, surprised.

"What is it? What's wrong?" Cinder asked, worried immediately by their reaction.

"Her *heart*..." I heard Seryn whisper to him softly. "Her entire *soul is...pulsing*."

"The queen is reacting to Astaroth," Winter murmured, nodding and glancing between me and my brother.

I didn't remember ever seeing him before, but there was no way that I couldn't *know* that he was my brother.

He and I...we looked so alike. The same hair and eyes, the same cheekbones, noses...it was as if our faces were both carved on one another's bodies, though mine was admittedly more feminine, of course.

Cinder gaped at the scene, even as my twin paid no mind to anyone around us, stepping forward hesitantly.

We stared at one another for a long moment, lost in one another.

There was something down in my bones that knew him. I recognized him.

I knew him in my heart of hearts.

We stared at one another for a few more moments in silence, before he flung his arms around me, burying his face in my shoulder.

"My sister," he sobbed. "*Kyeareth*. I thought...you were dead. This was all *my* fault! The entire thing. If I hadn't been so stupid, the duke would never have done all this, you wouldn't have been hurt!" His voice cracked as his body trembled. "My *love*," he whispered.

I could feel the guardians shifting uncomfortably at the scene, taking cautionary glances at the king, but I was undisturbed. I wasn't sure why, but I didn't actually care about his opinion over my brother.

I didn't care about anyone's opinion, and...

Something told me that my husband, somehow, already knew about this bond we had; this bond that I had no recollection of, but I felt it in my bones.

I knew well enough that the guardians could read my mind, especially since the bond had to be re-established.

Before, there would have been a wall of privacy there to protect my thoughts, but since my mind was broken, so was that wall.

I felt my body respond, even though my mind felt uncomfortable.

My heart raced, my cheeks flushed, and even though I didn't even think about it, my arms tightened around him.

"*Astaroth*," I said softly without even thinking, and he startled, pulling away from me, eyes wide and lips slightly parted.

The rest of the people around us looked on similarly.

I froze myself, realizing that even though I had been taught his name, I wasn't using my current mind to address him...his name had tumbled from my lips all on their own, absent-mindedly.

How could that be? For that matter, how could I know that? Was he just so engrained in me that I couldn't forget him? Then...

Then, what about my husband? Shouldn't he have been in that spot?

"My queen," Azoth whispered, kneeling next to me. "Your soul has established an official connection. You didn't speak with your current mind just then. You spoke with your true heart."

So...I wasn't the only one who thought so?

"What do you mean?" I asked.

"You *recognize* Astaroth. This is the first time this has happened since you have returned, and it is Astaroth whom has made the connection."

"What does that mean?" My maid asked.

Azoth glanced at my maid, before looking away, a bit embarrassed. "It means that they had a *particularly* strong bond before the incident; a bond strong enough that it survived through what happened. From the moment he spoke, her soul...it has been pulsing."

"I don't understand what that means," my maid said, stiff. "'Pulsing?'"

"Think of it as her heart is pounding, and her soul recognized him. She knows him. He and she are on the same wave lengths."

"Wait, wait a moment...Are you...telling me that it is *true*? That Duke Steel truly did all of this just because my lady seems to have some...some, unholy, sick, *unnatural* bond with her own twin brother?" She asked, scoffing. "My brother was a Palace guard who died in the coup attack!"

The room went eerily silent with a heavy, heavy air...and she froze.

"No..." She grated out. "No, *no*, **no**," she said, tone getting thicker and harsher each second. "You *can't* be serious."

"You need to calm down—" Cinder started, but she wasn't having it.

"Are you just *joking*?" She asked. When there was still no answer, she threw up her hands. "So, my brother died for your sin!" She shouted, pointing a finger and glaring at us.

"You need to stop—" Cinder tried, but she whirled to face him.

She glared at the king. "Did you know? Were you aware that your wife is a disgusting whore who trapes around with her own brother? Is this whole kingdom cursed to serve a queen involved in incest?!"

"Shut your mouth!" Cinder snarled, and I flinched.

I was causing too much tension; I was causing more problems—

"It is true," Astaroth said, soft. "We have always loved one another, yes, but it transcends simple romantic or lustful affection. It always felt as if...we were *connected*. Almost as if we were the same person sometimes."

"See?! He admits it!" The maid shrieked, pointing.

Astaroth continued, glaring at her. "I will admit that romantic and lustful affection are there, but...it was so much deeper than that. My sister is no whore. She and I have never, even once, lain together intimately. The only man she's ever taken is her husband, and the only woman I have ever taken was my wife. She has done nothing wrong. Your brother died to save her, and his death wasn't in vain—"

"No!" My maid cried. "I am not willing to accept this!"

"What—"

"I cannot serve a queen like this!" She bent down, lifting a small pebble, and threw it at me with all her might.

I startled when my Keeper Knight stepped in, blocking the way, and shielding off the stone with his shield.

As she was escorted away at the command of the king, suddenly, we became aware of a new party in the room as they began to suddenly cry.

I whirled around, looking over to a woman who was holding an infant crying in her arms, and a young girl at her side.

She tried to comfort the baby, but I left my brother's arms and approached her on my own.

She backed up a bit, looking between my brother and I with wide, confused eyes.

My eyes were focused on the children, though. They seemed so familiar to me...but why?

The child who stood at the woman's side looked a lot like the woman, but her eyes were like mine and my brother's.

It was a young girl who looked a few years old.

The woman startled when she saw me get closer, and I looked upon the baby in her arms.

The child was wrapped in a pink blanket, with very light ashen-brown hair, and looking up at me with eyes that matched mine and my brother's.

The hair was a bit darker, but the eyes were the same. She had beautiful peachy skin, and rosy cheeks as she stared up at me.

Astaroth shifted uncomfortably for a moment, before finally, after a long moment, coming to my side.

"That's right...you haven't met, yet. When she was born, I sent her mother back to the Steel duchy as the duchess, under the condition that she never contact either of us again."

"But...why?" I asked. "Why send your wife—"

"Her father was the one whom started the coup, that led to your injury and your being missing for so long."

"...Oh," I breathed, startled, and overwhelmed.

"I let our mother care for my daughter, while I dealt with the situation with my ex-wife," he said, gesturing to the woman holding the baby.

"Astaroth, Kyeareth, is it true—" The woman started, but Astaroth gave her a solemn expression. She stopped midsentence, cutting off her question.

She handed the baby over to him, and stepped back, watching us with tearful eyes.

Astaroth faced me again, smiling at me. "I know you don't remember, but this is our adopted mother. Our father was killed during the coup, but *she* survived. While I sent away my ex-wife, I kept the child and didn't kill the mother, despite everything she caused. It was my last act of mercy toward her, when she could have been executed along with her father for treason against our family and the royal family, both. She graciously accepted her new role and fled, letting me file for divorce with no complaints. *This*," he said, gazing at the baby in his arms. "Is my daughter...Kynroth," he said, soft.

I gaped at him. "You...gave her this name in my namesake?" I asked.

He nodded. "Of course, I did. You named Asfaloth in my namesake," he chuckled.

My brother-in-law fell to his knees nearby, whispering pleas for this to not be true, before he gazed at my husband.

...Was that the appropriate reaction? I wasn't sure anymore.

My mind was positively reeling and spiraling and—

After a few moments, though—when finally, he noticed that my husband *hadn't* reacted this entire time—he stopped cowering and stood, slowly, as if my husband was a wild animal waiting to be released. "Cinder...?"

"What?" Cinder asked, looking confused.

"This...this truly doesn't offend you? How can you even be alright with this? How are you silent?" He asked.

I was curious myself, as I glanced at my husband with a hesitant, nervous gaze.

My husband shrugged, a confident grin on his face. "Because *I* know that they have never been intimate...and I know where they currently stand with one another. Kyeareth has had *many* opportunities, and has not once been unfaithful to me; my surveillance measures around the palace proved as much to me, and I was never concerned about their interaction after that. I am confident in my trust in her, and I trust my brother-in-law, too. I don't have anything to be concerned about."

His brother looked upon my husband with wide, surprised eyes.

Astaroth nodded. "Brother is right...so long as she is his wife, I will honor their relationship. I would never betray either of them that way. While you may feel that I am...overly affectionate with my sister..."

He glanced around, taking us all in.

"I do, surprisingly to you, I'm sure, know how far is *too* far. I have never been intimate with her, and I don't plan to be..."

"Right," my husband smiled.

Astaroth smile. "I will admit, though, I'm unsure what would happen if they were to ever *divorce*." He shrugged. "But I will never stop being affectionate and close with her. He and I have agreed to as much, privately."

My brother-in-law looked away, seeming to contemplate this, before he stood, coming over to us and looking at my brother.

"I had better not ever hear tales of you being intimate with your sister in such a way while she's married to my brother...or you won't have to worry about remarrying and having a *son* to run the duchy..."

The threat was clearly. If my brother became romantically intimate with me, my *other* brother would kill him.

Azoth cleared his throat. "My queen," he said. "Cassian has arrived, as was arranged."

I rushed to get away from the group, trying to calm my racing heart and my throbbing soul.

Cassian stepped into the room, stopping when he saw my family.

He spoke in surprise in his own tongue, and my brother startled...before speaking in the same tongue.

We gaped at my brother, and they conversed for a moment before my brother grinned from ear to ear, clapping Cassian on the back and pulling him into a hug.

I could imagine, from the tone and the expressions, that he was expressing gratitude.

"Do you two already know one another?" I asked.

"No," Cassian said. "I was just stunned to see how much you look alike, and I spoke in my tongue."

"Okay...?"

"Well, he understood me," he explained. "He, being a linguist, started chatting right away, knowing that the man from the Olivian Kingdom who came back with you was the one who found you and helped you."

"Ah, okay, that makes sense."

"You...*really* look like one another," Cassian said, glancing between me and my brother.

I looked to my brother. "I am impressed that you had the had the ability to speak other languages," I said.

My brother smiled. "Yes, I spent some time traveling around other kingdoms with father." He glanced to Cassian. "Thank you for saving my sister."

"Speaking of—I have a gift for you, Cassian," I smiled. "Actually, it has two parts, but the other part will come later. For now...I am naming you, Duke Cassian Ren Orion," I deemed him. He startled, looking between my husband and I as we smiled at each other. "My husband and I decided to grant you the title of Duke, the highest noble rank that we can name you, in repayment of helping me. You will have your own castle, a sect of land, and anything else you could want...but I am also deeming you as something else."

"Please, your majesty, this is all too much as it is—"

"I am naming you my best friend," I smiled. "I would like you to be at the palace often, to spend time with me. You are free to live whatever life you wish, Cassian."

He kneeled before me, taking my hand in his and kissing the back of it reverently. "My queen...I am honored. I truly don't know how to express my gratitude. I didn't do this for a reward, but I am humbled by this gesture."

"I know," I smiled at him.

"I swear my undying loyalty to you, Queen Kyeareth Renna Severing Ashland. I will follow you, serve you, protect you, and love you reverently...for the rest of my days. I swear my fealty to you, as her husband, your majesty, King Cinder Burn Ashland."

Cinder gave a respective nod. "As you will, then. And not to worry, your castle isn't very far from here. Only about an hour," he laughed.

"Wait...you didn't have time to prepare—"

"It was vacant already, but we restored it as soon as we arrived to be prepared as a gift for you. You are a new duke, so we will grant you a treasury aside to get you started. You are in charge of a small town, but I have an advisor and tutors to help teach you how to run your town and make the necessary adjustments to this new life."

"Thank you, your majesties."

"Congratulations, Duke Orion," everyone told him, giving him handshakes and hugs, thanking him for his deeds.

I glanced to my brother. "You are also being renamed," I said.

"What?" He asked, surprised.

"In honor of father's death, I decided to rename him as Archduke...so you are currently the Duke of Severing, but you will be deemed Archduke Severing soon. We will make it official."

"Sister, I..." He looked emotional. "I won't let you down," he said, kneeling.

I turned to the maid who had started an attempt to run away.

Thankfully, my Shadow Guardians had stopped her.

"As your first duty...I want you to silence her," I said. "That maid that they took away. She is to be banished from this kingdom, with her family. Please, see to her departure and have her set up in another nation. If she decides to go blabbering about any of this...get rid of her."

"As you will, my queen," he said, soft.

Chapter 21

Kyeareth...

Solaris's End, 317 Ashland Rule

It was the first day of the month when I awoke with a strong pain in my belly, and a rush of fluid between my legs.

I gasped, sitting up in bed, crying out.

"I—I think—!" I sobbed. "Cinder! Seryn!"

"My queen!" Seryn cried, rushing into the room from his part of the chambers, and Cinder waking up, lifting me, and carrying me to the medical room down the hall.

The rest of the early morning was a whirlwind, nurses and the doctor and maids rushing in and out, instructing me to breathe, to push...

I heard, vaguely, that Cassian, Gaia, and my own family had arrived and were waiting in the waiting area for me.

Flashes of a dead baby in my arms with screams and cries coming from me and my husband flashed in my mind, wracking my mind.

I started sobbing and crying.

"No!" I sobbed. "No, don't! Don't—Aagh!" I cried.

Cinder took me into his arms, asking me what was wrong, but I couldn't focus. "Kyeareth!"

"No! No, d-don't let him die! I don't want to lose him again! Asfaloth!" I cried, clinging to my husband even as the doctor and nurses clutched each other and cried softly, watching my post-traumatic stress episode.

"Kyeareth," Cinder shook me. "The baby is *fine*, darling. The baby is fine, and it is time to push! You have to push, now. Focus. Our baby needs you to focus."

"I can't!" I cried, rocking. "I can't, I can't, can't!"

"You *can*," he said, taking my shoulders in his hands. "You can do this. We've been through heartache. We've struggled, we've suffered unbearable loss. We can get through this. Take my hand, Kyeareth."

I focused on his words, and I took his hand.

"Now, bear down, and *push*!" He told me.

Finally, after a while of struggling and pushing, arching my back, crying, pushing...it was three o'clock in the morning hours when he arrived, on the day of Moon's Height.

Healthy lungs pushed out healthy, loud, boisterous cries into the early morning air.

He was wrapped in a deep, navy-blue blanket—knitted by Alice, I would learn later, as she had knitted a blanket in both lavender for a girl and navy for a boy as soon as she had heard that I was expecting.

It was her last gift to me, and had been found in her things after she had passed away.

My son was taken by the doctor, examined and washed up, before they wrapped and swaddled him, and lay him on my chest.

His thrashing and crying ceased almost instantaneously, soothed by my presence as he relaxed. His ear pressed to the naked flesh above where my heart lay in my chest, listening to the steady beat to soothe him.

He had brilliant, rich black hair, and I saw his eyes open slightly to see the striking grey-blue blurrily looking at me.

"He is stunning," Cinder said, pressing kisses into my hair and face, whispering praise and lavishing compliments upon me and our son.

"You t-think so?" I asked, sobbing out my love for him, and my mourning for the one I had lost, all at once.

Tears filled his eyes as he rested his face against the baby's thick tufts of dark hair. "He is brilliant. You have done such a splendid job, my queen. You did so well, love."

I hiccupped with sobs and cries even as I blushed, and the doctor and maids helped clean me up a little before moving me back to the King and Queen's chambers.

A fresh new mattress and sheets and blankets had been prepared there. They got me set up comfortably in bed, a new cradle beside of the bed on my side, and they slowly began to bring people in to see us.

The first were my guardians and Seryn, who had actually stayed out of the room during the birth.

He had told me that he wanted Cinder and I to have a more private, intimate experience together...and I think that we had.

Now, we were ready for visitors after a while with the baby alone. According to what I had been told, the room had been chaotic, filled with people, when Asfaloth had been born, and we hadn't had any privacy.

At least this experience was immensely better than that.

Not only had I not lost the baby, but we'd even had time alone with him.

I already knew what I would name this child, and I could only hope that he would approve of the name.

It was honorary, yet again, and I was pleased with the name.

When everyone had arrived, my family took turns gazing upon him, smiling at him fondly and declaring his beauty, how radiantly he was glowing.

It was when Cassian arrived into the room that I cleared my throat, and got everyone's attention.

"I have decided on a name for the prince," I said, soft. I gazed upon him lovingly. "I have decided that his name shall be, 'Castarion Renoth Scorching Ashland," I deemed.

Cassian gaped at me. "M-my queen, you can't mean—"

"Yes," I smiled. "I tried to combine the names, 'Cassian' and 'Astaroth,' in honor of the one who saved me...and the one who was able to establish their existing connection to me in my new mind, which is a testament of how much he must mean to me. My husband and I discussed this beforehand, and he agreed...with the tribute to his 'fiery' family and his last name added, of course."

They all stared at me, eyes wide and my brother coming and giving me a gentle embrace even as he smiled down at my son.

"He is fantastic, sister," he said. "Truly...and I am honored to share a namesake with yet another of my sister's sons."

I felt my face heat a bit, even as I watched my husband lift the baby into his own arms, looking down at him with affection.

The rest of the visiting was quiet, with everyone taking turns looking at the newborn prince and smiling, praising him...and soon, I fell asleep.

It was about midday when I awoke again, and Cinder noticed right away that I was awake. He came to me, pressing a gentle kiss to my lips, before he offered me a tray of lunch and wiped the sweat from my forehead with a cool wet cloth.

"Where is Castarion?" I asked.

He smiled. "He is with the nanny for a while. I just woke from a nap myself. We both needed some sleep and a meal."

"N-nanny...?" I asked, nervous.

"I assure you, she is highly trained and well-to-do in her duties," he told me, confident. "She is also being monitored by the Shadow Guardians at all times, who are watching over the prince like hawks. Do not fret, my lioness. She has passed all security clearances and has taken care of many noble children in the past, so she knows well how to do this job. She was my sister's nanny when she was a baby, so she is in her forties, now, but still in good shape and orderly. In case that isn't comforting enough for you, all six of our combined Shadow Guardians are watching over them both. She can't hurt him."

"I am sure, but...does he *have* to be with a nanny? I am a bit anxious having him away from me."

He paused, looking at me with wide eyes. "You...don't wish him to have a nanny?"

"What I mean is, what exactly does a nanny do? How often am I going to get to be with the baby if a nanny is in charge of everything?"

He smiled. "You can see him as often as you wish. I only insisted on a nanny right now because you desperately needed rest, and so did I. That, and I know that many mothers feel...strangely detached and upset when they give birth. It isn't something that I can understand, but I remember how detached and aloof and upset my mother was after my sister was born. It was as if she couldn't look at the child without bursting into tears. The nanny helped her greatly."

"...I see..."

"After what happened with Asfaloth, I just...I want to be sure to take the utmost care of your mental health."

Fondness and thankfulness flooded my entire being at his careful consideration of me.

He had me sit back in bed, and he fed me my food himself, letting me eat slowly and savor the food, informing me that he had actually cooked it for me himself. His skills weren't as great as the chef of the palace, but it was still tasty and nutritious.

When I was finished, he took me to the bathtub where a tub of hot water awaited me, and he helped me undress before he and I slipped into the tub together, easing into the soothing heat, as I sat between his legs. He washed me, taking care of me, massaging me as he went, and I found myself feeling more and more...in need of him.

I turned, looking at him over my shoulder.

"I...I love you," I whispered.

He startled. "W...what?" He asked, thinking he had misheard. "What did you say?"

"I said that I love you," I murmured.

"I...I still feel that I must not have heard you," he chuckled, looking a bit awkward. "Can you...say it one more time?"

"I love you," I smiled up at him, and he gave me a triumphant grin before he pressed his lips into my own.

"I think that may just be the first time you've ever said it first yourself."

Veras's End, 318 AR

It was nine months later, and our son was growing rapidly.

He had begun crawling at seven months, and had started walking...if you could call his toddling and stumbling "walking," in any case, just this month.

He was babbling well, and some words were quite coherent and easy to understand. His hair was rich and thick, his eyes healthy, bright...

Also, he was quite the lady charmer.

Prince Castarion and Lady Kynroth were practically joined at the hip already.

She was two-weeks older than he, but he seemed older than her, with his advanced motor skills for his age.

It seemed that the magic hadn't just helped him be born a little sooner—three weeks before his due date—but it had also helped him pass milestones sooner, as well.

He was very smart. He was a great help to Lady Kynroth.

My husband, brother and I were discussing this already, setting our children up together.

While sibling relationships were frowned upon, cousins of nobility often married.

Cinder and I were a prime example.

Technically, he and my father were cousins.

Though it was not encouraged, many royals married cousins to keep bloodlines strong and pure for generations. Unlike defects that could occur with direct incest, that would not happen with cousins.

It was when my son was just shy of ten months that I heard a piercing shriek as I was getting dressed, and I rushed into his bedroom across the hall, half-naked, to find the nanny and a maid up in the air, screaming and flailing while my son laughed and waved his hands around even as they flew wherever he swung his arms.

I gasped, crying out in shock even as Lord Winter and Azoth rushed past me into the room, and Seryn rushed to cover me with his cloak, helping me back to my room to get finished getting dressed.

"What on earth happened?" I heard Cinder's voice ask, and I gasped, looking over to see him stride into the room.

When I relayed the events, Winter brought Castarion into our chambers.

"We have a problem, your majesty..." Winter said. "The prince has no idea how to control his powers, and they are manifesting *far* sooner than we had anticipated. He used a floatation magic on the servants," Winter said awkwardly, drifting off.

Cinder gaped at him. "What?"

Winter nodded. "Yes, your majesty...he is only nine months in age, and yet he is already...quite powerful. That is advanced magic and requires quite a large amount of mana to perform. He seems to be a genius and a prodigy, which is amazing for the Mage's Faction, but..."

"Not for the Knight's Faction," I reiterated.

Winter sighed. "His magic is potent, certainly. It will be exceedingly difficult for him to learn to control and maintain this level of power. To be honest, he already matches a novice adult mage. Quite a feat for a baby, I must say."

"What would you suggest, then?" Cinder asked, lifting our son into his arms.

"I can only think to begin to implement light disciplining..." Winter said, hesitant. "He cannot think to use powers like this on people. It will be difficult to keep the servants quiet as it is," he said. "If rumors get out and spread, it could cause catastrophe."

Cinder nodded. "We will attempt to start this, then. We will begin teaching him not to behave this way right away. But, is there a more permanent solution? I know that he is almost entirely Mage Mana, and as it has been established...if the Knight's Faction finds out about this, it will be a nightmare. We can try to keep it silenced, but when he fails to produce Knight's Aura, people are going to talk. People will speculate."

"I am sorry to say this, your majesty," Winter said, looking away. "But the only permanent solution would be to...the only permanent solution would be for your majesties to bring forth another son, and name him the Crowned Prince rather than Prince Castarion."

We all got quiet for a moment, Cinder glancing at me with a guilty expression.

"Perhaps, but I—" I didn't get a chance to finish what I was about to say, however, because I heard someone calling out to me.

"Your majesty!" We heard my brother call, and we glanced over to see my brother approaching with his daughter in his arms.

"What's going on?" I asked.

"Kynroth simply was inconsolable, so I brought her here. She began to settle as soon as we reached the palace," my brother laughed, giving a shrug. "It seems that she prefers to be here, because she knows she will get to see her cousin," he smiled at her fondly when she beamed at my son.

They reached for one another, and my brother and the king set them down. They both moved to one another, clinging to one another, and playing in the floor as we watched, smiling at the scene.

"We should be especially careful with Lady Kynroth," Cinder said, a deeply contemplative look on his face.

This alarmed my brother. "Why? What's the matter?" My husband leaned over and whispered what happened in his ear, and my brother startled. "What?" He asked. "He's...he's—?"

"You *must* keep this information secret," I stressed to him, and he nodded gravely. "You know what would happen if you don't, I am sure."

"I know probably better than you," he told me.

"...What do you mean?"

"Oh...I mean, that you don't remember our childhood. I remember how we grew up, and the difference in how we were treated, you and I."

"So...you mean, I was treated poorly...?"

He sighed. "We are a Knight Faction family."

"Right..."

"It was risky enough for father to have a woman of the Mage Faction of another nation to give birth to us in the first place, but...then, you were Mage-Born. So, of course, as the Duke of the Severing duchy, I am well aware of the consequences of..." He trailed off.

"Yes," we murmured, serious.

"Wait. Wait a moment," he said. "Wait a moment! I think...I might have a solution."

"A solution?" I asked.

"Make Castarion the next heir to the *dukedom*," he said, holding out a hand as if offering a gift. "I can pass the title to him. Rather than making me remarry, and then having my daughter marry into the royal family, becoming the Crowned Princess for Castarion...why not have Castarion marry into the Severing family as the next archduke?"

"...Would that work?" I asked.

"Sure, it would! It would also mean that the title was still staying in the family, even though I don't currently have a son."

"And that would mean you get to remain single, as you wish," Cinder nodded, smiling.

"Exactly. It was difficult enough to marry Lady Steel. Doing this, I wouldn't have a need to remarry and father a son. My daughter doesn't qualify to inherit the title because she's a woman, but if she had a man marry into our family instead..."

"Then the title would pass on without making you marry, and without bringing in someone of a different surname who would refuse to be renamed for the title," I said.

"That's right. We were discussing marrying the two of them, as it were. The people might be disgruntled, a bit, but if he married a woman who is Knight-Born, it shouldn't be an issue."

"But, could we really do that?" I asked. "Won't the vassals get angry about it?"

"Eh, I'm not too concerned."

"...But how?" I asked. "Why?"

He shrugged. "Why not? It isn't like I intended to marry or have any more children, anyway. Let me announce him as my heir to the dukedom. You two can try to have another son in the meantime."

I contemplated this, before glancing at Winter. "Can I undergo some tests and treatments to be sure that my fertility is high and my ability to conceive is actually working?"

"Of course, my queen."

"Then we are in agreement then," I said.

We all nodded, and we began to set things into motion to get things quiet.

We would protect the prince at all costs.

I was stressed and worried, but we would just have to make it work...

~ *Fin* ~

……...Stay tuned for the exciting conclusion coming in:

The Apathetic Knight, Part 3 – The Freezing!

Coming soon!
In honor of the Relaunch of The Royal's Saga, I am doing a Rapid Release!
The Apathetic Knight, Part 3: The Freezing, will be released in just a couple of days!
More information to come!

Book Excerpt to follow

Kristen Elizabeth

The APATHETIC Knight

PART 3

The Freezing

3RD AND FINAL REVISION
EXTENDED AUTHOR'S ART EDITION

1.5

Book 1.5 Excerpt...
Kyeareth

When we reached the door, he gave me a slight bow, gesturing for me to enter first.

I gently opened the door, peeking inside, when I gasped, stepping fully inside, and gazing around the room.

Beautiful, healthy dandelions were everywhere, making the room extremely fragrant.

The sheets were freshly washed and made, candles lit and burning around the room...

"Oh, wow," I breathed.

I looked at a side table, noting a bottle of apple cider wine, and a plate of quiche, beside of a box of gourmet chocolates.

I turned to face the king, but found him on his knees, a small box presented in his hands.

Breathing shallow and quick—like small gasps—I stepped over, wordlessly, and lifted the lid off of the box to find a red tulip, propped up, with a ring hidden in its center.

I sniffed the tulip even as I slipped the ring out of the flower, and he took my hand after he sat down the box, slipping the ring onto my middle finger.

It was a beautiful silver, with a stone of onyx surrounded by small, delicate turquoise pieces.

I knew it was to represent ourselves.

"Do you know the *meaning* of a red tulip, my queen?" He asked, his voice husky.

I somehow knew it, even though I didn't.

Then, I remembered that one of my listed favorite hobbies had been "Symbolisms", so I knew, somewhere in my mind, the symbolism behind almost everything in court language.

"It means—"

"*Passion*," he whispered, standing, and hesitantly taking me into his arms.

"You...?"

"I...I have been patiently waiting for you, Kyeareth. It has been...so very long," he said, his voice thick with emotion. "So long since I have held you, since I have had you the way a man should have his wife."

I gulped. "C-Cinder..."

"I have seen your lingering eyes upon me lately, my queen. I have seen your signals, your blushes and giggles, your batting lashes...I have felt this growing bond between us since you returned. Unless, I have perhaps misinterpreted?" He asked.

I shook my head. "You...you haven't misinterpreted," I murmured. "You are right, I have been watching you."

"Might I please, my love, please...have you again?"

I gaped at him, before I glanced at the flower again. I sat it down on the table nearby, before I grabbed a cherry stem, holding two cherries.

I stepped back over to him, before I lifted the stem to my mouth, lifting one cherry to rest between my lips, and I moved to push the other to his lips.

He took it, and at the same time, he and I both bit into our cherries.

He took the stem of his into his mouth, twisting and turning it before he presented a tied knot on his tongue.

I blushed heavily, before he pulled the knot out of his mouth and kissed me deeply.

Sharing dual cherries meant "sex" in court language.

Accepting them and eating one was a very clear, resounding permissive on my part.

He led me to the bed, and I was awed by his beauty as we became bare to one another.

His muscle was rounded and soft, but thick. His abs were well defined; I could six, leading to a deep muscular "V" that dipped down to his—

Oh...oh, my...

He was already stiff, hanging heavy over his thighs, and my cheeks flamed.

I knew that I'd seen it before; rationally, I knew that...but...

I was seeing it for the first time.

He was *beautiful.*

Sizeable, to be sure.

It wasn't something that I was used to seeing, but I liked it.

He was so handsome, and I flushed at the thought that this wasn't the first time that I'd had him in such a manner.

He chuckled at me as I studied him.

"Is it that fascinating?" He asked.

"Well, I...I don't *remember* it," I said, subdued. "It is as if I am seeing it for the first time. It is...amazing," I said. "It is definitely holding my attention."

He smiled, letting out a husky laugh under his breath.

He leaned forward, taking me into his arms and I flushed as his length brushed against my thighs.

The skin was warm and silky smooth, like velvet steel.

He kissed and touched me everywhere, and when I thought that it couldn't get better...it did.

"*Submit to me*," he whispered into the shell of my ear.

I trembled, and I didn't know how I knew, but I fell to my knees. He gasped as I took him into my hands, stroking him, kissing the tip. He flinched, moaning.

"Good **girl**," he groaned.

I opened my mouth for him, and he drove in with force for a few minutes.

I pushed myself not to gag, but I couldn't let him push in very far before he hit the reflex.

"What do you want, sweetheart?" He asked me. "Tell me what you want from your king."

I glanced up at him, pulling him out of my mouth with one last lick to the under ridge of his shaft, and kissed the tip.

"I want you, Cinder...inside of me," I whispered.

Extra Content

Books by Kristen Elizabeth

>The Royal's Saga<

The Apathetic Knight, Part 1 – The Crowning
>The Apathetic Knight, Part 2 – The Burning<
The Apathetic Knight, Part 3 – The Freezing
The Villainous Princess, Part 1 – The Trapped
The Villainous Princess, Part 2 – The Freed
The Disregarded Dragon
The Hidden Queen
The Conquering Empress
The Abandoned Prince
The Decoy Duchess
The Empathetic Brother
The Anonymous Writer
The Luxurious Slave
The Incensed Guardian Novella
The Royal's Behind the Scenes Finale Novella

The Shifter's Saga

The Rejected Lady Book 1: Parts 1 & 2
The Rejected Lady Book 2: Parts 3 & 4

…Further titles coming soon!

The Lover's Saga

Titles coming soon!

The Spell-Caster's Saga

Titles coming soon!

The Dreamer's Saga

Titles coming soon!

The Queen's Saga

Titles coming soon!

The Knight's Saga

Titles coming soon!

The Immortal's Saga

Titles coming soon!

The Villain's Saga

Titles coming soon!

The Children's Saga (PG13)

Titles coming soon!

Acknowledgments

A special thanks to my proof reader & good friend, Trisha, for reading through the novels and helping me with the grammatical and spelling aspects. Without your help, there were a lot of mistakes that would have made it into the books, and you encouraged me a ton. Thank you for your interest and investment in the story! I love you.

A thanks to the Ghost-Writer who helped me with some editing, some of the ideas, and some of the bonus content added to the original story. You rock, and I appreciate that. Thank you so much!

A special thanks to those who supported my work, including but not limited to, Sammie-Anne, Shannon, Amber, and so on. Several people who really encouraged me to write, publish and seek higher things. You guys inspired me to make this possible. I appreciate it so much. Special thanks goes to my most avid of fans, including Christine, Jeanna, and a few others who had been following my work and have gone to extra measures above and beyond to support and read my works.

All of you aforementioned people make writing the books so much more exciting so that I can see your reactions and give you good books to read!

Thank you all for being amazing. Without you, there is no way I would have gotten such a great start!

A special thanks to my husband, Reece, for allowing me to take so much time to write and keeping everything running, and not complaining a ton.

You wanted me to pursue my goals, and I needed that extra push because I'm bad about procrastinating on things. I love you, handsome ;)

Lastly, I want to give a special thanks to my mom. You don't read my work or really think this will go that far, but you love me and try to support me the best you can. Thank you for everything, and I love you.

Thank you all so much <3

About the Author

Kristen Elizabeth is now on social media! Follow on Instagram and Tiktok! Handle for both apps is

lovelymadness92

She also has an author's page on Facebook! Check her out at

Kristen Elizabeth
(Lovely Madness Fantasies)

Follow for more bonus content, updates, and publishing schedules!

Kristen wants to share her unique worlds with those around her. She hopes someone out there will enjoy her creations as much as she does and use her creations to escape from the mundane everyday life. Kristen's biggest goal is to fit somewhere outside of the norm, and to broaden horizons in the world of fiction.
Life isn't always happy endings, sunshine, and rainbows. Sometimes, life is an utter freakshow and things don't work out the way you hoped.
That's something that Kristen wants to bring to her writing.

Let Kristen help you fall into her world of Lovely Madness ;)

None of this happens without the readers! Please help me by sharing and spreading the word means so much to me! Thank you so much!

I hope you tune in for Book 1.5:
The Apathetic Knight – Part 3 – The Freezing!

About this Book

The Apathetic Knight, firstly of all, is a self-publication made possible by Amazon Self-Publishing KDP.

The author spent two years putting together this novel.

The original drafts and storm-boards were crafted in five-subject notebooks, before being made into manuscripts.

Most of my typing is done between 8pm and 12am, as my children are the light of my life and I do not take time away from them to work. (When they are in school, of course it is a different matter, though, and I have normal working hours until they get home.)

Overall, typing up the story took about one year.

This work is entirely fiction, and is entirely original material from the author.

The original 1st edition of—

"The Royal's Saga, Book 1: The Apathetic Knight" was published as a single installment novel of the series on December 21st, 2022.

It had a dandelion photo as the cover.

The original book almost 700 pages long! In fact, the spine was actually giving out for multiple buyers that the author knew personally, and so, she decided to publish it as two separate installments.

The 2nd edition of The Apathetic Knight was made into Books 1.0 and 1.5, Part 1 and Part 2, with new covers included.

There was a revision for extra editing, as well. This new version edition was released January 10th, 2023, and was 379 pages long!

Finally, last but not least, this new edition of <u>The Apathetic Knight – Author's Art Edition</u> is the final release of the self-published version of the novel, and has over 100 pages of added dialogue and author's hand-drawn art featured! This version was published as Books 0.5, 1.0, and 1.5!

No other release of this novel will take place unless it is brought into a publishing house and released with tons of new features.

Thank you again to all of you readers!

You are amazing, and I hope you enjoy the rest of the novel series!

Please review the story, and please share with friends! One of my biggest dreams is to see people unboxing my story and enjoying the worlds that I take them to within it.

Much Lovely Madness to you all!

#TheRoyalsSaga

#TheApatheticKnight

#SteamyRomance

#KristenElizabeth

#LovelyMadnessFantasies

Kristen Elizabeth
Letting you fall into a world of
Lovely Madness

Reader's Observing Questions:

Q: Who was your favorite character? Why?

Q: What do you think will happen in Part 3?

Q: What do you think will happen to the Female Lead?

Q: Who do you believe the Female Lead will end up being with, in the end, if not Cinder?

Q: Did this novel turn out the way that you thought that it would?

Q: What did you think the novel would be like, based on the cover?

I hope you enjoyed the book! I hope you keep following the journey that this story takes!

Kristen Elizabeth

The Royal's Saga

In honor of Relaunching
The Royal's Saga,
I will be Rapid-Realeasing the novels
throughout the remainder of the
year 2023, in anticipation of the
release of
The Shifter's Saga
Coming January, 2024!
Follow me for more!
@ lovelymadness92
Insta & tiktok!

Lovely Madness Fantasies

Kristen Elizabeth
Fantasy Romance Author

Made in the USA
Columbia, SC
27 May 2024